Publis

wwv

ISBN (eBook): 978-1-83756-214-5
ISBN (Paperback): 978-1-83756-215-2
ISBN (Hardback): 978-1-83756-216-9

THE KILLING GROUND

A DI CROW NOVEL

HJ REED

INKUBATOR
BOOKS

1

I'm halfway along the path to the church entrance when the horizon takes a sudden tilt and I'm locked in place, terrified of taking another step and falling over. It doesn't happen that often now, but when it does, usually in stressful situations, my therapist tells me I should simply stand still, relax and wait for it to pass. My therapist, I think bitterly, has probably never had an attack of vertigo in the middle of a formal procession at an official police funeral.

'Bugger it,' I mutter to myself, and try to take some deep breaths. Out of the corner of my eye, I see an oversized figure in an undersized dress uniform lumber across the gravel.

'You all right, Al?' Sergeant George Saint stops at my elbow, smelling faintly of mothballs, but wisely makes no attempt to help me along.

'Sod off, George,' I reply, trying to unclench my teeth.

He grins. 'You realise, Al, if you stay where you are, you run the risk of getting arrested for obstructing the pall-bearers in the course of their duty?'

The angle of the path is slowly righting itself, and I suck

a good dose of air into my lungs, risk lifting my left leg. Thankfully, I stay upright. 'That should please the chief constable,' I tell him as we resume our progress into the church, 'bump his success rate up no end.'

A low chortle rumbles from George's ample stomach, but it doesn't last long. 'I bloody hate these things,' he says. 'At least you were lucky enough to miss the last two. This one, though ...' He catches the look on my face, presses his lips together and retreats into his own thoughts. Meanwhile, my mind has tumbled back to the first of those funerals, for my sergeant Joe Bailey, shot dead by a drug dealer in the pits of West Hill. It's true, I didn't attend his service. I was in hospital at the time, having the same bullet that shattered his skull taken out of mine. The second death is the one that, these days, gives me the biggest twinge of guilt. I suppose I simply didn't want to face the parents of the young PC who died – poisoned by a psychotic killer while protecting my ex-wife and grandson. I was still on sick leave back then and managed to conveniently slip through the net on the grounds of ill health.

This time, though, I'm out of excuses. I'm back on the job – if you can call a dingy office dealing with the serious and burgeoning crime of designer dog theft anything resembling 'the job' – and so I'm dutifully in attendance at the third final farewell to a serving West Hill officer in less than three years. The circumstances in this case, however, are a little different. DS Vicky Brent wasn't killed in the line of duty. She'd just got off the last bus and was walking home to her flat in Weston-super-Mare when some arsehole, probably drunk or drugged, decided to drag race down the Locking Road, mounted the pavement and ploughed into her at three times the legal speed limit. Forensics identified the make of vehicle from the paint flecks on her clothing, and the car, stolen naturally, but so old the teenage owner didn't even bother to report the theft, was found burned out on waste ground four miles away. Whoever was driving knew how to cover their tracks.

We finally make it into the church, and I squeeze into the corner of the back pew nearest the door. George, after a struggle, manages to ease his bulk down beside me, and we sit quiet for a while, taking in a rear view of the assembled manpower of West Hill police station. Most have made the effort to dust off their best uniforms, the sunlight glinting off polished tunic buttons, making the congregation look like a shoal of serge goldfish in a medieval aquarium. The side pews behind the choir are taken up by senior ranks, mostly from head office, including the chief constable displaying his newly acquired MBE – for services to the British paper industry, George suggested when the word got out – and next to him, looking as if she's swallowed a golf ball, my boss, DCI Grace Helston, practically choking on the starch in her white shirt, hat crushed under one karate-honed bicep.

'Bloody hell,' I mutter to George, hunching into the black overcoat that just about covers my only decent grey suit.

He grunts his agreement, but any further comment is stalled by the arrival of the cortege, and for the next hour or so we sit through the inevitable string of eulogies, few of which, I suspect, have any recognisable connection with the occupant of the flower-strewn casket in front of the altar. The fact is, DS Brent had officially been attached to West Hill less than three weeks, and at the time of her death had yet to put in an appearance in the station, owing to some kind of refresher course at head office. Our only other information is that she had transferred from Newcastle to fill the gap left by the newly promoted acting DI Polly Sillitoe who, to the delight of those who put money on it, is currently leading what used to be my team. At that thought, I zone out of the proceedings to spend a while nursing my resentment towards Sillitoe, who is capable enough to take over permanently if I don't get myself out of the back office within the next few months. Understandably, I suppose, head office are also objecting to a senior officer taking back a job at the sharp end of policing while still being treated for PTSD.

A nudge from George pulls me back to the present and a slow procession of uniforms following the coffin out into the churchyard. He reaches down to retrieve his shoes, which at some point he's kicked off, revealing a threadbare pair of socks and one naked big toe.

'For God's sake, George!' I can't help hissing as he squeezes his way back into his footwear.

'They were bloody killing me,' he replies, and then, with a sidelong look adds, 'Besides, you looked as if you were going to swear out loud during that last hymn, and I thought I might need a sock.'

Before I have time to absorb that thought, he's on his feet and shuffling to the end of the pew, one hand delving in the top pocket of his jacket for what, if I know George, is a sausage roll. I follow him out into the chilly March sunshine, where he, reading my expression, pats my shoulder and wanders off to commune with the rest of the squad at the graveside. I retreat to the corner of the church under the bell tower and watch from a distance, trying to construct an image of a young Geordie lass who, just a few weeks ago, was well on her way to a successful career in law enforcement. As the gathering begins to break up, I turn to go and almost bump into DCI Helston, who, I realise, must have been standing behind me for some time.

'Bloody awful business,' she says, and then, 'Any chance of a lift back to West Hill, Al? I had to come in with the ACC, and I don't think I could stand another twenty minutes of chapter and verse on his golf handicap and his wife's asthma – not to mention his daughter's place at Oxford – classics, apparently.'

'Be my guest,' I tell her as we detour to the back entrance, avoiding the crowd at the main gate. 'At least he won't have to worry about his kid joining the police, unless she's after a posting where the villains speak Latin.'

'Don't you believe it,' Grace answers with a grim smile. 'He's got her name down for Hendon already – wants her to join the Met.'

'Jesus bloody Christ,' is all I can think of to say to that. We turn into the side street where I've parked my old Ford, deliberately well away from the church car park, and Grace slips into the passenger seat, gives a long sigh and chucks her battered hat onto the back seat. 'Where to, ma'am?' I ask as I key the ignition and hope the engine starts first time.

'The Rifleman's,' she says as the engine sputters into life. 'I don't know about you, Inspector Crow, but I damn well need a drink.'

2

The Rifleman's Arms isn't the roughest pub in West Hill by any stretch, but even so, the sight of a uniform generally results in a fair few ruffled feathers.

'Are you sure about this?' I ask Grace as she brushes the debris from my passenger seat off her freshly dry-cleaned uniform jacket.

'Bloody right I am,' she says, making a start on the trousers. 'It never hurts to give the local population a reminder that we take community policing seriously. Jesus, Al – don't you ever clean out your car?' She plucks a mint humbug that's been in the footwell so long it's leaked out if its wrapper from the sole of her shoe. 'Besides,' she goes on, 'I need to have a serious talk with you, and this is one way of making sure we get some privacy.'

My stomach takes a lurch at that revelation. Just over a year ago, when I walked back into West Hill after eighteen months of sick leave, I had expected it to be to pick up a quote for early retirement – the sort with no alternative. As it turned out, there *was* an alternative, and even though the prospect of spending the rest of my career chasing over-priced lost dogs didn't have the job satisfaction of drug raids, riot control and murder cases, it was marginally better than sitting at home with a 'painting by numbers' kit. It was, as they say in the movies, an offer I couldn't refuse. Now, though, with all the cutbacks, I suddenly have a vision of the long, slow climb back up to what I used to be kicked into free fall by the size twelve boot of police bureaucracy.

I realise I'm almost trembling with the effort of not spitting out the first words that come into my head – the gap in my brain where the bullet used to be still causes a few problems when it comes to restraint between my language centre and my mouth. Finally, I manage, 'Jesus bloody Christ, Grace! If this is your idea of softening the blow, I'd rather we just went to the station and made it official – or are you afraid I'll end up putting a dent in the oak panelling?'

She gives me a sidelong glance and lifts an eyebrow, but before she has a chance to reply, there's a scuffle in the pub doorway. A gang of youngsters, the eldest no more than fifteen by my calculation, scatter in all directions across the car park like rats escaping a sinking ship, and disappear into the surrounding streets.

'Well, Inspector,' she says drily when the tumbleweed settles back over the tarmac, 'I'll put a fiver on the landlord offering us a complimentary double, so we might as well go and give him chapter and verse on identity checks, seeing as we're here. What do you say?' She doesn't wait for a reply, but sets off towards the door. 'By the way,' she adds as we head for the bar, 'it isn't oak, it's MDF – I thought you were a detective.'

A couple of minutes later we're sitting in an empty bar,

each nursing a double Scotch and soda, which Grace has insisted on paying for despite the landlord's protestations. The threat of prosecution for serving alcohol to schoolkids has had the desired effect, and he's retreated to the deserted snug where, I suspect, most of the minor drug deals take place of an evening. Grace pulls off her cravat, undoes the top button of her shirt, takes a slug of her Scotch and starts massaging her temples. Whatever is coming, it's not good, but I understand my DCI well enough to know there's no point trying to push her, so I simply sit back, sip my drink and wait for her to drop the bombshell. Finally, she folds her arms on the table and looks me in the eye.

'Before we go any further, there are two things you need to understand, Al. Firstly, this has nothing to do with your job – at least, not with your position as a police officer. As far as I'm concerned – and it's also the chief constable's opinion, by the way – that's safe, no matter what you decide. I want to make that clear, okay?'

For a moment I can only stare blankly at her. The initial flood of relief at having an office to go back to in the morning is quickly overshadowed by the way Grace has worded that piece of news. *No matter what I decide?* What the hell is that supposed to mean? When I find my voice, though, I just say, 'And the second?'

'This conversation never took place.'

Now she's really got to be joking. 'For God's sake, Grace – we're the police, not MI bloody 5!' I can see, though, from the look on her face, that whatever it is, it's far from a joke. I spread my hands in a resigned shrug. 'Okay, ma'am, perhaps you'd like to tell me what the hell is going on here?'

Grace gives a slow nod and gestures for me to wait while

she hauls the barman out of the snug and gets our glasses refilled. Once he's disappeared again, she takes another dose of Dutch courage and makes a start.

'DS Brent,' she says, with deliberation, 'was not killed in a hit-and-run.'

That makes me sit up. 'Then what …'

'She was tied by the wrists to the tow bar of the vehicle and dragged over a rough surface – not tarmac apparently – several times, according to the pathologist.'

'Sweet Jesus!' I mutter, and suddenly feel grateful that Grace had the foresight to top up my whisky. I swallow a decent mouthful. 'Where? And why?'

'Not on the road where she was found, and not where we found what was left of the car either. More likely it was a piece of waste ground not too far from Weston, but there are dozens, if not hundreds of possibilities. We've got forensics working on it, but nothing so far. It looks like they kept at it until they finally killed her, put her body in the boot and staged the hit-and-run on the main road where someone was bound to witness it and call us in.' She pauses to drain her glass. 'They wanted us to get thrown off by the hit-and-run, and hoped the body would be mangled enough to disguise any other injuries. Plus, if there were witnesses about, they would simply confirm the picture they wanted to paint.'

The questions that have been forming in my head don't make it any further as it dawns on me what Grace is saying. 'She was under cover,' I mutter under my breath, and then louder, 'She was under cover, and her cover was blown. That's what you're telling me, isn't it?'

She nods. 'Only five people so far are aware of the true

circumstances of Vicky's death – me, DI Sillitoe, the chief constable, the pathologist, and now you.'

'Why? I mean, why keep it quiet? Surely we have enough to go after whoever did it on a murder charge regardless of whatever else they were up to? Which was what, by the way?'

She gives me a snort of disgust. 'Drugs, guns, child prostitution, you name it. We're up against an organisation with a finger in just about every pie. Yes, we could go after the ones who tied the knots and sat behind the wheel, but they're the bottom feeders, Al. We'd be doing no more than sticking a very small pin into a tentacle of a very large octopus – one that can scuttle under a rock at a moment's notice and stay hidden, virtually anywhere, and possibly for years. We got a heads up from Birmingham a month ago that one of the "board of directors" of this particular organisation was coming over to check on their various businesses and supervise a large shipment of heroin somewhere along our coastline in the next few weeks. As for why we're keeping the details of Vicky's death quiet ...'

She takes a deep breath, presumably deciding how far I'm in the 'need to know' circle, decides, and carries on. 'There are a number of reasons. First, if we can make them think we're stupid, they might not be as careful as they should be. Even the smallest mistake will work in our favour. Secondly, you know what happens when an officer bites the bullet ...' My expression must have changed, because she holds up a hand. 'Sorry, Al – bad choice of words. But you get my meaning. We can't have the whole station frothed up into a gung-ho frenzy and crawling all over places they shouldn't on their own time. As long as they're looking for a random death by dangerous driving, it buys us time to root out the real bastards – the ones who gave the orders.' Again she pauses and shakes her head by way of apology. 'I know, Al. I don't like the deception any more than you do, but the people we're up against are responsible for hundreds, if not thousands of deaths, from drugs, shootings, stabbings, you name it, and West Hill is right in the middle of it all. We have to stop them, and if we want to do it legally, we don't have that many options.'

I can't disagree on those points, but I get the feeling my DCI is still working up to what will be the real killer. I give myself a minute to absorb the information so far, and end up asking the most obvious question. 'Why are you telling me all this?'

She hesitates, glances round as if considering dragging the unfortunate landlord out of his hiding place to get us another round. Thankfully, for both of us, she decides against it and settles back in her seat, looking as if she's about to attend a second funeral in a single afternoon.

'The thing is ...' She stops, wipes a hand across her brow, and without warning brings a fist down on the table, so hard I jerk backwards and almost upend my chair. 'Jesus Christ,' she hisses at the empty room, 'I never thought I'd be saying this.'

'Saying what?' I ask. 'Come on, Grace, spit it out!'

She tries again. 'The thing is, Al, apart from the people I've mentioned, nobody knew why she was here, or what she was doing. Security around the whole operation has been tighter than the ACC's wallet, and she was a very experienced officer. There's no way she would have given herself away, not at this early stage. We've looked at it every which way, and there's only one conclusion.'

It takes me a couple of beats to realise what she's suggesting, and when I do, the shock hits me with the force of the bullet that punched a hole in my skull. 'You can't be serious!' is all I manage to say. Grace doesn't reply, just keeps her eyes on mine, watching the cogs of my thoughts click into place. Eventually I add, 'Sodding hell!'

She nods. 'My thoughts exactly. I don't want to believe it, but the only way they could have found out is if someone tipped them off – someone on the inside.'

'But nobody knew,' I protest, 'just you, Polly Sillitoe and the chief, and he might be a pen-pushing arse, but I can't see him as a stool pigeon for an organised crime group, can you? Plus, I don't believe for a minute Polly is bent. What about Birmingham or Newcastle? It could be someone there?'

Her gaze doesn't leave my face. 'No. The whole plan is down to us – they didn't know anything about it – still don't. The bugger of it is,' she adds, with more than a touch of bitterness, 'we'd just found out where part of the gang were holed up, in a flat in Weston, but now they've cleared out, and we're going to have to start looking all over again.'

While she's been talking, I've finally caught up with the real reason we're sitting in a deserted pub well away from West Hill nick, and why she's telling me all this. 'Not a chance,' I say, and emphasise the words with a painful jab of my index finger on the table between us. 'Not a chance in hell, Grace.'

She doesn't answer straight away, but leans forward again, elbows on the table, hands clasped together so tightly the blood has drained from the tips of her fingers. When she does speak, her eyes are fixed on the glass between her arms. 'I believe – and for what it's worth the chief constable also believes – that you are the only other officer we can trust, Al. You know your way around like no one else, you're sharper than anyone else, and you're based at the station with nobody looking over your shoulder.'

'In other words,' I snap, 'I'm a liability that's been relegated to the broom cupboard and given a crap job to keep him out of the way. Thanks for the vote of confidence, ma'am, but I prefer being a glorified dog warden to spying on my friends and colleagues. So you can trot back to the chief constable and tell him to stuff it up his—'

'That's enough, Inspector,' she says, in a tone that is a sharp reminder that she's pulling rank. 'Listen, Al,' she goes on, more softly. 'It's possible the information came from elsewhere, and it's in our interest to make absolutely sure we're clean. Otherwise we'll have the anti-corruption mob crawling all over us like lice, and any chance we have of bringing in a major crime gang will be dead in the water.'

'In other words,' I say, 'you don't think the information came from elsewhere. If you're worried about internal investigations, it must have gone way beyond a hunch.'

She sidesteps that one. 'This is your chance, Al. I know how good you are, and I've been trying to persuade my bosses to give you a more active role for the last six months. Or do you want to be chasing pedigree poodles for the rest of your career?'

One thing I can say about DCI Helston – her interview technique is second to none. If gentle persuasion doesn't work, try blackmail. I finish my Scotch in a single gulp, slam the glass on the table and get to my feet.

'One more thing, Al,' she says as I pull my overcoat from the back of my chair, 'the guy we're after, the real boss of the operation – we think he's the same person who put that bullet in your head and murdered Joe Bailey.' She gets up, dusts off her jacket and takes a step towards the door. 'No need to decide now,' she says. 'Go home, think about it, and let me know in the morning. Don't worry about me – I can walk back to the station from here.'

'Jesus bloody fucking hell,' I mutter to her retreating back.

3

I've got the key in the ignition and am about to turn it when I catch sight of the landlord peering through the snug window. I meet his eye, and he wags his index finger, accompanying the gesture with a sly wink. I swear under my whisky-scented breath and pull out my mobile. Half an hour later my ex-wife, Chrissie, slams the door of her cab and marches across to me, wearing a very familiar expression – the one that warns me not to attempt an explanation until she's taken a couple of swings with the verbal equivalent of a baseball bat. I get out of the car and brace myself. She's around three feet away when she stops, and the look of impending doom melts into genuine concern.

'Jesus, Al – you look bloody awful! Exactly how drunk are you?'

I straighten up and attempt a smile. 'Probably not half as drunk as the DCI is by now,' I reply, hoping the statement is true and, what's more, that after Grace's performance in the pub, she ends up with a healthy hangover in the morning. 'I didn't want to risk it – you know how it is.'

She glances at the pub, the landlord still staring out the window, waiting to give the all clear to his regular clientele, and rolls her eyes. She knows from bitter experience exactly how it is. Without a word, she gets into the driver's seat and doesn't speak again until we are on the other side of the river, well away from West Hill.

'It can't have been easy for you,' she says finally as she drives straight past my house, heading for the leafy streets of Clifton and the Georgian terrace she shares with Joyce, my former mother-in-law. I glance across at her, and for once I can read her thoughts as clearly as if she had spoken them aloud. It could so easily have been Chrissie attending my funeral nearly three years ago. Every so often she reminds me of that fact – of the sleepless nights by my bedside, waiting for me to wake from the induced coma after the surgeons extracted the bullet from my brain. It was touch and go. Although, thankfully, I wasn't aware of any of it, and it was only much later that she told me she had been there at all. It's why we're not back together – that, and all the other sleepless nights I put her through before she finally told me she couldn't cope anymore, and that love wasn't quite enough. What I can't tell her now is that having to show my face at the church has become the least of my worries, and if she knew about Grace's proposal, she probably would have left me to pick up a conviction for driving over the limit.

I reach across and touch her hand briefly, before she has the chance to pull away. 'I'm sorry, Chris.' The frown that appears tells me she has heard the two words I didn't add – *for everything*.

She pulls up at her front door and turns to me with a long-suffering sigh. 'Come on. I promised Mum I wouldn't let you go back to your house alone until you'd had at least two strong coffees. Plus, we're looking after Ben, and he wants to show you his new drawings.'

'In that case,' I say, bowing to the inevitable, 'how can I refuse?'

I'm hardly across the threshold when Joyce rushes up, pecks my cheek, then stands back and gives me an appraising look. 'God, Al, you look terrible! Go on through and I'll bring the coffee straight in.' She glances over my shoulder at Chrissie, her expression transmitting the clear message, '*Go easy on him or you'll have me to answer to*'. I don't get the chance to go anywhere, though, as a series of loud clatters and thumps on the stairs announces the descent of my six-year-old grandson, Ben, who wriggles past his great-grandmother and glues himself to my left leg.

'Hey, Grandad,' he yells at a pitch high enough to shatter a window, 'you've got to come and see my picture – I've drawn you and Granny and the dog.'

'Hey, Ben.' I hoist him up to detach him from my leg, and set him down firmly on the hall carpet. 'I'll come up in a little while, okay? I'd better drink my coffee first; otherwise I'll be in trouble.'

'Yeah,' he agrees, nodding wisely. 'You'd better, or you'll get arrested.' He scampers back up the stairs, stops on the landing and shouts, 'Laters!' before disappearing back into his room.

'What dog?' I ask as Chrissie shoos me into the living room.

She slumps into an armchair and groans. 'The one Ben's been pestering for since Rosie got pregnant. He wants a bloody Alsatian, for God's sake – because it's what Grandad's got in the police force.' Her glare indicates that without doubt this is another problem I'm responsible for. 'John and

Rosie have put their foot down, of course. They'll have enough on their plate with a new baby, and with them both working, it's just impossible. We're trying to persuade Ben a guinea pig would be a better bet, but you know what kids are like.'

Joyce brings in a big pot of coffee and invites me to stay for dinner before diplomatically leaving us alone – 'Things on the stove,' she mutters as she stages her retreat.

'How is Rosie?' I ask, filling my mug and adding three heaped spoonfuls of sugar. 'And how come Ben's here? Isn't her husband supposed to be helping out?' I know before the words come out that the question is both unfair and uncalled for. John Larson, Rosie's other half, is a good man and a good father – much better, probably, than I ever was. He's also brilliant at what he does – the kind of computer tech I will never be able to grasp. Without his help, I have to grudgingly acknowledge, Chrissie might well have become the victim of a grief-crazed killer a couple of years or so ago, and Rosie would be serving a long prison sentence as an accessory to murder. Since then, I've spent a long time trying to work out exactly what it is about Larson that trips my unreasonable switch, and in those rare moments of self-honesty, I have to admit it is the one fear all fathers must have when their daughters fly the nest – that the more Rosie loves him, the less time she'll have left for me.

'Rosie's fine,' Chrissie replies, adding pointedly, 'and so is John. Rosie's starting to get a bit fed up now, I think. If she's anything like me when I was eight months pregnant, she won't be getting much sleep either. Remember how you used to have to massage my ankles every night?'

'How could I forget?' I say, grabbing at the moment of connection.

It swerves, too quickly, out of my grasp and back into the murk of history as Chrissie goes on. 'John's just been given some sort of new job, and he's been working late the last week or so. It's not ideal, but with circumstances as they are, and Rosie back at university, they're going to need all the income they can get. Besides, we love having Ben here, and we're happy to help out. What else are grandparents for?'

She pauses, working up to the real reason I'm sitting in her living room. 'I want you to have a word with Rosie, Al,' she says finally.

'Why? Is something the matter?'

She shakes her head. 'As far as you're concerned, probably not, but ...' She takes a long breath and spears me with a determined look. 'I don't like it, Al. I don't like what she's doing. Working in a mental hospital was one thing – at least the patients were – well, under some sort of control. Prisons are different. People get attacked; there are riots, drugs; anything could happen to her. It's too dangerous – she doesn't know what she's getting into. It was bad enough worrying about you every hour of the day, and I don't think I could bear to go through it with Rosie. Will you talk to her – please?'

'And say what, exactly? Chris, she's not a child, and you know as well as I do that she'll do exactly what she wants, whether we like it or not. Besides, if she won't listen to you, she sure as hell won't listen to me.' What I don't add is that Rosie's decision to ditch mental nursing and retrain as a forensic psychologist is scaring me, too. I've seen the inside of enough high-security prisons to know that Chrissie's assessment is about right. I drain my mug and get up. 'I'd better go and look at Ben's drawings before he sends out a search party. And don't worry, Chris – I'll talk to Rosie, make sure she knows what she's getting into. It won't make any difference, but I'll talk.'

Around an hour, an art gallery tour and a plastic truck race later, I'm sitting alone on the floor of Ben's room while he goes on a vain quest for biscuits in the kitchen. The door opens quietly, and my daughter steps – or rather waddles – across to me.

'Hi, Dad.' She starts to lower herself, but I push myself up before she gets too far, and guide her over to Ben's toy chest, which doubles as a window seat. 'Don't be silly, Dad,' she says, laughing. 'I'm not that fragile.'

I settle beside her and kiss her cheek. 'Even so ...' I shrug. 'You can't blame me for worrying – I'm your father; it's my job.'

After a short silence, she says, 'I take it Mum's sent you to do her dirty work? She's told you to put me off prison work, hasn't she? You won't, though – not a chance!'

'I know that.' I squeeze her hand. 'I promised I'd do my best, though, so if I don't, she'll see right through it – and she does have a point. Don't forget, I've put away plenty of the kind of criminals you'll be dealing with – they are the worst cases, and the last thing on their minds is rehabilitation and therapy unless it's to gain access to the drugs cabinet.'

She bristles at once and draws herself up as far as the enormous bump that is about to be the next Larson family member will allow. 'And don't *you* forget,' she counters, 'that I spent weeks as one of those cases. I've been on the inside – you haven't.'

'But quite apart from being innocent,' I protest – weakly – I know I'm on a hiding to nothing, 'you were on remand, not in the main prison. Believe me, sweetheart, it really isn't the same – you never saw the real thing, thank God!'

'No,' she agrees, 'but there are plenty who do – and some of them are innocent, too, whatever you say. In fact, there was a story going round while I was there about a policeman who was convicted of taking bribes, and your lot only found out he was framed after he'd committed suicide in the showers. If he'd had someone on his side, who'd listened to him, given him some hope, maybe he'd have lived to go back to his family. I'm sorry, Dad, but things aren't always as black and white as you want to make them. I know I can do more good in a prison than simply nursing the ones who are already broken and drugged to their eyeballs in a hospital. I've made up my mind, and not you, or anybody else, is going to change it.'

I reach across and pull her into a hug, hoping she hasn't caught the look on my face. 'I know, sweetheart,' I say, 'and whatever you do, you'll be bloody marvellous at it.'

Thankfully, she is oblivious to the effect her little speech has had on me. For a few minutes I'd managed to forget my conversation with Grace, but now it comes back with full force, and the implications are starting to hit hard. She wants me to spy on my own people – my friends, people I've worked with, in some cases, for more than twenty years. And if I make a mistake ...

At that moment, Ben steams into the room to inform us that dinner is on the table, and if we don't come right now, he's going to eat my slice of pie.

4

At around 5am I give up trying to sleep, make myself a strong coffee and sit, staring out at my back garden. It's a lot neater than it used to be since Rosie started to visit again, usually with Ben in tow. Larson has taken matters into his own hands and cleared away the jungle of vicious brambles that used to cover my patio, installed a little table and chairs and a colourful plastic child's slide on the reclaimed patch of grass by the back fence. For once, though, my son-in-law's interference in the smooth running of my personal life isn't uppermost in my mind. Instead, it's a dark shadow at the end of a hallway – one that never quite resolves itself into anything more than a vague human shape. In my nightmares, it rushes towards me, a toxic, faceless black haze that grows to gigantic proportions, spitting poisonous liquid fire that fills my eyes, nose, mouth, and jerks me awake, choking and fighting for breath, just as I realise the slime that is dripping down my face is a mixture of blood, bone and human brain.

'Shit,' I mutter to myself, and again, 'Shit!' I've broken out in a sweat, and the hands clutching the mug are shaking so much the scalding coffee is spilling over my fingers. 'Damn you to Hell, Grace.'

THREE HOURS later as I walk through to the station's front desk, the jitters have worn off, which is more than I can say for my fury at Grace, which is still on the fast-boil setting in the back of my mind. George is on duty, and I grab his attention with a sharp rap on the vandal-and sneeze-proof Perspex that has become the public face of community policing.

'Where's the boss?' I ask as he comes across to join me at the counter, his breath misting the polycarbonate and turning him, for a few seconds, into a blur.

'Meeting,' he says and, looking at his watch, 'for the next twenty minutes. If you're wanting to see her, though, be warned – by the look on her face when she came in this morning, someone's let off a serial killer with a parking fine.'

'Good,' I tell him. 'If anyone asks, I was never here.' I leave his raised eyebrow to draw its own conclusions, and head up to the cubbyhole that serves as my new office. Top of the pile on my desk is a report of a litter of stolen puppies from a breeder out near Whitchurch. I grab it and make my way back out to the car park, using the stairs, just in case the DCI's meeting finishes early and things get awkward in the lift.

The drive out to Whitchurch, a pleasant outer suburb of Bristol bordering open countryside, goes some way to distracting me from the unpleasant thoughts that have been plaguing me since the previous afternoon. I pull into the gravel driveway of an old farmhouse at the end of a single-track road just outside the village. A carved wooden plaque at the entrance announces:

Chalmers Charmers: Home of championship Rottweilers and Dobermans

In case there is any doubt, the minute I open the car door, my ears are battered by a series of earth-shattering barks and howls, and before I can put a foot on the gravel, a black shape the size of a small pony emerges from the side of the house, racing towards me so fast all I can see is a massive blur of fur and bared teeth. I manage to get my foot back inside and slam the car door just in time, as the monster crashes into the metal, setting the suspension creaking, and head butts the driver's window so hard I think, for one terrifying moment, the glass is going to smash, and the massive jaws are going to take my head off in a single bite. Luckily, when the car stops rocking, it's still intact, and all I can see out the side window is a thick film of dripping saliva.

Some way beyond the curtain of drool I hear a woman's commanding voice. 'Heel, Daffodil! Heel, Daffy – good girl!'

The owner of the voice, a small but formidable-looking lady, probably in her late sixties and dressed in combat trousers and wellington boots, appears at my front windscreen. The dog, to my relief, has obeyed her command and trotted round to stand at her heel, but what completes the picture and sends another spike of terror through my already fragile gut is the shotgun, broken, admittedly, balanced in the crook of her elbow. After a few long seconds frozen in my seat, I gain enough presence of mind to pull out my ID and press it to the glass in front of me, at the same time attempting a reassuring smile, which I'm sure comes out more as a death-mask grin.

She peers forward to read the card and visibly relaxes. 'I'm so sorry, Inspector. Please, do come in.' When I don't move, she adds, 'Don't worry, it's perfectly safe.' I risk opening the door a crack, and see the muscles in the dog's shoulders tense, but it doesn't move, so I take my life into my hands and get out, slowly, just in case her canine bodyguard changes its mind. She strides towards me and sticks out a hand. 'Susan Chalmers,' she announces. 'I'm so glad you've come. I'm afraid we're a bit on edge – I'm alone here, you see – apart from Daffodil, of course. It's all been a bit ...' She pauses, and I see the hard-woman image start to crumble. 'They took all of them – all except Daffy, and God knows what's happening to them now. You've got to find them before ...'

She finally cracks and starts to sniffle. The dog, who up to now has been a silent sentinel behind her, makes a sudden movement, and I jump backwards, catching my shin painfully on the front bumper. To my surprise, though, it rears up on its hind legs, rests its front paws on her shoulders and sets about licking the tears off her face. 'There, now, Daffy,' she coos at it, 'get down, there's a good girl.' She ruffles its massive neck, and the beast reluctantly drops back onto all fours, glaring at me as if its mistress's misery is all my fault.

I clear my throat and take what I hope looks like a confident step forward. 'Don't worry, Mrs Chalmers – perhaps we could go inside and you can tell me exactly what's happened. We'll do our best to catch the people who took your animals and get them back to you, I promise you.'

I follow her through a long hallway into a traditional

farmhouse kitchen, complete with Aga and polished copper pans suspended from a wooden trestle above an open fireplace.

'I'm sure you'd like some coffee, Inspector,' she says, directing me to a seat at the table while the dog, sensing that my status has been elevated from intruder to honoured guest, curls itself in a basket the size of a bath at one end of the fireplace and occupies itself cracking an enormous thigh bone.

'Daffy's a lovely girl,' Mrs Chalmers comments, joining me at the table with mugs of coffee and a plate of chocolate biscuits. 'She's getting on a bit now, but she makes a good guard dog. She belonged to my husband – he was the expert on the Rotties. He died two years ago, and I couldn't cope with them and the Dobermans, so I stopped breeding them, and when Alfie died, there was only Daffy left.'

I get the feeling Chalmers ('Please, call me Susan') is about to embark on a long, complicated life story, so I head her off at the pass. 'Perhaps you could tell me exactly what happened, Susan? When did you become aware that the dogs were missing?'

'Last night, around 3am,' she says, her lower lip starting to quiver again. 'Daffy started to bark, and wouldn't stop. I knew someone was out there from the way she was howling and scrabbling to get out. I ran straight down, got the gun from the cabinet and went out. I know it was stupid, but ...' She dabs her eyes with a chunk of kitchen towel. 'I was so frightened for the pups. Daffy went straight to the kennel, and as soon as we got there, I could see it was empty. The fence had been ripped open with wire cutters, and they were all gone – all my babies ...' Again, she falters, shaking her head. I try to look sympathetic – no point trying to rush her – and after a minute she recovers and goes on, 'Daffy chased off down the drive, and I saw lights come on and an engine start. Then they were gone, into the lane.'

'Did you see what type of vehicle?' I ask. 'And which way they turned at the end of your drive?'

'A van of some sort, but I didn't see the colour or number plate – it was too dark. They turned right, towards the main road, but they could have gone anywhere from there. You will try to find them, won't you? The pups are only seven weeks old, far too young to be separated from their mother, and you hear so many stories ...'

I cut to the chase. 'I'll do all I can, Susan, I promise,' I say, knowing full well that I probably haven't got a chance in hell. 'Can you give me a rough idea of what the animals are worth?' I've got my notebook out, and when she answers, I come very close to snapping the pen in half.

'We're a championship kennel, Inspector. They took two adults, the parents of the pups. Briar, the male, won Crufts a few years ago, and I've been offered around twenty thousand for him. Mayflower, the dam, was best of breed twice in a row and is still of breeding age, so probably about the same, although I'd never sell her. There were eight pups – five bitches and three dogs, and at current prices, they were due to be sold at between four and five thousand each.'

I choke back the expletives on the tip of my tongue, and in the process manage to spill hot coffee from the mug I've just lifted over the cuff of my shirt. Mrs Chalmers whips out a clean linen handkerchief and hands it to me. I swallow another curse and dab at the stain while Daffodil watches me with the canine version of the expression my ex-wife uses when I've royally fucked something up.

When I've finished, I offer the cloth back, but Chalmers smiles politely. 'Please keep it, Inspector. I have plenty more.'

I stuff the handkerchief in my pocket and pull myself together. 'Good God!' I say finally. 'You're telling me these animals are worth perhaps a hundred thousand pounds? That's incredible!'

She shrugs. 'It's about the going rate these days. People will pay for quality, and Dobermans in particular are in very high demand worldwide. We sell to Europe, the US and even the Middle East. Of course, we're careful who we sell to. Our dogs are show animals and family pets, but as you know, the breed has a reputation among certain types, and we don't believe a dog should be used as a symbol of violence. Of course, the figures I've given you are for legitimate sales – on the black market, who knows?'

'Christ!' I can't help muttering, thinking that at those prices, dog thieves could probably give drug dealers a run for their money. I get to my feet with renewed enthusiasm, causing Daffodil to jerk her head away from the bone and glare at me accusingly. 'Believe me, Susan,' I say, keeping one wary eye on the dog, 'I'll do my very best to find and return your' – I almost say 'property' – 'your pets,' I finish. 'Don't worry, I'll see myself out, and as soon as I have news, I'll be in touch.'

She sees me to the door, but thankfully leaves it at that, Daffodil eyeing me suspiciously from behind her as I make my way to the safety of my car.

I SPEND the drive back to West Hill preparing myself for the inevitable meeting with Grace, at the same time cursing my blunted instincts for not latching onto the importance of lost dogs a lot earlier. The more I think about it, the more insistent the prickle at the back of my neck becomes. The dog thieves knew what they were doing – this wasn't some opportunistic crime. They knew Chalmers would be alone, and that her Rottweiler would be inside the house. From my brief meeting with the ludicrously named Daffodil, I'm pretty sure the alarm would have been raised the moment the van turned into the drive, and Chalmers, given a couple of minutes to unlock and take out the shotgun, would have been outside with her canine protector too quickly to give anyone time to search the grounds for the Dobermans. And yet, the thieves were already on their way back to town when the front door was opened and the dog let loose. This was planned, organised, and if my hunch is correct, the dogs were stolen to order for someone – someone perhaps with, as my DCI put it yesterday, fingers in a lot of pies.

I've hardly put a foot inside the main door when George flags me down. 'The DCI's been looking for you since she got out of her meeting this morning,' he says through a mouthful of bacon sandwich. 'She didn't look too pleased either – told me to tell you to go straight up to her office as soon as you got in. I don't know what you've been up to, but it must be serious.'

He leans forward hopefully as I cross over to the desk. 'I tell you what, George,' I say, keeping my voice low, 'I'll tell you my secret if you tell me yours.'

'Deal,' he says. 'What do you want to know?'

I give him a confidential wink. 'Simple – how the hell have you managed to get this far without having a heart attack, given all the crap you eat?' His resigned sigh follows me all the way to the lift.

I head directly to my own office, but as soon as I open the

door, I know I'm out of luck. Grace is installed at my desk, riffling through my pile of unfinished paperwork and looking as if she's a whisker away from handcuffing me to the table leg. She makes me wait a good minute before shifting her attention from the mess of crime sheets to me, and leaning back in my chair, arms stiffly folded.

'Well?' she demands, giving me the feeling that I'd rather be fending off the attentions of Daffodil. 'This had better be good, Inspector.'

I meet her gaze as levelly as I can manage. 'I thought so, ma'am.' Before she has the chance to interrupt, I launch into my organised dog theft theory, which, if I'm honest, sounds slightly less convincing than it did in my mind during the drive back to the station. 'So I'm wondering,' I end, a little lamely, 'if there might not be some connection between the gangs responsible for other kinds of trafficking – drugs, slavery, whatever. After all, it sounds like the market for some of these dogs is pretty high value.'

To my surprise, she doesn't laugh. In fact, she gives a little self-satisfied smile. 'I agree with you,' she says after a pause, 'and it's good to see you haven't lost your instinct. And sit down, for God's sake, Al. I'm getting a crick in my neck!'

I perch myself on the plastic chair on the other side of the desk, and wait. She's got the look that tells me I've just backed myself right into the corner she was aiming me at.

'You're right, of course,' she says. 'Someone is bringing together the local outfits, organising them in a big way. Like I said yesterday, we're dealing with an octopus, and we're not going to come anywhere close until we can cut off a few tentacles. As long as they're one step ahead of us, we're left looking stupid every time.' She looks away and adds quietly, 'Except it's not just about looking stupid anymore. An officer is dead, Al, and she's dead because somebody in this station served her up on a plate.'

'There's no proof ...' I start, and she rounds on me, slamming the flat of her hand on the table.

'Then bloody well find me some, Inspector – or are you going to let it happen to somebody else? It could be one of your friends next, someone you've worked with all these years, and you're telling me you want to bury your head in the sand, you're not going to do anything to stop it?' There's a long silence, during which I scrabble for some kind of argument that's going to cut through the truth of what she's saying. I can't find one. Finally, she adds the final nail. 'Al, you've already lost Joe Bailey to these people. Damn it, we nearly lost you. Do you really think Vicky Brent is going to be the end of it?'

'I want full access to all Brent's reports,' I tell her, 'everything you've got so far. And I want a completely free hand – I do this my way, Grace, or not at all.'

'I wouldn't have it any other way,' she says, getting to her feet. 'There is one thing, though. You're going to need some expert help with the electronic side of things – if someone is messing us about on the inside, they may well have doctored files, records, goodness knows what. I've arranged for a new digital forensic expert to be assigned to you for the duration – a civilian, not directly connected to West Hill station, and vetted by the chief constable. You will be in charge, of course, but understand, you work together. It's not negotiable, okay?'

I know that arguing will be useless, so simply nod, defeated.

'Good,' she says. 'He's waiting in my office. Come along, and I'll introduce you.'

I follow her up to the third floor, feeling like a sacrificial lamb on its way to a ceremonial banquet. She opens her office door, and I stop on the threshold, frozen with disbelief. The 'digital expert', who has clearly been pacing up and down nervously between the desk and the window, turns, and I'm staring at a very familiar face, blond hair drooping over one eye, mouth opening and closing like a startled fish. Grace moves to one side, enjoying the moment.

'Jesus bloody Christ!' is all I can come out with, fixing her with my most withering glare. 'Larson? You've got to be bloody well joking!'

5

I catch the fleeting smile on Grace's face as she heads for the door, mumbling something about an 'urgent case' needing her immediate attention. It leaves me in no doubt as to how neatly I've just been stitched up. From the look on my son-in-law's face, he's just as much a victim as I am. For a moment there's a standoff, the two of us glaring at each other like bad-tempered kids in a playground. To my surprise, it's Larson who breaks the impasse, sinking onto the edge of Grace's desk with a snort of frustration.

'Damn and bugger it!' He runs a hand across his brow. 'Is your boss always like this?'

I follow his lead and perch myself on the opposite side. 'Believe me, son, you don't know the half of it.' I ignore his rising hackles. 'More to the point, what the bloody hell do you think you're doing? If this is about you and me ...'

'Of course it bloody well isn't,' he snaps. 'Believe me, this wasn't my idea. If you've got a complaint, take it up with your

DCI. She's the one who seems to think we make a good double act.'

'God knows where she got that idea,' I hiss under my breath, but as soon as the words come out, I see exactly what is in Grace's mind, and before I can stop myself, I'm laughing out loud.

At once, Larson bridles. 'You really think this is funny?'

'No,' I say, although I'm still struggling with the grin. 'No, son, I don't think it's funny, at least not in the way you think.' I finally get my expression back under control and cut to the serious question. 'So when were you planning to tell me about all this? I assume Rosie knows what you're doing – did you tell her to keep quiet as well?'

'Rosie knows nothing about it,' he protests, 'and until an hour ago, neither did I – and even then, not that you would be involved.' He lets out a long sigh. 'Listen – as I said, this is all down to your boss. You remember, when we were working to get Rosie out of prison, and I had to do a bit of delving into places I shouldn't?'

'I remember,' I say, 'and I also remember Grace saying she was prepared to turn a blind eye under the circumstances. So what about it?'

He nods. 'That's true enough. What you don't know is that she came to me afterwards, asked me to consider working in digital forensics – said it might be *in my interest* to help you lot out from time to time. It doesn't take a genius to work out what that meant. She also said that owing to the nature of some of the things I might be doing, I couldn't tell anybody, including you and Rosie – data protection and so on. I couldn't really refuse, and to be honest, the work appealed to me. I've only done a couple of jobs for her over the last year on a consultancy basis, and then, a week ago, it all changed.'

For a moment I almost feel sorry for him. When it comes to the ruthless exploitation of weaknesses, Grace can go straight for the smallest chink with the precision of a surgeon's scalpel. Even I have difficulty getting around her, and Larson wouldn't have had a hope in hell. 'Go on,' I say. 'What changed?'

'A permanent post came up – only part time, but it fitted with the other work I'm doing. She asked me to go down to Portishead to discuss it and, well, to be honest, I didn't need that much persuading. You know what our financial situation is like, with the baby coming and Rosie studying again – but even so, it's fascinating work, and I jumped at it. It was only after I'd signed the contract I was told that for the time being, nobody could be aware of my position within the police because I'd be working on a sensitive case. I didn't know until an hour ago that it involved an internal investigation, and I certainly didn't know who I'd be working with until you walked through the door. That's it. I'm sorry if it makes things awkward.'

'You and me both, son,' I say, and carry on before he has the chance to get his insults in a row. 'Looks like Grace has the pair of us over a barrel, and I can tell you from experience there's no point arguing the toss. One thing we need to be clear on ...'

'Don't tell me – you're in charge, right?'

'Damn right – whether you like it or not. It's nothing personal, it's just ...'

'It's just,' he finishes for me, 'that you're a much better arsehole than I am – at least, that's what you told me last time.' He gives me the ghost of a grin.

'True enough,' I agree, 'but more importantly, civilian or not, I outrank you, and I've got the experience – it's the way things work.'

He shrugs. 'Okay – you're the boss. Or do you prefer "sir" – or "guv"?'

'I prefer,' I say, through clenched teeth, 'that you don't piss me about.'

Larson, tight-lipped, focuses on a large seagull dropping obscuring Grace's view of the station car park. Given my unreasonableness, it is, I have to admit, a fair response, and bickering isn't going to get us anywhere. I try again. 'Listen to me, John ...' He lifts an eyebrow – calling my son-in-law by his name is another of the things my rewired brain still struggles with – possibly, my therapist has suggested, an unconscious aversion to becoming too familiar with the man who shares my daughter's affection. When I do manage it, it's a clear signal that things are getting serious. 'You don't have to prove to me how good you are at what you do – I know it, and so does Grace.' He opens his mouth, but before he can speak, I press on. 'You do realise, though, it's not the only reason you're sitting here?'

Now I've got his full attention. 'Meaning?'

'Meaning,' I say, 'that good as you are, there are others who are just as technically qualified. Grace could have simply brought someone in from another force. Instead, she creates an invisible job, shoehorns my daughter's husband into it, and swears him to secrecy. Does that tell you anything?'

He gets up and starts pacing again. It takes a minute for the bulb to light up, and then he actually laughs. 'Jesus – she's got a nerve!'

'That's one way of putting it. If you want to find a bent

officer, the quickest way to let them know you're onto them is to bring someone in who's already in the job, especially if they're transferred from elsewhere. We've tried that already, and Vicky Brent paid the price. If there is someone here passing information to the gangs, it's likely he or she is keeping a close eye on everyone in the station, including me. Grace hopes that as far as they are concerned, I'm simply meeting up with my son-in-law, so you will be firmly under the radar. It's perfect – except for one thing.'

'And what's that?' he asks, although I'm pretty certain he already knows the answer.

'It's going to be bloody dangerous, son. Last time you got involved, you nearly ended up in the morgue, and we were dealing with a single psychopath. Organised crime is a different level of shit altogether. One wrong move, one word out of place and these bastards won't just kill you, they'll make sure they do it in a way that sends the worst possible message back to us. I'm not sure I want to be the one to tell Rosie she's a widow and her unborn child will never know its father.'

He's silent for a long time and finally looks me straight in the eye. 'You say I'll be under the radar,' he says, 'but what about you? If everyone in the station is being watched, then surely you'll be a sitting duck the minute you start poking around. Or maybe it hasn't occurred to you that it works both ways?'

'Don't you worry about me, son,' I say, but it's a good point. 'I'm ugly enough to look after myself. Plus, I have the perfect cover.'

'Oh?' he says, 'And what might that be?'

'It may have escaped your notice, but I'm the brain-damaged station idiot who's been put in charge of lost dogs.

Talking of which, I have somewhere to be. It would be safer if we don't meet here – I'll see you at my place, say seven o'clock?'

'So what do you want me to do in the meantime? And where are you going?'

'I'm sure you'll think of something,' I tell him. 'Use your initiative. As for me, I'm going to see a man about a dog.'

6

Kelvin Draper is probably the least successful burglar and hard man this side of the Bristol Channel. The first time I nicked him, I had to read him his rights in the back of an ambulance after a post office heist resulted in him tripping over a revolving confectionary stand straight into a plate-glass window. The second, equally disastrous, involved an abortive cash machine theft from the wall of a local garage. A beginner with explosives, the machine stayed stubbornly where it was, but the wall didn't, and Kelvin was arrested once he'd been dug out of the rubble. The third conviction not only raised a titter among the jury – even the judge was forced to take a 'comfort break' before sentencing as Kelvin, just two days after his release for the cash machine incident, got drunk and tried to punch his long-suffering wife, Sonya, who responded by clocking him squarely with a cast-iron frying pan and fractured his skull. She left the court with an unofficial caution and a bright smile. He got six months. At that point, Kelvin gave up his life of crime, discovered a love of small furry creatures, and was given the chance to redeem himself with a job at a local wildlife rescue centre. A few years down the line, he's risen to the lofty heights of assistant manager. He also expresses his gratitude to his arresting officer by keeping his ear to the ground and passing on whatever he thinks might be useful.

I find him out back, sitting on an upturned bucket, hand-feeding a baby hedgehog.

'Afternoon, Inspector,' he greets me, rising to his full six feet five and sticking out a meaty hand. I take it cautiously – each of his tattooed biceps is thicker than my thigh, and solid as concrete. The hedgehog is cradled tenderly in the palm of his other hand. 'Ain't he a beauty,' he says, holding it up. 'I've called him Al, seeing as he's so prickly.' He chuckles at his own joke and jerks his head towards the reception shack. 'It's my guess you haven't come round to talk about this little fella. Come on through, and I'll get the kettle on.'

'That's what I've always liked about you, Kelvin,' I reply. 'You're so quick off the mark. By the way, how do you know it's a boy?'

'If it were a girl,' he says, chuckling again, 'I'd have to call it Alice, wouldn't I?'

KELVIN CHEWS ABSENTLY on a handful of nachos from the giant bag he's dumped on the table between us. 'I don't know nothing,' he says for the third time. 'I'm not involved in that kind of stuff. You know me, Inspector Crow – I wouldn't take an animal, and I won't have nothing to do with people who do. Cash, yes, back in the day, and the odd TV, that kind of stuff, but not even that anymore. You're sniffing at the wrong lamppost, if you get my meaning.' He's well and truly spooked, that's clear by the way he's desperately trying to avoid my eye. 'I don't know nothing,' he repeats, and I see, with a little jolt, that his massive hands are actually shaking in his lap.

'Come on, Kelvin,' I say, trying to sound encouraging, 'that's a lie and you know it. Surely you want to help an old widow get her pets back? How would you feel if someone broke in here and made off with that poor little mite you've got there?' I point at Al the hedgehog curled in a shoebox at his feet. 'It's my bet you know exactly the sort of shits who would do something like this, so just give me a name and save us both a lot of time. Otherwise I'll have to keep coming back, and one of these days someone might notice the kind of company you keep.'

'Fuck you,' he hisses under his breath, and then, 'You're all the same, you lot – load of fucking wankers.' He raises his eyes, and I realise he's not just nervous – he's absolutely terrified. 'You don't know what you're asking,' he says, a note of pleading in his voice. 'It's not just me, Inspector Crow, it's Sonya as well – she's pregnant you know, three months along – taken us long enough, but we're just getting straight, and we don't want nothing to do with that life anymore. If anybody finds out I've talked to you, we'll be totally fucked – both of us. I want to help, but ...' He shrugs helplessly.

'Look,' I say, 'I tell you what – tell me what you know, and I give you my word, I won't come here again. As long as you're not pissing me about, I'll leave you and Sonya alone and forget I ever knew you, okay? You try to spin me a line, though ...'

'All right, all right,' he spits, 'but you do what you just said. You forget you ever knew me, and you don't come back. Deal?'

'Deal,' I say. 'Now get on with it. The sooner you give me something, the sooner I'm gone. That's a promise.'

'Fuck you,' he says again. 'Okay, it's like this. Those dogs, they were a special deal – private sale, not for the open market or puppy farms, you get me? The instruction was, get the breeding pair and the pups, like someone was wanting to start their own kennel, know what I mean?'

'Who?' I ask. 'Who was the buyer?'

He gives me a humourless laugh. 'No chance – I'm not that fucking stupid. You'll have to get that from someone else.'

'Okay, Kelvin, sorry I asked. Which particular someone else am I looking for, then?'

He hesitates, as if debating how much his life is worth. 'Sharkey,' he says finally. 'Shark. He knows. Go and ask him. He won't tell you nothing neither, but he's the one you want to talk to. Now you can fuck off and leave me and Sonya alone, like you promised, right?'

'Right,' I say, and get up, knowing I'm not going to get anything else out of him. I pat his shoulder as I move past him to the door. 'You go carefully, Kelvin. Look after yourself and that family of yours – and Al, too, of course.'

As I reach the door, he says, 'Inspector Crow?'

'Yes?'

'You go careful, too, you hear me? Everyone's scared. Even Shark is scared, and he ain't scared of nothing. It's all different now, not like it was. So you look out for yourself and watch what you're asking, and who you're asking. It ain't safe anymore, not even for you, okay?'

'Thanks, Kelvin. I'll bear that in mind.' As I leave, I look back and see him scoop up little Al the hedgehog and cuddle it to his chest as if to protect it from the storm he knows is coming.

AN HOUR later I'm on the Cabot Rise estate in West Hill, heading for Vista House, one of the more run-down blocks, left to fester by a consortium of rogue landlords collectively styled 'Plimsoll Property Management'. Within five years of the block's construction back in the early 1970s, the locals had renamed it 'Vesta House' on account of the piles of empty fast-food cartons and smashed beer bottles piled up in the corridors, walkways and lifts. In those days it had windows. Now, even the wood and steel panels replacing the broken glass are rotted and rusting within weeks of installation. The whole place smells of mould, piss and cannabis, and most of the respectable residents, if there ever were any, have fought their way out, either to better social housing or simply to the safer option of a sleeping bag in a shop doorway. In short, Vista House has become the prime real estate of the local gangs, including a class A thug with the given name of Jermaine Johnson, otherwise known as 'Shark'. To say Shark and I have a gentleman's agreement might be stretching it a bit. The reality is that unless things get really out of hand, I leave him alone, and in return he does likewise. He's happy enough to let us deal with the everyday problems on his territory – domestic violence, minor drug skirmishes, unsanctioned stabbings, beatings and so on. Now and then our paths do cross officially, but whether it's a drug raid, a death or an out-of-control riot, Shark fades away like a phantom, without even a glint from one of the gold chains festooned around his neck. We usually get some of the small fry, his personal cannon fodder, but Shark Johnson himself has never been served with as much as a parking ticket.

I find him holding court on a wall above the entrance to the block's underground car park. I count three minders, each the size of Kelvin Draper and a hell of a lot meaner, one at each end of the walkway and one underneath, on my level, at the car park entrance. A dozen or so kids, some in school uniform, are milling around their local hero with bikes and skateboards, presumably picking up the merchandise they've been tasked to sell outside the school gates in an hour or so's time. I keep my distance and give the nearest minder a smile and a friendly wave. He saunters off up to the wall and whispers into Shark's ear. Within ten seconds the kids have disappeared. Shark dons his Ray-Bans, shakes out his dreadlocks, and with a gesture to two of the hulks to stay put, makes his way down the steps to the street, then down the ramp into the darkness below. It's my cue to make my way round the building to the car park's emergency exit, the door of which has been hanging off its hinges for at least the last ten years. The third minder follows me at a discreet distance, taking up a position outside the fire door, leaving me to feel my way down the pitch-black staircase.

Shark is leaning against a pillar under the only working strip light, putting the finishing touches to his roll-up. 'Hey, Bird Man,' he says, with a flash of expensive dentistry, 'looking good. How's the head?' He holds two fingers to his temple, miming a gunshot.

'Well enough, thanks for asking,' I reply, 'although how the hell you can see a thing down here with those fancy shades on is beyond me.'

He laughs out loud, takes the glasses off and hooks them over one of his gold neck chains. 'You know how it is, man –

got a reputation to keep up, yeah?' The grin vanishes – the small talk is over. 'Just so you know,' he says, 'we don't hold with it, none of us round here. Spraying bullets at our friends in the constabulary, it's bad for business, know what I mean? So no use you sniffing up my arse, yeah?'

'I wouldn't dream of it,' I reply. 'I never liked the smell of Chanel No. 5 anyway.'

His mouth twitches, but the grin doesn't quite reappear. Kelvin was right – Shark is nervous. He's hiding it well, but not completely. He nods an acknowledgement. 'So what do you want? Whatever it is, make it quick. I got places to go, and this' – he sweeps a hand round the car park – 'leads to rumours, know what I mean? Not good for anyone's health – especially yours.'

'Are you threatening me, Sharkey?'

'Me? Nah. Just friendly advice, that's all. You do your job, Bird Man, I do mine, and we know where things stand, you and me. But it ain't you and me, not anymore. You got bad blood in your family, and it's as bad for me as it is for you. You understand what I'm saying? So here it is. You ask your question and you go. If anything happens on your way home, just remember it ain't down to me or any of my people. And if you see any of your crew around, you tell 'em the same. We do things by the rules round here – you win some, we win some. But right now, nobody's winning, not you, not me.'

'You tell me who's screwing around on my side, I'll sort it.'

Now he does laugh, and it's a frightening sound. 'You think if I knew, they'd still be here? Thing is, whoever it is, they ain't just fucking you around. People are closing their doors all over, not just on my territory. It's affecting my business and everybody else's. As for rooting them out, that ain't my job, Bird – you find 'em, you get a free pass from me. In the meantime, after today, you're just another face with a target for a nose.'

'Jesus bloody Christ,' I say under my breath. Shark knows – he knows who, what, why and possibly where – everything except the one thing I really want to know. He sniffs and flicks the butt of his roll-up onto the concrete. 'What about dogs, then?' I ask. 'Dobermans, stolen last night. Two adults, eight pups, from out near Whitchurch. Worth getting on for 100K. I take it that was nothing to do with anyone you know?'

He's already rolling his second smoke, and takes his time licking the paper, lighting up with a retro gold Ronson, and then hawks elegantly, hitting a fire extinguisher on the wall ten feet away. He doesn't look at me as he walks away, but says, as he reaches the ramp up to where his minders are keeping watch, 'I like you, Bird Man – but if you don't want a beak full of worms, you back off and stay off, and you tell your people to do the same.'

I don't know if it's just my imagination, but I think I catch a slight tremor in the hand holding the roll-up as he disappears back up into the failing daylight.

7

It's gone half past seven by the time I finally arrive at my own front door. A soft clicking coming from the lounge tells me that Larson has let himself in and is busy on his laptop. I poke my head round the door with, for once, something far more important than my son-in-law on my mind.

'Don't know about you,' I say, 'but I'm bloody starving.'

He looks up from his screen and gives me a tolerant smile. 'Good to see you, too. You want me to send out for something?'

'Damn it!' As usual, shopping hasn't been top of my to-do list, and all I have in my fridge is a lump of cheese and half a loaf of bread, both now way beyond edible. 'I suppose you'd better,' I tell him, although he's already got his phone out, scrolling through menus on some home-delivery app or other.

'Curry okay with you?' he asks.

The automatic and completely irrational objection that

is halfway to my lips doesn't make it, and instead I just say, 'Sure, son. Knock yourself out.'

A shower, change of clothes and a very decent vindaloo later, we sit back with coffee – somehow Larson has managed to get milk for his latte delivered with the takeaway – and pool information. For me, three things are standing out. First, judging by the reactions of Kelvin Draper and Jermaine 'Shark' Johnson this afternoon, someone is stirring the mud and seriously disturbing the city's pond life. Second, my hunch about the theft of Susan Chalmers's Dobermans looks to be correct. There's a link between these dogs and whoever is scaring Bristol's underworld shitless. They were a private sale, Kelvin said – for personal use. Even Larson can see the stupidity, from a criminal's point of view, of trying to conceal the sudden arrival of two large, distinctive, and probably very noisy animals and their eight equally noisy offspring.

'That's insane,' he comments. 'Where the hell would they keep them? Even if they went out into the country, to a farm or something, surely someone would notice? I mean, rural communities are tight-knit – nobody can keep a secret for more than ten minutes.'

'That's true,' I agree, 'but it's not impossible. We've dealt with enough cases of human trafficking and modern slavery to know how difficult it is to locate some of these gangs. They could be anywhere by now, but somehow I don't think so. I think they're connected to whoever's spooking the local lowlife, and you can't create this much fear at a distance. They're somewhere close, son, believe me.'

'What about microchips – isn't that a requirement for all dogs now?'

'Yes, but it only helps if one of them escapes or is taken to a vet, and I can't see that happening. Besides, the pups weren't due to be chipped for another couple of weeks, according to the owner. We'll just have to keep our eyes open, or hope someone notices and reports the sudden appearance of a cartload of dogs in their neighbour's backyard.'

Larson gives me a look that suggests he thinks I might have lost the plot. 'I know this is probably a stupid question,' he says, with some hesitation, 'but if it's such a lost cause, why focus on the dogs? How is it going to help us find out whether or not there's a mole in your outfit? That's what we've been asked to find out, isn't it?'

'A mole? Jesus Christ – are you and Grace members of the same book club? Like I said to her yesterday, this is the police force, not something out of John le bloody Carre.'

He's not going to be diverted from what was a very good question. 'Okay then, pick a word. Same thing, isn't it?'

'If you say so,' I have to grudgingly agree, and move on to the third and most serious point. 'It isn't a question of whether or not – not anymore. I spoke to two people – both were scared, both warned me off, and Shark sent the message loud and clear that one of our lot is screwing us over. He wants us to sort it out, and that means wherever their paycheck is coming from, it's not from him or any of the local gangs. The feeling I got was that they are at as much risk as we are, and that's a frightening thought.'

'And the dogs?' Larson persists.

'Think about it, son. As far as West Hill station is concerned, I'm simply bumbling around doing what everyone thinks I'm supposed to be doing. If I trip over someone's feet, with a bit of luck, nobody will take me seriously.'

'And if you run out of luck?'

I decide it's time to change the subject. 'So what about you? Anything useful?'

He shakes his head. 'On the face of it, no. I've been through all DS Brent's reports. DCI Helston sent them over as soon as you left and asked me to bring you up to speed as soon as you got back. It didn't take long – she'd only been on the job three weeks, and it looks like she hadn't got very far. As I understand it, she was posing as the layabout daughter of a rich jeweller from Newcastle. Her main target was a guy by the name of Eddie Hall ...'

'What? You've got to be bloody joking, right?'

He blinks at me, confused. 'That's what it says here – why? Do you know who he is?'

I almost laugh. 'I think everyone between Bristol and Exeter does in one way or another – at least, if they don't know him, they know his father. I expect you've heard of the Honourable Gerard Hall-Warner, prospective Tory MP for Mendip North? His father was Lord Reginald Hall-Warner, QC, until his death a few years ago.'

Larson nods. 'Yes, I've certainly heard of Gerard. He caused a riot at a rally six months or so ago, talking about bringing back capital punishment and borstals, that sort of thing.'

'That's the one,' I say. 'He's standing on a law and order ticket at the next election, and from what I hear, he's getting a lot of support from the local country set. He's not so popular with the Somerset force though – every time he opens his mouth, he costs a bloody fortune in crowd control. He's a regular hard-line lunatic, but what a lot of people don't know is that his eldest son, Edwin Earnest Icarus Hall-Warner, fell out of the crib on the other side and has been nothing but trouble since the day he started to walk. I blame the parents – I mean, *Icarus*, for God's sake!'

'I can see how that might make him feel resentful,' Larson agrees, 'so you think this Eddie Hall is ...'

'I'm sure of it. It's one of the names young Edwin goes by when he's slumming it. What surprises me is that he might be mixed up in something like this. He's got a record, but it's mainly for vandalism, petty theft and minor drug offences. His father gets it hushed up, of course – friends in high places. It also fits with Brent's cover. Daddy restricted his son's allowance years ago, so it's my guess he'd go for anything attractive and solvent to fund his lifestyle. If he is involved with the outfit we're after, he could be in way over his head. It might be worth you delving into his activities – can you do that – I mean, more than the stuff on the police computers?'

Larson gives me a look. 'Are you asking me to act outside the law, Inspector?'

'Far be it from me, son,' I say, holding my hands up. 'But put it this way – the guest of honour at Gerard Hall-Warner's summer ball last year was Somerset's chief constable, and he dished out over a dozen invitations to local judges and magistrates. If we're going to snoop around Junior's business, we'll have to be damned careful about it. Still, you're right – given your position now, you can't breach data regulations without getting into a lot of trouble. We'll have to run it past Grace in the morning and hope that unlike his counterpart in Somerset, our chief constable wasn't on Hall-Warner's guest list.'

'Okay,' he says, with obvious relief. 'If I can get hold of DS Brent's phone record, there may be more information there – the phone is missing, probably destroyed, but the carrier should be able to recover any text messages and so on. The only other thing I've been able to establish is that, as far as I can tell, the only people who have accessed any of the files are DCI Helston and the chief constable, using their logins. Up to now, the only other person in the loop, DI Sillitoe, hasn't opened any of the files, at least not using her own login details.'

'What if she used someone else's?' I ask.

'Then it would have to be one of the other two, as the files are restricted,' he says, 'and she would need their password and to have logged in from their office computers. It's not impossible, but very unlikely.'

'So what's the next step?'

'Brent's laptop. I'll be picking it up first thing tomorrow. All her stuff has been under lock and key since her body was found a month ago, seeing as nobody has any idea who's a security risk and who isn't. Hopefully it will tell us a bit more about her movements – personal as well as professional. It's surprising how sloppy people can be when it comes to securing their own machines.' He closes down his own laptop and gets to his feet. 'I need to get back to Rosie. I'll see you in the morning.'

I have a sudden urge to ask him to let me know when he's home safely, just like I used to ask Rosie – and still do, much to her amusement – but manage to keep my concern to myself. I'm not quite ready to admit to myself that I actually worry about my son-in-law, and that, sod it, a part of me actually likes him. I watch from the doorway until his tail lights disappear round the corner, then head back to my armchair and a much-needed (but not medically recommended) glass of Scotch. I've just taken my first sip when the house phone rings.

'Christ, Grace – do you know what time it is?'

'Bugger the time, Al. We had a report an hour ago of a double murder on the New Park estate – husband and wife, both beaten to death. We've got a unit down there now, and by all accounts, it's pretty bad.'

'So why call me?' I ask. 'Is it DI Sillitoe's night off? Or was the killer a drug-crazed cocker spaniel?'

'Don't get smart with me, Inspector.' There's a short silence, a sigh, and then, 'I thought you ought to know. Polly's there now, with SOCO. The victims were Kelvin Draper and his wife, Sonya. From what we've been able to ascertain so far, it looks very much as though you might have been the last person to see Kelvin alive.'

'Bloody hell.' For a minute I can't think of anything to say. 'Sonya was pregnant,' I come out with after a long pause, 'three months, according to Kelvin. He was doing well, Grace – turning his life around, was starting to get somewhere ...' I try to pull myself together. 'You want me to go down there?'

'Absolutely not, Al. As you said, it's not your shout, and I don't want you going anywhere tonight. Is Larson still with you?'

'No. He left a few minutes ago.'

'Okay. Call him, make sure he got home, and I'll see both of you first thing. You come straight up to my office, and I'll set up a video link for him to join remotely. Meanwhile, try to get some sleep. There's nothing else you can do tonight. Oh, and by the way, take your bloody mobile off silent. I've been calling it for the last ten minutes.'

I give it a quarter of an hour and then ring Rosie. Yes, John's back, looking in on Ben, and is everything all right, and is there anything she should be worried about? No, I tell her, everything's fine, I was just concerned, as there was a traffic holdup in town, and I knew he was working late. She knows something odd is going on, but seems to accept my less than adequate lie. I hang up and make my way upstairs. As I drift into an uneasy sleep, the image in my mind is of Kelvin Draper sitting on an upturned bucket, little Al the baby hedgehog curled neatly in the palm of his hand.

8

After an hour's sleep and five mugs of coffee, I arrive at the station wondering just how many more nightmares will fit into the part of my brain that still works. Grace, who looks as if she's had about as much sleep as I have, gives me a nod as I walk into her office, and we both sit in silence, munching on the DCI's preferred breakfast – a bag of chocolate croissants from the deli down the road. She's already filled Larson in on last night's events, and has arranged her computer screen so that he can see both of us. We're brushing away the pastry crumbs when there's a loud ping that almost sets off one of the hand tremors that still plague me now and then. Larson's face appears, looking, if anything, more dishevelled than either of us. For someone who, as a rule, takes pride in his appearance, the sight of my son-in-law's red-rimmed eyes and uncombed hair reminds me, not for the first time, that as far as police work is concerned, he's a toddler who's wandered into the big kids' playground and has just realised he might be mown down before he can find the way back out.

Grace shifts in her chair and kicks off proceedings by stating the obvious. 'This is a real fucking mess.' There's not a lot we can add to that, so after a pause she goes on, 'Nobody's blaming you, Al. I want to make that clear – understood?'

'Nice of you to say so, ma'am,' I reply, without any conviction.

I get a curt nod in response. 'Right. I have some information on that – I'll explain later, but first I want a progress report from both of you. Al – did Draper say anything to you yesterday that might have put his life in danger?'

'It's possible,' I reply, 'but I didn't think so at the time. He was scared, certainly, and he knew more than he was saying. All I could get out of him was that the Dobermans had been stolen to order, and if I wanted to know more, to talk to Shark. It's possible Shark could have worked out who pointed me in his direction, but it's not his style, Grace. Sure, he might have sent one of his minders round to give Kelvin a thumping, but attacking a woman for no reason – and especially a pregnant woman – is way beyond his code of ethics. Besides, if he'd wanted to teach Kelvin a lesson, he would have taken him somewhere quiet – murdering an entire family in their own home would be the equivalent of professional suicide – the other outfits wouldn't stand for it. Plus,' I add, 'he was as frightened as Draper and as keen as we are to find out who's passing information.'

'Agreed.' Grace reaches for another croissant and listens while Larson tells his story. I can tell by her expression that something in his report isn't quite sitting right, but she doesn't interrupt, and when he's finished, she simply nods and sits for a while, eyes closed, rubbing her temples between finger and thumb. 'Okay,' she says finally, sitting up straight. 'John, you can pick up Brent's laptop this morning from Portishead. As for Edwin Hall-Warner, we've been keeping an eye on him for a while. It's my guess he's being groomed as the prime patsy for whoever is running the outfit. The little sod never did have much sense. We figured he would be Vicky Brent's best way in, posing as the stupid rich kid's even more stupid girlfriend. Still, perhaps that stupidity saved his life, that and his money and connections. I do think it's time someone had a quiet word with the Honourable Gerard, though. He can only bail out his son so many times, and not even his legal friends can smooth this one over. I want you to pay him a visit, Al, and make it clear there's a good chance the next time he sees his son and heir, it may well either be in court on a murder charge or in a body bag. If that doesn't work, remind him of the effect it would have on his political career.'

'It would be my pleasure,' I say, 'although I'm pretty sure it's a toss-up which is most important to him. But what about the chief constable? Aren't they both in the same funny-handshake brigade?'

She gives me a sly grin. 'Actually no. If there is one person our CC really can't stand, it's Somerset's CC. They've had a hate-hate relationship for years, on and off the golf course. Hall-Warner is Somerset's pet and, therefore, by association, also on his hit list. Nothing will give him greater pleasure than rubbing both their noses in it, and having young Edwin involved with an organised crime group is the perfect opportunity.'

'Right,' I say, deciding that when it comes to noses, keeping mine firmly out of force politics is top of my list. There's another silence, which stretches until I break it with, 'So what is it you're not telling us, Grace?'

She lets out a long breath. I glance at Larson, who, even though he's watching through a screen and doesn't know Grace as well as I do, senses something coming that definitely isn't good.

'When the shout came in,' she says, 'Sillitoe's team dashed off to New Park, and I took the opportunity to send George Saint to the wildlife trust. They have CCTV – now I have it – the only copy.'

She brings up a video on the screen, confirms that Larson can see it, and runs it forward to just past 2pm. The view is of the entrance to a large metal barn, the trust's main building. For a minute or so, nothing happens; then Kelvin Draper comes into view, walking across from the animal pens carrying a bucket from which, presumably, he has been feeding his charges. He enters the barn, and a few moments later, another figure comes into view from the opposite direction and goes inside. It takes a couple of beats to realise the figure is me. Grace forwards the video again by around five minutes, and a third figure appears, small, wearing jeans and a hoodie pulled low over the face. Whoever it is also goes inside the barn. Grace stops the playback and raises an inquiring eyebrow at me. Larson simply looks confused.

I replay the events in my mind, trying to pinpoint my movements precisely. 'I found Kelvin in the barn,' I tell them. 'We spoke for about a minute, and he invited me down to his shack. We went out the back way, so unless there's a camera there, we wouldn't have been seen. We were both there for around fifteen minutes, and Kelvin was still there when I left.'

Grace nods and starts the video again, moving through at triple speed. We count another twenty minutes, and she pauses. 'There's no sign of you leaving,' she points out.

I have to think for a minute before I realise. 'I went out the back way – there's a path from the shack running along the back of the barn to the car park. That's the way I left – I didn't go through the barn. If I had ... Jesus Christ!'

'You had no way of knowing,' Grace says quickly, 'but it's possible you and Kelvin could have been followed and overheard, yes?'

'It's not impossible,' I have to agree.

'Okay. Now for the punchline.' Once again, the video rolls, this time at normal speed, and we watch as the hooded figure emerges from the barn and turns towards the car park. There must have been a noise or some kind of disturbance from the animal pens because the figure suddenly pauses and looks back. It's only for a fleeting moment, but in that instant, the face is partially visible – still shadowed by the hood, but it's enough. Grace freezes the frame, and the three of us stare at it, not wanting to believe the evidence of our own eyes.

'This has got to be a bloody joke,' I say finally, 'or faked somehow.'

'Is that possible?' Grace asks Larson.

'Not impossible,' he answers, 'but I would say extremely unlikely. The technology is there, and so is the expertise, but it would be very difficult and time consuming. It would also depend on a number of things, like whether there is a cloud backup of the original footage, how up to date the CCTV system is, and how much the Trust invested in it. I can analyse it if you want to be sure.'

'Do it,' Grace says, 'and make it a priority.'

'And if it turns out to be genuine?' I ask.

'Then DI Sillitoe was somewhere she shouldn't have

been yesterday afternoon, and we've got a problem.' She dismisses Larson and turns to me. 'Your thoughts, Al?'

At the risk of sounding like a parrot, and for want of anything else to say, I simply repeat my boss's earlier sentiment. 'It's a fucking mess, ma'am.'

She gets up, goes over to the window and sighs. 'I've asked maintenance to clean that bird shit off my window three times now. You'd think I'd have some clout round here.' She turns to face me, leaning back against the sill. 'It was Polly's day off yesterday – what the hell was she doing there?'

'Whatever it was,' I say, trying to measure my words carefully, 'maybe we shouldn't jump to conclusions. I mean, she was off duty, so she could simply have been making a donation to animal welfare?'

'Oh, for Christ's sake, Al! You saw the footage. She was deliberately keeping her face covered, avoiding the camera. It's only by chance we managed to get a view of her. Who the hell does that if there's an innocent explanation?'

I don't have an answer – or, at least, the answers I have are only likely to make things worse. What's worrying me most is how Sillitoe managed to tail me from the station to the Wildlife Trust without my noticing, and if she was able to do that, whether she also followed me to Cabot Rise and my meeting with Shark. I decide to keep those misgivings to myself and instead voice what I know is foremost in Grace's mind as well as my own.

'I can't believe for one minute,' I say, 'that Polly Sillitoe is bent. There has to be another explanation, Grace – there just has to be.'

'Then find it, Al,' she says, just a hint of desperation in her voice. 'Until you do, she's out of the loop, although God knows how I'll manage that without rousing her suspicions. Meanwhile, go and see Hall-Warner and then hook up with John Larson and see what he's managed to get on that recording.'

'Yes, ma'am.'

I get to the door, and she adds, almost under her breath, 'And for goodness' sake, try to make sure you're not followed this time.'

9

It's around an hour's drive from West Hill to Oakwood House, the ancestral pile of the Hall-Warner family. I spend a good portion of the journey anxiously peering through my rear-view mirror and treating any vehicle that sits behind me for more than a mile with suspicion. It's not as if I would be able to shake off a tail, though, as most of the route is via winding country lanes, single track in places, and with very few junctions. If I do have even the slightest hint of pursuit, my only option will be to simply drive past and try to circle back. However, by the time I arrive at the gated entrance to the Honourable Gerard's private estate, just outside the market town of Frome, I'm pretty sure there's no one following me, so I pull in and announce myself over an intercom beside two eight-foot iron gates topped with spikes and barbed wire. I can't help thinking that if young Edwin Earnest Icarus ever gets convicted for anything, he's going to feel right at home in a high-security prison. After a series of unintelligible crackles, the gates swing open, and I make my way along the perfectly manicured gravel driveway to a forecourt, in the centre of which sits a fountain of spitting dolphins and pissing cherubs, all in full flow. Clearly, his lordship's obsession with law and order doesn't extend to a concern with saving the planet.

For the second time in two days, my arrival is greeted by a chorus of barks and howls and the sudden appearance of not one, but three dogs. 'Oh, for Christ's sake!' I mutter to myself and prepare to barricade myself behind my already dented driver's door. This time, though, the noise precedes a trio of spaniels fawning around the legs of the master of the house. The prospective parliamentary candidate for North Mendip is in his late fifties, thickset but running to fat, and is treating me to a look that could curdle milk at twenty paces. He is also gripping a very stout walking stick, the main purpose of which, by the look of it, is to beat off troublesome peasants who stray onto his land. He waits at the top of the steps, looking down his bulbous nose at my rust bucket, and as the dogs clearly don't think it's worth adding to the scratches on my paintwork, I take the risk, get out and go to meet him.

'Inspector Crow, I take it,' he says as I reach his level. One of his spaniels sniffs at my leg as though it's a lamppost, thinks better of it and pees against a terracotta pot a few inches from my trouser leg. With a curt, 'Follow me,' Hall-Warner turns and strides back inside, ignoring my outstretched hand. I can't help thinking that Edwin's descent into a life of crime has as much to do with the father as the son.

I follow him – and his spaniels – down the hallway into a sparsely furnished reception room, bare except for two sofas facing each other, a coffee table between them, and one wall lined with tightly stocked bookshelves. There's an almost overpowering smell of damp wood and musty paper, and the sunlight trickling through the French window serves to highlight the general shabbiness of the furniture, the mould creeping under the wallpaper. It's still early in the year, cool enough for a small fire to be burning in the hearth, and the dogs make a beeline for it, jostling for position on the threadbare hearthrug. Hall-Warner waves me to one of the sofas and takes the other for himself.

'I understand you are in charge of the investigation into the theft of Susie Chalmers's animals, Inspector,' he says before I have a chance to speak. 'I should point out that her late husband and I were good friends – Stanley and I were members of the same golf club, you see, as, of course, is ACC Bryce, so it's very important that this matter is successfully resolved as quickly as possible.' He gives me a sickly smile. 'I'm sure you will agree that we must get these thugs under control before they move on from helpless puppies to innocent women and children?'

I manage to stop my fist from clenching, and return what I hope is a smile rather than a snarl. 'And innocent men as well, I hope,' I add, thinking that as far as thugs go, his lordship is pretty near the top of my list. 'I can assure you,' I tell him, 'that everything possible is being done, but unfortunately I am unable to discuss an ongoing investigation with a member of the public. I'm sure you understand.'

The smile falters. 'In that case, Inspector, I fail to see why you are taking up my valuable time.'

'I'm here, *sir*,' I say, letting the emphasis hang for a beat, 'to discuss another matter.'

'Oh, really?' He leans back, prepared to be bored. 'In that case, you'd better get on with it. As I said, my time is valuable, and I would like to waste as little of it as possible.'

'Of course, sir. I'm sure we all have better things to do.' He stiffens, but before he has the chance to spit any more vitriol in my direction, I press on. 'It's really just a courtesy call to inform you of some concerns we have about the recent activities of your son, Edwin.'

I expected a reaction, but Hall-Warner's, when it comes, is what I can only describe as disproportionate. For a moment he just stares at me as if I'm some strange species of poisonous ant, and then leaps to his feet, spluttering with pure rage.

'How dare you!' he hisses, jabbing a finger so close to my face I start to wonder whether a charge of threatening behaviour leading to actual bodily harm would stand up in court. 'How dare you mention that name in my house,' he continues, warming to the theme and spraying spittle onto the coffee table. 'I've made it quite clear that I wish to have nothing to do with that – that *person* – and have no wish to hear about his so-called *activities*. This is a clear breach of the agreement I have with you people, and I won't stand for it. You will stay there, Inspector – what was your name? Inspector Crow, is it? Well, we'll see how long it is before you're back to being the oldest constable in the West Country. I'm going to call your superiors right now, and you can be sure they won't take kindly to this outrageous intrusion.'

He storms out, the dogs on his heels, and slams the door behind him, leaving me to compile a mental list of the many and varied ways in which I can officially make his life unbearable, from parking tickets upwards. He's gone around five minutes, and when he comes back, he's carrying a silver tray with a decanter, two glasses and a jug of water. The dogs rearrange themselves by the fire, and he pauses at the table, looking distinctly – and satisfyingly – uncomfortable. Finally, he sets the tray down and clears his throat.

'I hope you will ... er ...' He searches for the word. Clearly, apologies are not a part of his skill set. 'I hope you will forgive my outburst, Inspector Crow. It's just that ...' He sighs and flops back into his seat. 'It's been very difficult, you know, with Edwin. He's been such a great disappointment, and – we never got on, right from the beginning. I'm sure you understand – you have children, Inspector?' Without waiting for a reply, he lifts the decanter and hovers it over the glasses. 'I'm sure you could do with a drink – I know I could.'

'Thank you, sir, but no,' I say, enjoying the moment. I look at my watch – it's just gone ten thirty. 'It's a little early for me, and in any case, I'm on duty, as they say.'

'Of course, of course.' He hesitates and then pours himself a stiff one and takes a slug. 'So what is it this time?' he asks. 'Drugs, vandalism, dangerous driving? Whatever it is, I'm sure we can – er – come to some arrangement? He only does these things to get back at me and what I stand for. You do your best, but when they reach a certain age ...'

He trails off again, and I can't help thinking of Rosie and all those years of waiting, hoping she would call me, would realise I was still there for her after the divorce and the insidious whisperings of her criminal stepfather. It took a near conviction on a charge of accessory to murder to bring us back together – the only good thing that came out of that episode in my life. I have no doubt Hall-Warner's parenting skills leave a lot to be desired, but even so, I feel just a touch of sympathy for him and recognise the despair in his voice as he talks about his son. It highlights another of the many differences between us – I never gave up hope.

'I'm afraid it's a little more serious than that,' I say, 'as I'm sure was made clear to you just now.' His lip curls in annoyance, confirming my assumption about the outcome of his phone call, but he says nothing. 'Your son has associated himself with some very dangerous criminals, Mr Hall-Warner,' I continue. 'You need to be aware that he may be involved in a number of serious crimes, including the murder of a police officer.'

The air of superiority finally disappears, replaced by pure shock. 'Oh, my God!' He wipes a hand across his brow, which is starting to look distinctly damp. 'You have evidence for any of this?' he demands, making an effort to pull himself together.

'For some of it, yes,' I reply. 'For the murder, not yet, but believe me, sir, it's only a matter of time.'

He's quiet for a long time, mulling things over, although whether his concern is for his son or his political career, it's hard to tell. Finally, he says, 'I can assure you, Inspector, that should Edwin come here, or if I hear of his whereabouts, I will contact the police immediately. I can promise no more than that.'

'That's all I ask,' I say, and get to my feet. He follows me to the door, and as I leave, I hand him a card. 'When you do contact us, make sure you call this number and ask for either DCI Helston or myself. If we are not available, simply leave your name and request an urgent callback and don't speak about this to any of your golf club friends. If you do, it may well make things worse for your son.'

He looks confused, but doesn't argue. I leave him at the top of the steps, the card gripped in his hand, the dogs milling around his feet, and head for my car. I've just fired up the engine when my phone rings.

'Can we meet up, Inspector? I've found something I think might be important.' I can't quite tell whether Larson is excited or nervous.

'Where are you?' I ask.

'Still in Portishead. They've given me a temporary office at headquarters to make it a bit easier to access what I need, and it's far enough away from West Hill to keep me under the radar.'

'I can get there in around an hour,' I tell him, 'and while you're waiting, see if you can swipe some of the chief constable's smoked salmon sandwiches. After the morning I've had, I need a decent lunch.'

10

'What the hell do you call this?' I squint at the plate on Larson's desk, piled with cubes in a garish assortment of colours, reminding me of Ben's collection of Lego bricks.

He gives me an apologetic shrug. 'It's the vegan option,' he explains. 'They didn't have anything else left in the upstairs restaurant. It's actually quite good, but' – he almost grins at my expression, but thinks better of it – 'I thought you'd prefer something else.' He opens a drawer, brings out a foam container and hands it over. I risk lifting the lid and catch the unmistakeable scent of bacon rising from the sandwich inside.

'If you're trying to get on my right side, son ...'

'Perish the thought,' he finishes for me, 'and you're welcome, by the way.' He spears something purple from the plate and chews unenthusiastically while I take the edge off my hunger. He's still looking pretty ragged and, if anything, worse than earlier in the day.

'Okay, son,' I say when my stomach allows me to concentrate, 'what have you got?'

'A few things.' He twists his computer screen so I can see, but hesitates.

'What is it?' I ask.

'Nothing, really. It's just ... well, nothing. I'm fine.'

Like hell he is. 'If you're fine,' I tell him, 'I'm in training for the London bloody marathon. The thing is, son, we have to work together, and if I'm working with someone, I need to know they aren't going to flake out on me when I need them.'

'Have I let you down so far?' he asks, sticking out his chin and trying to look a little more alert.

'No, you haven't,' I reply, 'but if you carry on like this, you will, I damn well guarantee it. So the sooner you tell me what's bothering you, the sooner we can get on with the job, and the happier I'll be.'

There's a short stand-off before he slumps back in his chair, hands up in surrender. 'The murders yesterday,' he starts, his voice a little unsteady, 'the guy you went to see and his wife – she was pregnant.'

I nod. 'Yes, son, I know. Shit happens every day.'

'In your world, yes. Not in mine. When I got home last night, I started to think about Rosie and Ben – and Rosie about to have a baby, you know? And that woman, the one who died, she was killed for no other reason than that someone saw you talking to her husband, right?'

'That's about it. And you're thinking, what happens if whoever is giving information to the killers finds out you're working with me? Will Rosie and Ben be next on the list?'

'Yes. I know it makes me look a bit stupid, but it's something that didn't occur to me when I agreed to do this job –

not that DCI Helston gave me much choice. It was different before. Rosie was in trouble, and I – we – were trying to protect her. But what if I end up being the one putting her in danger?'

I can think of a number of unreasonable comments, but for once the sensible part of my brain takes charge. Besides, I sense he hasn't quite said all he wants to say, and like any good interrogator, I know that interrupting a suspect in full flow is never a good idea. It takes a while, but he finally works up to it.

'How on earth do you cope? I mean, you've been a policeman most of your life. It can't always be like this, can it?'

The naivety of the question almost makes me laugh. 'Son, you're asking the wrong person. I've lost my wife, my home, a decent portion of my brain, and my daughter, at least I did for a while. But no, it isn't always like this – sometimes it's worse.'

He shakes his head in frustration, trying to work out whether I'm being serious. After a little thought he decides I probably am, and says, 'If that's true, why the hell do you keep on doing it? Rosie told me ...' He falters and gives me a nervous glance.

'Go on,' I say. 'Don't stop now – Rosie told you what?'

He takes a deep breath. 'Rosie told me that Christine wanted you back – you know, after all that happened – that she hoped you'd retire and she could stop worrying about you. You wanted that too – so why are you still here?'

I'm hit by a sudden jolt of fury at the idea that he and Rosie spend their time discussing my relationship with Chrissie. I can feel my hands bunching into fists, and make a conscious effort to uncurl my fingers, take a few deep breaths. Larson tenses, very aware that the only thing separating us is two feet of fragile veneered chipboard. He doesn't back down though – just stares at me, waiting for an answer. It takes me a minute, but I'm finally forced to the conclusion that of course he and Rosie are going to discuss family affairs, and in all honesty, it's a question that deserves an answer. If not for his sake, then for Rosie and my grandchildren. As he's pointed out, I'm not the only one in the line of fire – he is too, and, by extension, our shared family.

'I'm here,' I say slowly, 'for the same reason you are. Yes, I've been in the job a long time – maybe too long. But being a police officer isn't just what I do – it's what I am, and I couldn't give it up, not even for Chrissie. Yes, I'm probably a complete bastard, and yes, it's my fault my marriage broke down, but it's also true that if I hadn't been a policeman, Rosie might be in prison now, and Chrissie might be dead. The thing is, son, the world is full of even worse bastards than me, and if I can stop them hurting other families like mine, at least I can say I'm good at something.'

He opens his mouth, but I cut off whatever he was going to say. 'You say you didn't have a choice – that's complete bullshit, son. Grace is a wily fox, and she knows how to turn a screw better than anyone else I know, but you could have said no, and don't bloody tell me you couldn't. And don't tell me you don't know the score either – I'm not the only one who ended up in a hospital bed standing up for law and order, or have you forgotten being fished out of the floating harbour after your little tussle with a serial killer a while ago? You've made the decision, and you knew damn well it would have consequences for your family, but you made it just the same.'

'And you don't think it was a good decision?' he asks.

'Sodding awful,' I reply, 'but as much as you might hate to hear it, it's the same decision I would have made. So, are we going to get on with it or not?'

He nods and gives me the ghost of a smile. 'Okay, here we go. A question first, though – are we investigating a criminal gang or a bent copper?'

I smile. 'Is there a difference?'

'Right, then. I thought I'd focus on the night Sergeant Brent died – or at least when her body was dumped. There were two speed cameras on the route, one on Locking Road and another on the seafront. One wasn't working, and the other clocked the car, but not the driver. There was also CCTV footage from a number of shops, pubs and private houses. Again, some sighted the car, but not in any detail, because most were angled at the pavement rather than the road. It was first picked up just beyond the junction with the M5 and dropped off the radar at the southern end of Beach Road. It was finally found on waste ground in Uphill.'

While he's been talking, he's pulled up a map of the area and follows the route with the tip of his pen. 'So,' he goes on, 'the police have focused on any CCTV on or near the main Uphill Road, between the last sighting and the wrecked car. There are hardly any video security systems in the surrounding residential streets, so it wasn't considered worth the time and manpower. However, there are three pubs off the main road, a few streets back,' he jabs the map with his pointer, 'here, here and here. I thought one or more of them might have cameras, and I couldn't sleep, so went over there this morning before the meeting. I thought it was worth a shot.'

I suddenly see my son-in-law in a different light. 'You

went all the way over to Weston and back before nine o'clock?'

He gives me a tired grin. 'Not quite. I took the laptop and pulled into a car park for the meeting, then came straight here afterwards. I managed to get all the landlords out of bed. One didn't have CCTV, but the other two did. The Fighting Cock, the one closest to the road, only had it for the car park, and I drew a blank for that night. However, the Albion, four roads back, have just had a new system put in, and it covers both the car park and the front of the pub – they had a serious assault outside the entrance around six months ago and thought it was worth covering all bases. The best thing is, it covers both the bar entrance and a good portion of the road outside. Take a look at this.'

He brings up a video, crystal clear and with a wide-angled view extending from the pub doorway right out into the street. The time stamp is 12.32am, and as it plays, three vehicles move through the lens. It's the third, an old, battered Ford Focus, that makes me sit up. The front of the car has clearly suffered a hefty impact, leaving the bumper at an angle, one side of the bonnet crumpled inwards, and a broken nearside headlight. The rear of the car has a tow bar. To my frustration, there isn't enough light to see the driver.

'Bloody hell, son,' I mutter, 'that's it!'

The rear indicator winks, and the car turns left immediately after the pub.

'There's more,' Larson says, and we carry on watching. Just over two minutes later another car, a BMW saloon, follows the same route, turning left. This time, as it moves into shot, another vehicle comes towards it, and for a brief moment the driver's profile is clearly visible, face obscured by a hood. 'The pub car park is just after the turning,' he says, 'but neither car went into it. I'm guessing they knew or assumed it was monitored. The thing is, the installation of the camera on the frontage was only completed a month or so ago, so it's possible they didn't know about it. The next part is the most interesting, though.'

He skips through around five minutes and then, to my utter surprise, a recognisable figure walks into view, coming towards us, face lit up by a streetlamp just out of shot. 'Jesus bloody Christ,' I can't help bursting out, 'Edwin Hall-Warner!'

'You're joking!' Larson says. 'Okay – wait for it.' We don't have to wait long. A minute or so later, the Focus re-emerges from the side street, this time turning right, straight into the same glare from the streetlamp. 'I'm pretty sure that's the same guy who was driving the BMW a minute ago,' Larson says, 'although I will have to do a comparison to confirm it. That's not all, though.'

We fast-forward five minutes, and the BMW reappears, also turning right, into the light. The driver is a different man altogether, stockier in build, with long hair that looks as if it's pulled back into a ponytail, although it's hard to be sure. It's not so much the sight of the driver that suddenly sets off the jitter in my right hand, forcing me to suck in a few deep breaths to calm myself down. It's the sight of another figure in the back of the car, head thrust between the two front seats – the unmistakeable muzzle of a Doberman pinscher. I realise I've leaned forward, gripping the edge of the desk. The words of Kelvin Draper come into my mind – *a special deal, not for the open market, like someone was wanting to start their own kennel.* Kelvin was terrified, and with justification considering how he ended up. So was Shark. Could this possibly be the man everybody is so scared of? At the very least, he could well be a man who has no misgivings about declaring open season on the police, and who is quite happy to take his family pet along to a clean-up operation. It's not one of the stolen animals – the timescale doesn't fit, but even so ...

'Christ almighty,' I say, with genuine feeling, 'have you ever thought of becoming a detective?'

A touch of colour comes back into his face as he recognises the compliment. 'I'm afraid the number plate was blanked out, but I managed to enhance the image a bit, and there's a printout for you to take away.' He closes the file and picks up a book. 'This is probably much less interesting – DS Brent's diary. She didn't keep it on a computer, maybe because she was worried it might get hacked into.'

'Where did she keep it?' I ask.

'In a locked drawer in the apartment she was using as part of her cover. Forensics went over it and found no evidence of tampering, or that anyone else had used the key. That's not to say they didn't, though. Someone could have gotten hold of the key and used gloves, or she might have forgotten to lock it. In any case, whoever it was would have been a guest, as there's no sign of forced entry to the apartment itself.'

'Okay – and you say there was nothing of interest in the diary itself?'

'Nothing I could see – it's all pretty routine stuff, dates of meetings, appointments with doctor, dentist, friends and so on. Even if someone had read it, there's nothing to give any clue she wasn't what she was pretending to be. Maybe you should take a look at it as well, though, just to be sure.'

'I will,' I say, 'although you're probably right. It looks like she did everything by the book as far as covert operations are concerned. If you can print off scans of, say, the two months before her death, I can go through them later. Anything else?'

He nods slowly. 'One more thing. It's a bit …' He hesitates.

'Awkward?' I suggest.

'Difficult,' he concludes. 'Grace wanted another source of evidence on the whereabouts of DI Sillitoe at the time you were visiting Kelvin Draper, so I got hold of the location history for her mobile number. It puts her at the rescue centre at the same time as the image on the CCTV.'

'Shit! I suppose that puts the lid on it, then.'

'It looks like it,' he agrees, 'but there's more. On the night DS Brent was killed, she – or her phone – was less than half a mile away, at the other end of Locking Road. There are also a large number of records locating her on Cabot Rise and the New Park estate. I suppose they could all be perfectly legitimate – it is the main area served by West Hill station, but I think you should know she was on Cabot Rise at roughly the same time you were visiting Jermaine Johnson – that Shark character.'

'Oh, Jesus!' I feel as if one of Shark's minders has just punched me in the stomach. 'Does Grace know?'

'Not yet. I thought I'd run it all past you first.'

I think about this for a minute and make a decision. 'Don't tell her yet. I'd like to take a good look at everything first, okay?'

'If you say so,' he says, 'but are you sure she'll be happy with that?'

'Don't you worry about Grace. That's the thing about the police force, son – there's a hierarchy. She's in charge of me, and I'm in charge of you, so if I tell you to do something and she doesn't like it, it's my fault. What I do want you to do is try to find out where that BMW went. There must be other traffic cameras, both in town and on the routes out of Weston in most directions. Or is that too difficult?'

'Not difficult,' he replies, 'but probably very time consuming if I'm doing it on my own.'

'In that case,' I say, 'you'd better get started. But make sure you get a couple of hours' sleep first – if you go home looking like that, Rosie's going to think you're spending your evenings in a brothel.'

'If she does,' he says, deadly serious, 'I'll simply tell her I was there keeping an eye on you.'

11

I get back home mid afternoon, dump the pile of papers Larson gave me on the coffee table, and head to the kitchen and the coffee jar. It's empty, just like the fridge and most of the food cupboards. After a suitable period of what Dr Rogers, my therapist, would label 'inappropriate language', I grab my coat and head off to the local minimarket a couple of streets away. I've just turned the corner when a group of youngsters on bikes steam towards me at full pelt. I've got more serious things on my mind than chasing after a bunch of kids riding on the pavement, so I thoughtfully step aside, pressing myself against the wall to let them through. By the time I process the fact that one of them has peeled off and is heading straight for me, it's too late. I take the impact on my left shoulder, my head hits the wall with a painful crack, and the next thing I'm aware of is a helmeted head looming over mine, a series of muffled, unintelligible grunts issuing from it.

'What?' I mumble, blinking to clear my blurred vision. 'I don't understand you.'

The helmet disappears, replaced by a woman's face. 'Sorry. Can you hear me now? Are you okay? I've called an ambulance. I saw everything – that kid deliberately went for you. I've called the police as well, and I'll give them a statement. Those little vandals from West Hill ought to be locked up, they've been nothing but trouble since they started coming down here. My name's Becks, by the way. What's yours?'

I can hear the piercing wail of a siren, coming closer, and try to raise my head, only to drop it back as a red-hot poker rams its way through my skull. This time my head makes contact with something soft – my rescuer's leather jacket, I realise. 'Thank you,' I manage to say as the paramedics arrive and bundle me into the ambulance.

'No problem,' I hear her say. 'I'll follow you down, just to make sure you're okay.'

'No need,' I tell her, and then, as if it explains everything, 'I'm a policeman.'

I'M in the middle of a full-blown argument with a duty doctor in the infirmary's A&E – I want to discharge myself, and she doesn't think it's a good idea – when a third contributor to the debate barges through the curtain. 'For God's sake, Al – what the hell have you been up to now?'

The doctor gives me a triumphant look and, with a knowing smile at Chrissie, leaves us to it.

'I got mugged,' I say weakly, 'on my way to the shop.'

'Jesus!' Chrissie dumps her bag on the end of the bed and pulls up a chair. 'You frightened the bloody life out of me.' She sighs and takes my hand. 'Are you all right? What did they say?'

'I'm fine – or I will be as soon as I get back home. Just a bit of a headache, that's all.' I gingerly explore the back of my head and discover a lump the size of an egg around halfway down. 'How long have I been here?'

She checks her watch. 'It's just after seven now, so around four hours.'

'Christ! I have to get back, Chrissie. I need to ...'

At that moment the curtains part again, and Larson walks in. He pecks Chrissie on the cheek and then turns to me. 'I've just had a word with the doctor. She's agreed to let you out as long as there's someone to keep an eye on you for the next twenty-four hours.' He gives me an apologetic shrug. 'I volunteered.'

The stab of gratitude that runs through my mind translates itself into, 'Is Rosie happy with that?'

He rolls his eyes, but he's grinning. 'She's fine with it. She took a pile of groceries and some of my things round when she picked Ben up from school.'

For once, the object of Chrissie's displeasure isn't me. 'For God's sake, John, you're as bad as he is! He needs to be in a hospital bed, where someone can keep a proper eye on him.'

'He'll be fine with me, Chris,' Larson says. 'Don't worry. I'll lend him my watch.'

This statement means nothing to me, and I'm starting to get annoyed at being spoken about as if I'm not here, so I squeeze Chrissie's hand and slowly haul myself upright. 'I'll do as I'm told, I promise,' I say.

Chrissie grunts. 'You'd bloody well better, or you'll be back in here before your feet touch the ground!' She turns to my son-in-law. 'I'll tell Rosie to come over to us tonight.' She gives him the sort of glare she usually reserves for me. 'After all, somebody's got to look out for her.' With that, she sweeps out, leaving Larson gaping after her, shuffling his feet like a schoolboy.

I can't help but laugh, even though it sends needles of pain through my long-suffering brain. 'Don't worry about it, son,' I say, trying to slip my feet into my shoes. 'You'll get used to it.'

'I'm not sure I want to,' he replies, staring apprehensively at the still fluttering curtain. 'You want any help?'

Thankfully, I manage to fumble through tying my shoelaces. 'No. It's all good. Come on, let's get out of here – I only went out to get coffee!'

A COUPLE of painkillers and a bowl of my ex-mother-in-law's chicken soup later, I finally get my mug of coffee. Larson finishes up in the kitchen and joins me in the lounge, my jacket in one hand and a puzzled expression on his face.

'You say you were mugged by a gang of kids, right?' he asks.

I try to nod, but give up as the lump on my head reminds me that any sudden movement is a bad idea. 'I definitely got that impression. Why?'

He reaches into my jacket and pulls out my wallet. 'Looks like they weren't very good at it, then.'

He hands it to me, and I can tell before I open it that nothing is missing, not even the fifty quid or so in cash. 'It doesn't make sense,' I say, turning the wallet over in my hand. 'I know the way those kids operate – stun and run. They can knock a victim over and lift a wallet in seconds, sometimes watch and jewellery as well.' I open it, just to double-check. 'Everything's here – what the bloody hell is going on?'

While I've been talking, Larson has been rifling through my jacket, and brings out a neatly folded sheet of paper. 'What's this?'

He starts to unfold it, but when I realise it isn't anything I recognise, instinct cuts through the fuddle in my brain, and I shout, 'Stop!' He freezes, startled, and I point to the coffee table. 'Put it down – right now!'

He does as he's told. 'Why?' he asks, and then, realising, 'Oh, shit! Sorry.'

'There should be a few pairs of surgical gloves in one of the kitchen drawers,' I say, and, when he raises an eyebrow, 'There's nothing worse than getting called out to a crime scene in the middle of the night and having to stand and watch like a bloody idiot because SOCO claim they haven't got any spare gloves.'

'I can see how that might be annoying,' he says, and fetches two pairs of gloves from the kitchen, together with a clear plastic freezer bag.

It's clear, once Larson has laid the paper out flat, that it's a page from a book – a pretty hefty textbook if the size and density of the print is anything to go by. It's also definitely not in English. Most of the letters are in a script that looks totally alien. 'Don't take it the wrong way,' I say, 'but is this all Greek to you?'

He nods. 'Yes, I'm pretty sure that's exactly what it is.' He pulls his laptop out of its case, and while it's firing up, he takes a photo of the page that's face up. I decide not to ask him what the hell he's doing, but he tells me anyway. 'We should be able to translate the extract and find the exact book from a scan of the page,' he says. 'I guess we can assume that the text itself is important in some way, as there are no other markings.'

'Agreed. Plus,' I add, 'it hasn't been torn out. It's been very carefully removed, probably using a razor blade. Whoever did that might have been keen to conceal the fact that a page was missing. So what the hell is this about?'

'Greek mythology, by the look of it,' he replies, with an expression that tells me he's as mystified as I am. He taps at his keyboard for a minute or so and then looks up with a grin. 'Got it. *The Concise History of Greek Mythology*. But why? If it's some sort of coded message, it has to be one the sender was confident we could work out. Otherwise, what's the point?'

'Jesus bloody Christ,' I mutter under my breath. 'Have we just joined the Secret sodding Seven? We'll be making ourselves badges out of coat buttons next!' Larson gives me a confused look, clearly wondering if the bang on the head has had more serious consequences than he thought. 'Don't worry, son,' I tell him. 'I suppose you're far too young to have grown up on Enid Blyton.'

'Ah,' he says, with a grin. 'I was more into the Famous Five myself. I doubt if either is going to help us answer the question, though.' He goes through a few more mouse clicks. 'It's a page from a chapter entitled *The Graeae and the Gorgons*. The section is on the Gorgons, and Medusa in particular. Mean anything?'

I try to think, but end up shaking my head. 'Not a bloody thing. All I know about Medusa is that she had snakes for hair and turned anyone who looked at her to stone, and I only know that because of Ray Harryhausen.'

'Yeah, I saw *Clash of the Titans* too.' He muses for a moment. 'I wonder ...'

Whatever he was going to say is interrupted by a sharp rap at my front door, making both of us jump. 'Check who it is before you open it, son,' I tell him.

'Yes, *Dad*,' he replies with a smirk, and leaves me seething on the sofa. He really is starting to get above himself.

A few seconds later, Grace bustles into my lounge, looking distinctly rattled. 'I called the hospital,' she says, in a tone that is, if anything, more accusing than Chrissie's. 'They said you had discharged yourself – against medical advice.' She sniffs and folds her arms. 'Bloody idiot!'

'I'm recovering nicely, ma'am, thanks for asking,' I reply, 'and if that's a bag of grapes in your hand, you're welcome to share them with my nursemaid.'

She snorts out a laugh. 'Grapes?' She drops the bag into my lap. 'It's a get well present from George – what do you think?'

I risk opening it, and count four very unhealthy-looking Cornish pasties. 'Tell George it's probably the best death threat I've had in a while, but if he's after my job, it won't work.'

'I'll pass it on,' she says, with a grin. 'Meanwhile, perhaps we can catch up on progress, seeing as I'm here – if you're up to it, that is.'

Larson comes back with more coffee, and I let him take Grace through the evidence he's managed to gather. She's going to find out what's happening with her acting DI sooner or later, and I've run out of reasons to explain Polly's actions. When he tells her about Sillitoe, she's quiet for a long time, simply shaking her head in disbelief. Finally, she comments, 'Fucking hell!' and nods for him to continue. He replays the videos from the CCTV outside the Albion pub.

'Dear God,' she whispers under her breath, and then, 'What the bloody hell is happening here? Edwin Hall-Warner might be a toerag, but I would never have put him down as a murderer – he's a two-bit delinquent, for Christ's sake, and you're saying he killed Vicky Brent?'

'We're not saying anything,' I say. 'There's no evidence he actually killed her, and all this footage tells us is that he was in the same place as the car involved in the so-called hit-and-run. It's all circumstantial, but whatever else he did, I'd put money on him being the driver who ran over her dead body. Not only that, I'd say he was most likely present at her death.'

Grace nods and picks up the enlarged images of the BMW driver that Larson gave me earlier. 'So who's this guy – the one with the dog?'

'We don't know,' Larson puts in, 'at least, not yet. I'm running the image through various UK databases, but nothing's come up so far.'

'Okay.' She turns to the latest puzzle, now safe in a plastic bag. 'Al, are you sure this was deliberately put in your pocket?'

I give her a look. 'Do I look like I'd be carrying bits of a Greek textbook around?'

She grunts. 'Fair enough. So what does it mean, if anything?'

'We don't know that either,' I say, 'except that it's a page from a book on Greek mythology, and the subject is the Gorgon Medusa.'

'And if I click my heels three times, I might end up back in the real world?' She gets up and goes over to the French window, stares out into my garden. 'What the fuck is going on, Al?'

I don't have an answer, and neither does Larson, so we sit, huddled in our own thoughts, which in my case extend as far as the pattern on the rug under the coffee table.

Suddenly, Grace straightens and snatches up the CCTV images. She pulls one out and hands it to Larson. 'Can you clean this up any more?'

'I might be able to. Is there a particular area you want to look at?'

'Here.' She sets the picture down on the table and points at the steering wheel. 'His hand,' she says. 'He's wearing a ring, a signet of some sort, with a design engraved on it. Can you tidy it up?'

He squints at it, considering. 'It's possible, but I'd have to use some software to fill in the blanks. At least half of it is obscured, so the result would only be an approximation.'

'Do it.'

He nods and sets to work on his laptop. Grace sits next to me and blows out a long breath. 'I know it's a lot to ask, Al, but ...'

'But you're going to ask anyway,' I say, and reach across to squeeze her hand. 'You want me to trail Polly.'

'It's a shit job,' she says, 'but you're the only one in a position to do it – a glorified dog catcher on the trail of a Doberman. If she gets wind, at least you have some kind of reason. Plus, you can track a suspect better than anyone else I know.'

I stifle a laugh. 'Sod off, Grace.' Then, meeting her eye, 'Assuming I'm still alive and not in a coma by morning, I'll do it. Like you say, it's a shit job, but somebody has to.' After a brief pause, I ask, 'What do you want to do about Hall-Warner?'

'Nothing, for now,' she replies. 'As yet we only have circumstantial evidence, and if we pick him up, it might spook the bigger fish. My only worry is that the longer he's around them, the more of a liability they'll think he is. I have a feeling he's pretty high on their redundancy list.'

I feel her body tense just a little at this last observation. 'People make their own choices,' I remind her. 'We just clear up after the bad ones. We can't afford moral dilemmas – it's not in our job description.'

We're saved from further philosophical musings by Larson, who sits back and exclaims, 'Bloody hell's teeth!'

Grace and I exchange a look. 'What have you got, son?' I ask.

He swivels the laptop so we can both see the screen. It's filled by a close-up image of the ring on the middle finger of the BMW driver's right hand. It's a contorted face, mouth open in a horror-movie vampire-like gape, wide eye sockets set with gemstones of some kind. The hair is a nest of stylised writhing snakes.

'What I've got,' he says, still looking stunned at his discovery, 'is the Medusa.'

12

I wake up around 8am with a clear head and a sharp pain in my wrist where Larson's smart watch has done its best to stamp a permanent indentation. The thing has apparently been transmitting my vital statistics to his phone all night, rigged to set off an alarm at the first sign I might shuffle off my mortal coil in my sleep. I hand it back to him at breakfast with an inward sigh of relief and an outward expression of thanks.

'Believe me,' he says, with a grin, 'my motives are purely selfish. If I hadn't got you out of that hospital, you'd have been impossible to work with by this morning.'

'Son,' I tell him, 'you're developing a very good talent for understatement.'

In addition to making scrambled eggs on toast, he insists on driving me over to West Hill, just to be safe. 'Besides,' he says, 'if I see you up to your office, it's a chance for me to get in and see Grace face to face without anyone realising what I'm doing.'

I have to admit he's got a point, so, an hour later, we turn up at the station doing a fairly passable imitation of a conscientious relative shepherding an unreasonable and slightly fuddled father-in-law who has insisted, against all advice, on getting back to work. When I catch George's concerned look as we go past the front desk, I can't help thinking the act is too close to the truth for comfort.

We're just coming up to the lift when the CID office door opens, and Polly Sillitoe emerges, a model of business-like efficiency in pinstripe trouser suit and stilettos, her blonde hair scraped into a neat bun. She pauses mid-stride, eyes widening when she sees us, and I feel Larson stiffen beside me. So far, since my return, Sillitoe and I have done a pretty good job of avoiding each other. This time, though, there's nowhere to go, and she recovers her poise almost instantly, paints on a smile and carries on towards us.

'Inspector Crow,' she says, with a nod, and then, to my son-in-law, 'It's Mr Larson, isn't it? It's good to see you again. Everything's okay with your wife and mother-in-law, I hope?' She holds out a hand.

Larson grasps it. 'Everything's fine, Inspector,' he answers smoothly. 'Rosie is about to have a baby, and Christine is fully recovered now – partly thanks to you, of course.'

'That's good to hear,' she says, 'although it's only acting inspector ...' she turns back to me before adding, 'for the moment.' Her expression melts into concern. 'I heard what happened yesterday. It's lucky you weren't too badly hurt – we were all worried. I've got one of my DCs helping uniform out, but you know what it's like trying to chase down a bunch of kids from Cabot Rise.'

'Thanks, Polly,' I reply, 'I appreciate the thought, but like you say, it's going to be a complete waste of time. You'd be better off putting all your resources into the Draper murders.'

The concerned look disappears. 'Thanks for the advice – I'll bear it in mind.'

She takes a step past us. 'By the way, Polly,' I call after her, and she stops, looks back over her shoulder. 'Any news on the Vicky Brent investigation? I'm a bit out of the loop up there in my little broom cupboard.'

She gives a bitter laugh. 'Chance would be a fine thing. They've handed it over to Weston and Worle completely – won't give us a look in, say we're "too involved", whatever the fuck that means. If I hear anything, I'll be sure to let you know – I'm sure the fastest route to the broom cupboard is on Google Maps somewhere.'

She clacks her way along the corridor and out to the front desk. Larson raises an eyebrow. 'Ouch!' he comments.

'Don't worry about it, son,' I say. 'She's only doing what all good newly promoted coppers do – marking her territory. Some decide to start off at a new station, with people who didn't know them in the lower ranks. Staying put means having to stamp your authority over both former equals and superiors, and that's not easy, especially as most of them are tough bastards like me.'

The lift arrives, and we are on our way up before he comments, 'And particularly difficult if your loyalties are divided, I would imagine.'

I call Grace as soon as we get to my office, and she comes down to join us. 'I'm fine,' I tell her before she has a chance to make a discussion out of it.

She glances at Larson for confirmation, but he just shrugs, so she shuts down the topic with, 'Glad to hear it,' and moves on. 'I've gone through the location pings on Sillitoe's mobile, and checked the timings against her duty records. All the relevant instances are when she was officially off duty.' She looks at Larson. 'I could ask you to go through the records of the rest of her team, just in case she wasn't alone, but I suspect it would take too long and not tell us more than we know already.'

'Perhaps not as long as you think,' Larson replies, 'and it might confirm that we are only looking at one person, for now at least?'

'I was hoping you'd say that,' she says. 'In the meantime, I have some interesting information. After I left you last night, I called an old friend in the National Crime Agency. I've followed up with an official request, but thought it may save some time.' She grins. 'He wasn't too happy at being pulled out of a family party – until I sent him a copy of that CCTV image. He called me back around two this morning. We should get the full file later today, but the bottom line is that several forces, including Interpol and Europol, have been after a group known as Medusa for a few years now, but with very little success. All they know is that it's centred somewhere in Greece, has probably been operating on a large scale in several countries for at least ten years, and started to make inroads in the UK around five years ago, mainly in Glasgow, Birmingham and Bristol – I suppose they figure the provincial forces are less of a threat than the Met, and so far, damn it, they've been right.'

'So if they've known about this group for at least five years, why haven't we picked up on it before now?' I ask. 'Or does the NCA think we're just a bunch of bloody yokels, too stupid to handle serious crime? For Christ's sake, Grace!'

Grace gives me a grim smile. 'I wish it were that simple, Al. But the fact is, they are operating an MO we haven't really come across before, not on the scale we're looking at. The truth is, they are too fucking clever, even for the NCA and Interpol. They don't give a toss about the police – in fact, I doubt we even register as a threat on their radar. That's because the first thing they do is infiltrate the local force, make sure they know where we are and what we're doing before we've so much as got out of bed. There's no way of knowing how long our movements have been monitored. It could be weeks, or years.' She pauses, shaking her head, unwilling to voice the conclusion we're all coming to. 'Their main targets,' she goes on, 'are the local gangs. It makes sense – I mean, why set up your own organisation when you can hide behind dozens of small-time kingpins. They learn their way around the local area and then make offers the gang leaders can't refuse. One or two do, of course, but the others snap into line when the bodies start turning up, usually in bits with evidence of a long and very painful death. Us plods have been happy enough to put it all down to local disputes – another dealer off the street and move on, yes? You can bet nobody is going to make a complaint, unless they fancy a few days of torture and a body bag. Meanwhile, Medusa has taken over, and the local police don't even know they exist.' She looks at us, the steely determination that I love her for clear in her eyes. 'Now we do know, and by Christ, we're going to get these bastards, and bugger the NCA!'

'So what about the BMW driver?' I ask. 'Any information on him?'

'Ah.' She shifts in her chair, preparing for another revelation. 'According to my friend, he's pretty high up in the organisation. Sightings are rare, and he only turns up where there is a problem that needs his – how can I put it – expertise? They haven't managed to get even close to his real identity, but they do know his nickname within Medusa. They all have monikers reflecting their function within the organisation. His is *Alastor*. He is, apparently, their head troubleshooter – the Greek god Alastor represents retribution, the male equivalent of Nemesis. He's essentially a globetrotting assassin sent to sort out difficulties with the locals. If a lucrative deal goes wrong, or someone decides to rip Medusa off, he sorts it out and disappears. Believe it or not, the screenshot I sent over is one of only two pictures anyone has of him, and both are very low quality. Still, better than nothing.'

'So something's gone wrong, and he's here to sort it out?'

She nods. 'My bet is that the West Country gangs aren't playing ball. He's been sent in to whip them into line.'

'And somebody,' I say, 'is resisting, to the point of knocking me over and leaving a hint in my pocket, hoping the police will help out. Jesus fucking Christ!'

I'm already pretty sure who that might be, but Grace carries on. 'I'm hoping to get fingerprints off that page – should be through any time now. Then we'll know for sure.'

Or not, I think sourly. Shark isn't that stupid. 'It's worth a try,' I say, 'but don't hold your breath. It does explain why all the local villains are so jumpy, though.' It takes me another minute to realise the full implications of what Grace is telling us, and all of a sudden my stomach is ice. 'Something went wrong three years ago, didn't it? That big drug deal on Cabot Rise was a Medusa operation, and me and Joe Bailey walked straight into it.' I grab the picture off the desk and stare at it, feeling a little sick. 'The locals tried to get one over on the organisation; this bastard turned up to straighten things out, and fucking well shot us without a second thought. Is that what you're saying, Grace?'

'It's highly likely,' she says quietly, 'but not certain. For my money, though, yes, Al, I think that's what happened, and yes, this piece of shit, whoever he is, is the one who put a hole in your head and murdered Joe.' She pauses, clearly struggling between sympathy and pragmatism. 'I know you want him, Al,' she goes on. 'So do I, but I need you to remember that it isn't just about you and Joe. The odds are he's responsible for Vicky Brent as well, and God knows how many others. I'm relying on you to keep your head well down and not do anything stupid, you understand me?'

I give her my most innocent look, which, to be fair, has never been that successful. 'You know me, Grace.'

Her response is a dubious grunt. Larson, meanwhile, looks as if he has something on his mind, but is prevented from sharing by a trill from Grace's mobile. As she listens, her brow starts to furrow, and when she ends the brief call, she turns to us, puzzled. 'The lab has lifted some prints off that page. There were two sets – one was yours, John, but we expected that. The others belong to an adult, but there's no match with anyone on our records.'

'So if it was the kid who ran into me, he was wearing gloves?' I ask. 'That sounds a bit sophisticated. It's possible, but I don't buy it.'

'Weren't you knocked out?' Larson puts in. 'Maybe someone put it in your pocket while you were unconscious.'

'I was only out for a second – more stunned than anything else. I'm sure I would have noticed ...' As I'm talking, I replay the incident in my mind. 'The motorcyclist – the woman who called the ambulance. She was there almost as soon as I hit the ground. She said she was going to give a statement. Did anyone get her details?'

'A PC took her statement at the scene,' Grace replies. 'I'll get him to bring her in. If she's got nothing to hide, she can't object to having her prints taken for elimination purposes; plus, if she was just an innocent bystander, she might have seen something that isn't in her statement, so it's worth pursuing.'

Larson, who has been fiddling with his tablet for the last ten minutes, finally gets his chance to butt in. 'You said you think Medusa have been operating in this area for around five years?'

Grace nods. 'About that, yes. Why?'

'I've just looked up Polly Sillitoe's record,' he says. 'I was thinking about what the inspector said, about officers moving to different forces when they get promoted. She started off as a DC in Birmingham and stepped sideways to Weston and Worle just over five years ago.' He looks at me. 'She made sergeant some six months before the shootings in West Hill, but even though there were three vacancies at the time in West Country divisions, she didn't apply for any of them. Sergeant Bailey's death left a post vacant at West Hill, and she was on it before the ink on the death certificate was dry.' He catches my expression at his poor turn of phrase and adds, 'Sorry, Inspector.'

'So what are you trying to say, son?' I snap, even though I see the implication well enough, and so does Grace.

He hesitates, his cheeks colouring slightly. 'I might be wrong ...'

'For fuck's sake, John,' I say, bringing him up short at the sound of his name, 'you don't need to spare my feelings – you should know by now I haven't got any. What you're trying to say is that Joe's murder wasn't the result of being in the wrong place at the wrong time. He was the target all along, and the tip-off we got about the drug deal was a set-up to get us out there, clear the path for Sillitoe to jump into his shoes.'

'Jesus bloody Christ,' Grace comments, and then adds, 'If that's true, it also means that the killer knew precisely who would be conducting the raid, and that he intended to get rid of you as well, Al. He probably couldn't believe his luck when he got both of you with one bullet – it added to the impression of it all being unplanned, and you getting caught in the crossfire.' She rubs a hand across her brow, frowning. 'No,' she says at last. 'It's too random – possible, and we have to consider it, but from their point of view far too much risk of things going wrong. Staged "accidents" are much more their style. Besides ...' Again, she shakes her head. 'I'm not prepared to draw any premature conclusions about the actions of DI Sillitoe – not yet, and not unless we have more evidence. Right now, she's a suspect, and I won't go any further than that.'

'Nevertheless,' Larson persists, turning to me, 'if you were a target back then, won't he see your survival as a failure, and you being back at work as a threat?'

There's a long silence, during which Grace glares at me, daring me to voice my thought. Eventually I say, with a grim smile, 'I hope so, son – I bloody well hope so.'

13

A couple of hours and several dire threats from Grace later, I'm escorted back home by my son-in-law. The official line is that, as the medics have recommended light duties following the bang on the head, I'm working from home, catching up on paperwork. Larson is staying over for a few days until the family is certain I'm fully recovered. Aside from continuing his electronic enquiries, his main purpose is to make sure I'm accompanied whenever I leave the house. Grace isn't taking any chances and can't risk assigning an officer to keep me under observation in case the true nature of our investigation leaks out. As if that weren't enough, she has also arranged an unmarked car from a neighbouring force for my use, figuring that my rust bucket is far too recognisable, and cars in our own pool might be too easily tracked to me. I did point out that if it was parked outside my house, and if my house was being watched, the whole exercise would be pointless. Undeterred, she's been in touch with my elderly neighbour, who doesn't own a car but has the rare advantage of a garage opening onto the small track that runs the length of the terrace behind the gardens, out of public view. Of course, like most of the law-abiding public, and much to my frustration on this occasion, he is always ready to assist the police.

I head for the kitchen to sort out lunch, and when I emerge, I find Larson pacing up and down in the garden. I go out to join him, and we both sit at the table with a plate of my speciality, cheese and pickle sandwiches, between us.

'Whatever's on your mind, son,' I say, when after five minutes he hasn't said a word, 'it might be a good idea to share – at least, that's what my therapist always tells me.'

He blinks, as if only just realising where he is. 'Sorry. It's just – it doesn't make sense.' I can see he's trying to get his points in order, so give him room to think. 'It's the dogs,' he says, reaching for a sandwich. 'Kelvin Draper said Chalmers's dogs were taken to order for someone high up the criminal food chain who specifically wanted Dobermans, or at least that's what he implied, right?' I nod, and he goes on. 'Okay. Then we see Medusa's resident assassin in a car with a Doberman, looking like they're best friends, and naturally assume it belongs to him – but have you ever heard of an international hit man who travels the world with his pet dog? It would be like putting a flag out with his name on it.'

It's a good point. 'So if it's not his dog,' I say, 'it has to belong to the other guy in the BMW. What do we know about him?'

'So far, nothing,' he replies. 'The image we have is simply a figure in a hood, and there's not much we can do with that.'

I mull this over for a few minutes and decide. 'I want you to go through all the airline records you can find of Dobermans being transported worldwide, but particularly into and out of Greece over the last, say, five years, and see if there are any frequent flyers out there.'

He almost chokes on his sandwich. 'You have got to be kidding me! Do you have any idea how many airlines there are, how many flights? Since the quarantine rules were relaxed, the world and his wife take their dog on holiday these days. It could take days or even weeks, if it's possible at all.'

'Better get started, then,' I say. He gives me a look that indicates I might have finally lost it. 'I haven't gone mad,' I reassure him, 'or I don't think so, not yet. I do have a feeling though – the kind of feeling that's kept me in this job for as long as you've been alive. It's a sort of itch in the back of my neck, and I've learned, over the years, not to ignore it. If I'm wrong, you can complain all you like later, but until we know for sure, just humour me – please?'

He sighs. 'If you think it's that important, I'll do my best. There's something else – I was doing some thinking ...'

'Be careful, son. I've got enough of a headache already.'

'I was thinking,' he repeats, an edge in his voice, 'that if my assumption is right, and you were a target in that raid three years ago, they could have been looking to replace you with one of their people as well as Sergeant Bailey. It could be worth following up, don't you think?'

Now that he's mentioned it, I realise we have to consider it, even though I'm not convinced. I'm not really worried about my own safety. As long as I'm no longer threatening the aims of the organisation, I'm likely way under their radar – for now, at any rate. The situation might well change, of course, if they get wind of what I'm trying to do. What does concern me is the possibility that there is more than one informant within the force, and that if Polly Sillitoe really is bent, she's not working alone – *if* Polly's bent, and *if* Larson is right – there are, I tell myself, just too many ifs.

'I suppose it's worth looking into,' I reply, and add, unreasonably, 'I didn't know you cared.'

His jaw tightens, but at that moment both our mobiles decide to burst into a duet of loud squawks, resulting in an echo of the old hand tremor as I try to retrieve mine from my trouser pocket. It's a reminder that I have my monthly therapy session with Rogers at two this afternoon. There was a time when I would have simply ignored it, just to wind him up. More recently, I've ignored it because grappling with sending a text message is more than my level of patience can handle. Undeterred, Rogers has now included a link in his messages, so all I need to do is tap on it to let him know I can't, or won't, make it. I tap on the link and turn my attention back to Larson, whose fingers are flying across the screen so fast they are almost a blur. After a minute of this, he jumps up, goes inside and comes back out with his laptop.

'Sillitoe is on the move,' he explains, and after another flurry of tapping, 'According to the duty record, she was working overtime all night, went home an hour ago, and now she's on her way to Weston-super-Mare.'

'It could be nothing,' I suggest, grasping at any reasonable explanation. 'People are allowed out when they aren't working – maybe she's gone shopping or something.'

'Would you, after a twenty-four-hour shift?' he asks. 'If I were her, I'd be ordering a takeaway and getting my head down.'

I can't argue with that, so I get to my feet and grab my jacket. Larson, predictably, objects. 'Wherever you're going, you can't go alone,' he points out. 'Those are the DCI's instructions.'

'And you have your instructions from me,' I snap, 'which you rightly tell me are going to take a good while, so bugger the DCI – I need to know what Polly is up to.'

'Agreed,' he says, 'but how exactly are you going to do that if you don't know where she is? Weston's a big place, and the tracking data is routed through to my mobile.'

He's got me in a corner, and by the satisfied look on his face, he knows it. 'Jesus bloody Christ,' I mutter under my breath, and wonder if he hasn't been taking lessons from Grace on how to target my weak spots, one of which, naturally, is technology. 'Sod it!' I manage. 'Come on, then, but if we both wind up murdered by the mob, just remember, you'll be the one explaining to Chrissie.'

AN HOUR LATER, we're in the warren of back streets behind Weston's seafront, edging past rows of parked cars taking up both sides of the streets, leaving inches to spare on either side. It's another twenty minutes before I spot Sillitoe's Toyota wedged into a gap between two transit vans halfway down a particularly narrow lane of two-up two-downs on one side, a builders' yard on the other.

'She's three streets away,' Larson tells me, without looking up from his mobile, 'or at least her phone is. Maybe we should go on foot from here?'

I nod my agreement, but it's easier said than done. In the first place, I don't want to park too close to Sillitoe's car and risk bumping into her when she returns to it. The streets are narrow, with no alleys to duck into if needed. Secondly, there simply are no spaces big enough to wedge the oversized saloon we've been assigned to. Even though it's still early in the tourist season, the area is close enough to the seafront to be bloated by the cars of visitors unwilling to pay the prices of the multi-stories closer to the promenade. We, on the other hand, have an expense account, and it's a short enough walk. Plus, it reduces the chance we'll be spotted. Larson keeps an eye on the blip on his screen while I head for the car park above the town's mall and grab a space closest to the lift.

'She hasn't moved,' Larson says as we hit the street behind the mall, 'three roads back, and according to Google Maps, it's a café of some sort. Maybe she's meeting someone?'

Somehow, that thought doesn't fill me with confidence. 'You can be that accurate?' I ask, not quite able to put the same faith in gadgets as my son-in-law.

He nods. 'More or less, yes. With a good signal we can pinpoint to within a few metres, and thankfully she hasn't turned off GPS. I doubt she's even thought of it – most people don't.'

We've reached the turning and stop at the corner, trying to look inconspicuous – easier for Larson, dressed in jeans and a sweater, than me in my regulation CID suit and tie. Luckily, the locals here are well used to unfamiliar faces wandering about consulting tourist maps and, these days, phones. The road is wider and busier than the older streets between the mall and the promenade. There is even a pedestrian crossing a hundred metres or so along, linking a small row of businesses on one side – minimart, off-licence, café and charity shop – with a row of run-down 1960s bungalows on the other and, further down, a modern terrace jammed into what probably used to be a patch of green space. The bungalows all have the telltale ramps and grab rails of council housing for the elderly and disabled. In other words, from a policeman's point of view, they might as well have 'Break in and help yourself' daubed across the front door in big red letters. The other thing that strikes me is that if Sillitoe is in the café and decides to come out as we are walking down the street, there's no way she won't see us despite the flow of vehicles and pedestrians.

Larson has clearly had the same thought. 'If we stand around here much longer,' he says, 'we might as well have blue lights on our heads.'

I'm thinking of an answer when the door to one of the bungalows opens, and two figures step out onto the street, one of them very familiar. 'Bloody hell – it's Edwin Hall-Warner!'

For a minute I'm frozen, but a painful nudge in the ribs jolts me into action as I realise they are walking straight towards us. Larson pulls me into a tiny boutique a couple of doors behind us, stuffed with 1970s-style Indian skirts and scarves, startling a woman hunched over a till in the corner, who eyes us suspiciously through a haze of incense smoke. I keep my eye on the street while Larson makes a show of browsing through a rack of gaudy scarves, selects one and takes it to the till. As he's paying for it, I see Hall-Warner and his companion stride past the window. Thanks to the billowing incense, I don't have to fake my warning cough, and we spill out onto the pavement just in time to see them head off towards the mall.

'What do we do?' Larson asks, clutching a bright orange chiffon scarf with green polka dots, the sight of which is making me wish I hadn't had lunch.

'Stick with Polly for now – and for God's sake, put that

thing in your pocket. What the hell did you buy it for anyway?'

He shrugs, embarrassed. 'I thought I ought to, just to be polite. Do you think Rosie will like it?'

'If you give her that,' I tell him, 'she'll be filing for divorce before she gives birth – that is, if we don't get arrested first. It's not a scarf, it's an offensive weapon!'

He shoves it into his jeans, and we head back to the corner. 'I'd bet that the other guy was the one on the CCTV, driving the BMW,' he says. 'He's the right build, and his face fits the profile, insofar as we have one.'

'It's likely,' I reply, 'and as long as he's with our Eddie, the regulars can keep tabs on them for now.' Hall-Warner fades to the back of our minds, though, as we reach our inadequate surveillance spot just in time to see Polly Sillitoe emerge from the café, cross the road and knock at the door to the bungalow he and his friend have just vacated. She's discarded the business suit and is dressed in the same jeans and hoodie as the image we caught at the wildlife rescue centre. We watch, mesmerised, as the door is answered by an elderly woman clutching a Zimmer frame, and after a short conversation, she goes inside, and the door closes.

Larson and I exchange a look and, by unspoken agreement, set off towards the bungalows. As we get closer, we can see a narrow pedestrian alleyway threaded between the last of the older, Victorian buildings and the bungalows. We cross and dive into it, praying that Sillitoe doesn't decide to use it as part of her exit route. The first section of the alley is bordered by high brick walls, but a couple of hundred metres down, we hit a transverse path running along the end of the back gardens of the bungalows, the boundary marked by a simple six-foot chain-link fence. The target property is third in the row and, by the look of it, the most neglected. Like the path we're on, the garden is completely overgrown, the back fence covered in brambles and bindweed. There's a large shed next to the fence, but unlike the rest of the garden, it seems to have been kept in reasonably good condition – suspiciously good, with what looks like brand-new bitumen felt covering the roof.

'I need to get closer,' I tell Larson. He nods, and we head along the fence, trying to keep our heads down, to the relative safety of the choking greenery, which effectively hides us from anyone looking through the back windows.

The first thing I notice is that the edge of the wire fence has been neatly cut where it meets a supporting concrete post, from the ground to a height of about four feet. The vegetation effectively conceals the break, but anyone who knew it was there could easily bend the fence back to enter the rear of the property, closing the gap behind them. It's Larson who alerts me to the second, far more serious addition to the old lady's back garden. He taps my shoulder and, with a finger to his lips, points upwards to the roof of the shed. I follow his direction and at first see nothing, but then, just visible in the afternoon sunlight, I see it – the tiny pulsing red light of a surveillance camera. Instinctively we both crouch down and watch as the pulse disappears, then reappears – the bloody thing is moving, sweeping from the back door of the bungalow, through the garden and across the fence we are hiding behind. It probably takes in the path we're on as well. I nod my understanding, and in a series of gestures, just in case it's rigged for sound as well as vision, Larson tells me that retracing our steps to the road isn't an option.

As we prepare to move further along towards the far end

of the path, hoping it isn't blocked off, a door opens, and we hear voices – two, both female. The thin, reedy tone of an elderly woman is saying something about lettuce and asparagus. The second woman replies – unmistakably Polly Sillitoe. Footsteps come towards us on the other side of the fence, and we both freeze, not daring to breathe. Thankfully, they stop, there's a good deal of rustling – pulling vegetables from the overgrown beds, by the sound of it – and they retreat up to the house. We hear the back door close, and silence returns. I give it another minute, then gesture to Larson, who nods, and keeping low, we make our way to the end of the path where, to my relief, there's a gap wide enough for us to squeeze between the fence and the start of a garage block out into a tarmac lane running parallel with the main road back towards town.

'Jesus bloody Christ!' Larson comments, trying to pick goose grass out of his expensive sweater as we walk back towards the car park. 'What was all that about?'

'I don't know, son,' I reply, 'but I've got a pretty good general idea. I'd give a lot to know what's in that shed.'

'Whatever it is, there's a state-of-the-art surveillance system installed on it,' he says. 'If it's the type I think it is, it's sending a live feed to a computer, which could be just about anywhere. I've only ever seen that kind of security on banks, high-end jewellers and military installations.'

We walk the rest of the way in silence and are on our way back to Bristol before I finish getting my thoughts in order. 'You've heard of cuckooing?' I ask Larson, and he nods.

'A criminal gang takes over the home of a vulnerable person, right? They use it as a base for drug dealing or whatever.'

'That's right. That old lady probably suffers from

dementia – she can't remember who's who, or who came round and when. If anyone asks, she probably tells them the visitors are her relatives or friends, coming to help with shopping or the garden. They've set up that shed as a store and come and go as they please, some by the front – probably the most expendable gang members, like Hall-Warner, posing as the owner's carers or grandchildren or some such, and the bigger fish who don't want to be seen sneak in the back way. It's lucky for us nobody important wanted to pay a visit to the shed this afternoon – we'd have been sitting ducks.'

'But what about Sillitoe?' He shakes his head. 'She went in through the front door and would have been caught for sure by that camera at the back. I mean, what the hell was she playing at?'

'I'm still trying to work that one out, son,' I say. 'Either she's known by the gang and has free access to the place, or she's being incredibly stupid, and she's practically signed her own death warrant, or at the very least suspension and possible demotion, whichever comes first. If I'm honest, I don't know which is worse.'

'So what do we do now?' he asks.

'We get home,' I say, cursing as we hit the Portway and its queue of crawling rush hour traffic, 'and you get on with those computer searches. While you're doing that, I'll be working out what the hell I'm going to tell the DCI.'

14

By the time Grace arrives, Larson has retreated to the spare bedroom, claiming that he needs peace and quiet to commune with his electronic equipment. That leaves me to deal with the inevitable flak from the DCI. As it happens, Grace is surprisingly calm and has to grudgingly acknowledge that our unsanctioned expedition hasn't been unproductive.

'At least we've got one of their bases now,' she admits, 'and you're right, we need to get some kind of surveillance on that shed. As for the old lady in the bungalow, I got in touch with the council and social services. Iris Browning, age eighty-nine, in the mid stages of Alzheimer's. She has a son living in Norfolk, and a carer in morning and evening. We're looking into the carer now, but Browning is a prime target for cuckooing, with no relations nearby and patchy communication with the neighbours. I'd send an officer round to interview the other residents, but we can't risk spooking the gang at this stage.'

'And what about Sillitoe?' I ask.

'For now, all we can do is keep monitoring her movements, and hope she trips herself up somehow. So far, we have no evidence of direct contact between her and any known suspects, and you can bet she will have neat explanations for all her actions. After all, what she does with her off-duty time is her own business if we can't demonstrate that she's broken the law, and her work record is spotless. She even attends all her psych sessions on time – unlike some others I could mention.' She gives me a pointed look.

'Psych sessions? What on earth for? She hasn't been in some sort of trauma I don't know about?'

Grace shakes her head. 'Not that I know of, but then, I'm not privy to that kind of information unless a recommendation for further treatment comes through. It's one of the new initiatives from headquarters, brought in when you were on sick leave, and you were already being seen by a private psychiatrist by then. Each station has been assigned a counsellor, and all frontline staff from sergeant up have to sit through a cosy little chat once a month to make sure they don't have any issues that could affect their performance. It's a complete waste of time and resources if you ask me, but until the desk jockeys in Portishead realise it, we're stuck with it.'

'Jesus bloody Christ!' The whole idea fills me and, I suspect, every other officer in the station with horror. 'Does that apply to you as well?' I ask, trying, unsuccessfully, to imagine Grace attending meetings with any sort of mental health professional.

She grins. 'It did, but not for long. It only took a couple of sessions to persuade him I had far better things to do with my time. He goes by the name of Donald Davis, but the rest of the station have christened him "Donald Duck" –

short legs, a long beak and walks with a definite waddle. He's been making a nuisance of himself for the last six months.'

I can't help but laugh, but then a thought strikes me. 'There was an entry in Vicky Brent's diary, an appointment with a therapist. Would she have been part of the same programme?'

'Yes,' Grace replies. 'She was assigned to West Hill, and even though she was working under cover – in fact, especially because of her assignment – she was given regular weekly sessions, both with me as her handler, and with Davis to pick up on any possible psychological problems.'

'So, were there any – psychological problems, I mean?'

'Not that I was made aware of, no. I saw her just two days before the murder, and she struck me as very level-headed. What she discussed in the counselling session is confidential, of course, but I was assured there were no causes for concern.'

I park that information for now. 'Okay,' I say, 'so what else have we got?'

'The note that ended up in your pocket,' she says, 'just came back from forensics. The second set of prints isn't on our database, so I doubt it was the kid on the bike who planted it. He's one of Shark Johnson's, by the way – a little bugger by the name of Clive Gingell, and we've got him on record. My guess is that it was his job to make it look like an accident to give someone the opportunity to make the delivery.'

'Don't tell me – the woman on the motorbike?'

'It looks like it. She was concerned enough to call an ambulance, but gave a false name and address. Rebecca Gripton of 23 Dragonfly Terrace doesn't exist. Turns out it's a shared student house occupied by three lads who have never heard of her.'

'It sounds to me,' I say, 'as though she was strong-armed into it by one of the West Hill gangs – and I think I might know who.'

Grace nods. 'So do I. Shark is definitely jumpy, and nobody is happy with this Medusa outfit muscling in on the local trade – honour among thieves and all that. Still, he was trying to give us useful information, so whoever this woman is, perhaps we shouldn't pursue it too vigorously – he might decide to give us more.'

'You mean get us to do his dirty work! It would suit Jermaine Johnson just fine if we get rid of the opposition so that he can carry on making junkies out of the local kids without any competition.'

'True,' she agrees, 'but right now I know who I'd rather be dealing with. Johnson might be a crook, but he's our crook, and we know his boundaries. At least he hasn't murdered any police officers or pregnant women.' She rubs a hand across her brow and shakes her head. 'As long as he's lying low, Shark isn't my main concern – knowing who goes in and out of that bungalow is. I want to know what's being stored there, and where the goods are going to. It could be drugs, guns, people, for God's sake, Al, and there's no way I can think of to find out. There are just three of us, and any surveillance operation doesn't stand a chance of staying out of the station gossip mill. It's bound to get back to Sillitoe ...' She pauses and adds uncomfortably, 'Or whoever it is we're trying to root out.'

I close my eyes, trying to recall the geography of the bungalow, and suddenly I think I see a solution. Unsure of my memory, I go to the door and call Larson down to join us.

'Do you remember,' I ask him, 'the buildings on the other side of the alley leading to the back gardens of the bungalows?'

He thinks for a minute and then nods. 'Two rows of Victorian terraces, side on, with back gardens or yards separating the rows – difficult to say which because the backs of the houses were behind a solid brick wall.'

'And the second row was roughly in line with the path behind the bungalows, yes?'

He nods again.

'Do you remember a very small window, right at the top, maybe the attic of the end house?'

He, in turn, closes his eyes, thinking, and then smiles. 'Yes, there was. The side wall of the first row, with the frontage on the main road, was all brick, but the next one back did have a window, right at the top.'

'And do you think,' I say, with an inward sigh of relief that my memory hasn't failed me, 'that given the height of the window and some of your fancy equipment, you could rig up a camera to zoom in on that shed?'

'I could do better than that,' he says at once. 'I could set up a live video feed just like the one on the shed roof – maybe not so sophisticated, but enough to do the job. It would need to be periodically monitored though, and I'd need to see what the space looks like from the inside, for access and so on.'

I turn to Grace. 'We need an extra body,' I tell her. 'If we're going to do it, we'll have to bring someone else in.'

'Too risky,' she replies. 'It's bad enough trying to keep the three of us under the radar, but four? That's more than half a netball team! Besides, we still have no idea who we can trust at West Hill, and it will only take one careless word or a deviation from the normal routine ... We've got away with it so far, but that's thanks to a lot of luck as well as careful handling.'

'Which could all be for nothing if one of us gets spotted prowling around the back streets of Weston,' I remind her, 'and I wouldn't say that any of us exactly fits in with the background, would you?'

'And you know someone who would?'

'Put it this way,' I say, 'who do you know who wanders about looking totally dozy when in fact he's sharp as a pin, has an obsession with pastry, is totally trustworthy and would never say no to a free holiday in the chip shop capital of the West Country?'

For a moment she simply stares at me as if I've lost my mind, but then bursts out laughing and digs out her mobile. 'If anyone asks, Al,' she says as she dials the number, 'it was your bloody idea, okay?'

As far as the rest of the world is concerned, George Saint's long-suffering, but much-adored wife has gone to visit her sister for a couple of weeks, leaving George free to take some of his built-up leave to take a holiday by the seaside. His choice of a resort just a few miles down the road doesn't surprise anybody – our only slight distortion of the truth is that he is not in the caravan at Brean Down that's been booked in his name, just down the coast from Weston. As far as our chosen surveillance spot is concerned, luck, it seems, is with us. The resident, Hardeep Khan, a single, middle-aged Asian man who lives alone with a Jack Russell terrier and two parakeets, makes a living offering bed and breakfast during the summer season, but currently has no guests.

After half an hour of Grace's relentless charm and an offer of generous compensation, he is only too happy to turn his guest rooms and attic over to us and not ask any awkward questions.

I spend a sleepless night listening to Larson pecking away at his keyboard in the spare room, and just about manage to haul myself downstairs as he's leaving to pick up George Saint, then head off to set up his equipment. He looks like shit and probably hasn't slept properly for days. If he's going to carry on with police work, I think to myself, he's going to have to find the 'off' switch. Not that I ever did, so I'm not the best role model. I'm about to slump onto my sofa, determined to take my own advice and switch off for an hour or two, when there's a loud knock at the door, followed by footsteps in the hall and a loud shout of 'Hey, Grandad! Granny says are you decent?'

'No!' I shout back as Ben bulldozes into the living room and makes a wild leap for my neck. Luckily I manage to catch him without falling over.

He's followed, more sedately, by Rosie. 'Get down, Ben, right now!' she growls at her son, in a tone that has developed a definite hint of her mother's no-nonsense approach to the men in her life. 'Didn't I tell you to be careful with your grandfather? He's hurt his head, remember?'

Ben climbs down at once. 'Sorry, Grandad, I forgot. Can I go out and play on the swing?'

'Sure,' I tell him. 'Just try to keep the noise down, okay?'

Ben scampers off, and Chrissie appears in the doorway, weighed down by several carrier bags. 'Mum thought you and John might want some decent food,' she says. 'I'll dump these in the kitchen and make some coffee. Then we'll talk.'

It's a delegation – and I haven't got a hope in hell of wriggling out of it. I give Rosie a hug and guide her to the sofa. 'How are you feeling?' I ask her.

'Like an elephant,' she replies, sinking gratefully into the cushions. 'My feet ache, and this baby thinks it's a whole rugby team – here, feel.' She grabs my hand and presses it to her bump. I sit beside her, and we spend a few minutes in precious silence while my soon-to-be-born grandchild shuffles and fidgets under my hand. It's gone quiet in the kitchen, too, and I look up to see Chrissie standing in the doorway with a tray, watching us with a motherly smile.

Inevitably, the truce doesn't last long. Chrissie takes the armchair opposite the sofa, placing the tray on the coffee table between us like defensive wall. There's coffee for the two of us, a glass of orange juice for Rosie and a plate of my mother-in-law's apple cake. I glance out the window to check on Ben, who is sitting contentedly on the swing, munching his way through an especially large slice.

'Okay,' I start, biting the bullet, 'it's lovely to see both of you, but my guess is this visit isn't just to check on my health. Maybe one of you should tell me what's on your minds?'

Chrissie gives our daughter a look, and Rosie draws in a deep breath. 'I'm worried, Dad,' she says, 'about John. He hasn't seen Ben for days, and before he came over here, he only came home twice in the last week, and then only for a couple of hours. He hardly spoke to me and then went off again, and he looks awful. He phoned me last night after Ben was in bed and, well ... he just didn't sound right.' She pauses, takes another breath and goes for it. 'The thing is, Dad ... I'm not very, you know, attractive at the moment, and ...'

'What Rosie is trying to say,' Chrissie puts in, with more than a little accusation in her voice, 'is she thinks John might be seeing another woman, and we want to know if you know anything about it.'

'What?' I almost splutter a mouthful of coffee and cake crumbs all over my carpet. 'Of course not! What gave you that idea?'

In a sudden movement that makes me cringe back in my seat, Chrissie snaps upright, marches into the hall and comes back clutching the God-awful scarf Larson bought in the hippy shop yesterday. 'If that's true,' she says, 'maybe you can tell us which of the pair of you this monstrosity belongs to?'

My ex-wife would have made a damned good prosecution lawyer. I try to ignore Chrissie and turn to Rosie. 'Listen, sweetheart, I promise you, he isn't seeing another woman. John would never do something like that. He loves you and Ben and that little one' – I put my hand back to her burgeoning belly – 'more than anything else in the world. He's just ...'

Chrissie interrupts again. 'He's bloody well working for you, isn't he? This new job of his is working for the police, and neither of you saw fit to tell us what you were up to. For fuck's sake, Al!'

'If it makes you feel any better,' I snap back, 'I didn't know anything about it either, and when I found out, I was about as pleased as you are. As for that scarf ...' I turn to Rosie and give her a smile, 'he was going to give it to you, but I persuaded him not to. After all, it is pretty horrible.'

She stares at me for a second, wide-eyed, and then bursts into laughter. 'Now I know he hasn't got someone else,' she says when she can speak. 'In the first place, no woman would ever buy a thing like that, and I told John years ago never to buy me anything to wear – he's got no taste at all!'

Chrissie, who has been watching us quietly, sits back in her chair with a sigh. 'I'm sorry, Al. I wasn't being fair. You can see why we're both worried, though?'

I nod. 'I'm worried too. He's working hard, and long hours, but I'm doing my best to make sure he doesn't overdo it. I give you my word, Chris, I didn't want him to do this, but the fact is, he's a brilliant computer analyst, and he was bound to be headhunted for this kind of work sooner or later.'

'He was,' Rosie puts in, 'a few years ago, just before we were married – by GCHQ. I managed to talk him out of it. Believe it or not, I thought it might be dangerous.'

'You didn't tell me that,' Chrissie says, but Rosie gives her a dark look, and she holds up her hands. 'Okay, okay. But he isn't in any danger, is he, Al? And what is he doing running around the streets? I thought your computer people just sat in an office all day – it's what you told me, anyway.'

'They do, as a rule,' I reply, 'but John is working here just now, while I'm on sick leave, and he's popped out to set up some equipment for Grace. I can't tell you what he's doing, and neither of you can say a word about it to anyone – even other officers. The only people who know he's working for us are me and Grace – and now you. If anyone asks, whether they are police or not, he's simply looking after me, okay? Nothing else.'

'Why?' Chrissie persists. 'Why all the secrecy? And you haven't answered my question. Is John in any danger?'

I take a deep breath and give Chrissie a look that I hope conveys that she should know better than to ask. She gets the signal and leaves us to go into the garden to see to Ben. I turn back to Rosie. 'There's no need to worry, love, I promise. John knows his stuff, and he's no fool. Plus, I'll be looking after him every step of the way. I'll get him to call you as soon as he gets back, okay?'

'Are you sure, Dad?' she says, searching my face.

'One hundred per cent,' I lie. I help her up. 'Go on home and let your mum look after you – and the minute he gets in, I'll tell him to take that scarf back to the shop and let me choose another one.'

I watch them go, Ben still nibbling on his third slice of cake, and finally settle myself on the sofa to wait for Larson's report.

15

I'm awakened from a dream in which I'm being stalked by a Doberman wearing an orange and green polka dot scarf, by the insistent trill of my mobile. By the time I've clawed my way back to consciousness and straightened out the painful kinks where the arm of the sofa has dug into my back, it's stopped. I look at my watch – it's more than three hours since Rosie and Chrissie left. I pull myself together, head to the kitchen, splash my face with cold water and check my phone. It brings up Larson's number. I call it.

'Everything's set up,' he informs me, 'and I'm on my way back.'

'What about George?' I ask. 'Do you think he'll be able to handle things okay?'

He chuckles. 'No problem – I get the feeling he's a lot quicker on the uptake than people give him credit for. I left him with a newspaper and a sausage roll, keeping an eye on the equipment. He knows what to do if anything goes wrong, and if there's a serious mechanical failure, he can contact me. I'm also sending you an email with a link to the video feed so you can check it out on your laptop.'

'You're dead right about George,' I tell him, 'but keep it well under your hat. He's spent thirty-odd years perfecting that image of a lumbering old fool, and we don't want to let the cat out of the bag – he's probably West Hill's best secret weapon!' I go on to tell him about the family visit. 'If I were you, I'd drop in to see Rosie and Ben before you come back here, and take her a bunch of flowers or something. Besides, if there is anyone keeping an eye on us, it will look pretty strange if you don't.'

I switch on my laptop and spend the next hour or so staring at Iris Browning's back garden. As I hoped, the little attic window gives a perfect view over the top of the chain-link fence, the lens taking in the back of the bungalow and the garden path down to the shed. The little alley behind the garden, with its concealed entrance behind the shed, is also clearly visible. I have to admit, Larson has done a good job. The only problem is, nothing is happening, not even the old lady pottering around among her overgrown cabbages. I decide that glaring at it isn't the best use of my time, and go upstairs to freshen up before Larson gets back. On the way, I take a peek into the spare room and freeze in the doorway, open mouthed. I count at least three computers, one of them with two screens, lining the walls, and a mass of wires all over the floor, presumably connecting it all together. One monitor is showing the same video feed I was watching downstairs, while on another a stream of data is cascading down the screen almost faster than the eye can follow. There are enough flashing lights to induce epilepsy. 'Fucking hell!' I mutter to myself, and make a quick exit to the bathroom.

It's dark when Larson finally makes it back, looking as if he's just gone five rounds with an all-in wrestler.

'Did Chrissie give you a hard time, then?' I ask innocently.

He gives me a tired grin. 'She tried, but Joyce and Rosie headed her off. Still, I don't think either of us are her flavour of the month at the moment. Rosie's fine though.' His grin transforms into a puzzled look. 'How on earth could she think I was having an affair? It's ridiculous!'

'Maybe,' I reply, 'it's because you're so tied up with your work you haven't been paying enough attention to things that are probably a hell of a lot more important?' He bridles at this, but I carry on quickly, 'Believe me, son, it's easy enough done – take it from one who knows. Rosie's no fool, and she's with you all the way, but so was Chrissie, back in the day. Just don't make the same mistakes I did, okay?'

He thinks about this for a minute and then nods. 'Okay. Message received. Joyce said Chrissie had left us a couple of her casseroles and some desserts. I'm bloody starving!'

'I'm on it,' I say, pushing myself up and heading for the kitchen. 'Go and get yourself sorted, and I'll see to dinner.' I can't help feeling, as I fire up the microwave, that my son-in-law and I perhaps have more in common than I'd realised. When I think about Rosie though, tough, resourceful, about to give birth, and with a husband involved with clandestine police work, I'm not altogether sure the thought is comforting.

WE'RE SITTING at the kitchen table in a state of silent contentment after a generous dinner of beef stew followed by one of Joyce's speciality rhubarb crumbles, when Larson's phone pings. He checks it and jumps to his feet, then grabs the edge of the table as exhaustion gives him a violent poke in the ribs. I reach out to steady him, but he holds up a hand.

'Sorry – I'm fine, honestly.'

'You're not,' I tell him, 'you're bloody knackered. Whatever it is, surely it can wait until you've had a few hours' sleep? If something goes down over in Weston tonight, you'll be in no fit state.'

'I guess so,' he replies, 'but there's something to do first. I set a program running yesterday, going through those flight records you asked me to look at, with an alert coming through to my phone if anything was picked up.'

'And that was it?'

He nods. 'It may be nothing, but it's worth checking.'

I think about it. 'Okay,' I say, 'go and look, print the information off or send it to my laptop, whichever's easiest, and then go and get your head down for a while. I slept earlier, so I can keep an eye on things. If anything happens, I'll wake you. To be honest, son, in your state, you're about as much use to me as a chocolate bloody teapot, so it's not advice, it's an order, yes?'

To my relief, he goes off without an argument, and a few minutes later comes down with a sheaf of papers. Despite hardly being able to put one foot in front of the other, he's grinning. 'You were right,' he says, 'and I think we may have hit the jackpot.'

He goes to sit down, but I stop him. 'No. You do as you're told and get some sleep. I'll go through everything, and we can discuss your police medal for nerdery later. It's not negotiable. And by the way, I can hear your keyboard through several walls, so don't even think about it!'

Defeated, he slopes off, and I make myself coffee and

settle down to go through the sheaf of documents he's left me with. The pile is in date order, starting with the most recent, and a single glance at the first page makes me freeze, mug halfway to my lips. A passport photograph is staring up at me, and the face is instantly recognisable. The name, on the other hand, isn't. Rebecca (my name's Becks) Gripton is, according to her passport, Alexia Galanis, citizen of Greece, arrived in the UK five weeks ago for the purposes of tourism, accompanied by her pet dog, an adult Doberman. The address of an Airbnb near the city centre is given, but I doubt she spent a single night there. Nevertheless, I give Grace a call and ask her to check. 'While you're at it,' I add, 'can you arrange for the kid on the bike to be brought in on some pretext or other? I want to have a chat with him, see if I can't set up a meeting with Shark.'

I hang up and turn back to the record of Becks's (or whatever her real name is) travels. Each sheet has a different name, country of origin, destination, but the face in the photograph that stares out at me, whether blonde, brunette, short hair or long, is the same. And always, she's travelling with her beloved pet dog. Larson has done a good job. The records go back five years, and the list includes visits to presumably fictitious relatives and friends in several South American and European countries, even St Petersburg and Moscow. The more I read, the more my hunch crystallises into a certainty – this well-travelled Doberman is giving us a map of the activities of Alastor, Medusa's elusive hit man.

I check my watch – it's gone eleven, and despite dozing off earlier, my eyes are starting to close. I decide that if anything goes down tonight, I'm going to have to rely on George to pass the word. On the way to the bedroom I look in on my son-in-law and find him stretched out on his bed, snoring gently, still fully clothed except for his shoes and oblivious to the raft of winking lights and the chorus of humming power units that make the room feel like something from an episode of *Doctor Who*. My own room, by contrast, is dark and silent and filled only with the threat of bad dreams, the ones I haven't got round to telling Rogers about in my therapy sessions. As I drift into sleep, the image in my mind is of a giant black dog with a muzzle formed of writhing snakes, and behind it, the shadow of a man pointing a gun at my head.

16

There is just one message on my mobile when I finally surface at around 8am the next morning. It's from George, informing me that nothing kicked off in the night, and he can thoroughly recommend Hardeep Khan's full English breakfast. When I get downstairs, Larson is already in the kitchen, sipping fresh coffee and communing with his mobile. I help myself to a cup from the large cafetiere on the table and hear Ben's voice floating out of the tiny screen.

'Can I talk to Grandad?' I hear him say.

'Sure,' his father replies, and hands me the phone so that I can see Ben's face taking up the whole screen.

'Hi, Grandad,' Ben says, waving at me. 'I'm Zooming with Daddy before I go to school.'

I wave back, feeling a bit awkward. 'Hi, Ben. Where are you zooming to?'

He giggles. 'No, silly! I'm Zooming, like on the phone. I'm not allowed on my own, but Mummy's here, so it's okay. I haven't got a phone yet, so I have to do it before I go to school.'

'Talking of which ...' Rosie's voice butts in from somewhere across the room. 'We need to get going, or you'll be late. Say goodbye, Ben.'

Ben scowls, but waves reluctantly. 'I gotta go. Bye.'

His image is replaced by Rosie's. 'Hi, Dad. Is everything okay?'

'It's fine,' I tell her. 'Don't worry about us. I'll make sure John gets in touch this evening. Are you managing okay?'

'Of course,' she answers, and rolls her eyes. 'I've got Mum and Grandma clucking round me like a couple of broody hens. I know they're only trying to help, but I swear, if I don't give birth soon, they're going to drive me mad!'

'Hang in there, kid,' I say, and pass the phone back to her other half, taking my coffee into the lounge so that I can finish waking up in peace. It's a vain hope, as no sooner have I slumped onto the sofa than my mobile rings.

'A constable has just picked up the Gingell boy,' Grace says. 'As luck would have it, he got caught lifting a four-pack from the newsagents this morning. We can't do anything with him 'til his appropriate adult gets here, and if I know his mother, that will be at least a couple of hours. It will take her that long to sober up. In the meantime, if you get yourself down here, you could maybe have a quiet fatherly chat.'

'I'm on my way,' I tell her, gulp down the rest of my coffee and grab my jacket. Before I leave, though, I check in with Larson, who, thankfully, is looking a lot better than he did last night. 'I'm going over to the station,' I tell him, 'and I won't be needing a minder, whatever Grace says. I'm sure you've got plenty of other things to be getting on with.'

He gives me a dubious look, but has the sense not to

argue. 'In that case,' he says, 'I'll go over and join Sergeant Saint for breakfast and check up on the equipment. Then I'll do some more digging in the records, see if any other officers were angling for a transfer to West Hill at the same time as Sillitoe. There's also the question of the guy we think is the Medusa hit man. The searches are still coming up empty, but if he's travelling, he must be on record somewhere.' He scratches his head. 'I don't understand it.'

I give him a pat on the shoulder. 'I'm sure you'll find him, son. It's just a matter of time. With luck I'll be able to set up a meeting with Shark and we'll learn more. Meanwhile' – I give him a hard look – 'I hope you're making sure you go in the back way. If anyone sees you, they might put two and two together and actually make four.'

I leave him and his exasperated glare, trying to push down my envy at the thought of him and George chewing the fat – literally – at Hardeep Khan's breakfast table.

WHEN I ENTER the interview room, young Clive Gingell draws himself up to his full four feet six inches, backs away a couple of paces and sticks out his chin. I set a Barry's Burgers bag and an extra-large Coke on the table.

'Morning, Clive. Thought you might want some breakfast.'

'Fuck off!' Clive bares his teeth and jabs his middle finger in the air for emphasis. His nose is twitching, though. 'If you reckon I'm going to tell you anything just because you brought some crap burger in, that bang on the head must have knocked your brain right into your arse! Besides, you can't do nothing 'til I got my appropriate adult here. I know my rights.'

I move round and sit down, the table between us. I give him an indulgent smile. 'If I wanted information,' I tell him, 'I'd simply beat the shit out of you and save myself the fiver. It's just the two of us here, Clive. Nobody's watching.' I see a hint of doubt flit across his face, and carry on. 'Thing is, son, I thought maybe you and me could do each other a favour.'

'I ain't no snitch,' he replies, without hesitation. 'You can go fuck yourself.'

'I'm not asking you to snitch,' I say. 'But I reckon Shark isn't going to be too pleased when he hears about that four-pack you tried to shove down your trousers this morning. Bad for his business, I'd say. What do you think?'

He's uncertain now, and I see a flash of real fear. 'Thing is,' I tell him, 'I could have a word, make sure you just get a caution, and Shark need never know you got nicked. Plus, I could decide not to press charges for assault on a police officer ...'

'That was an accident – you can't do me for that!' he interrupts.

'I can do you for whatever I like, son.' I give him my sweetest smile. 'But I'd rather you did me a favour, so ...'

'What favour?' His voice cracks into the rasping squeak of approaching adolescence.

'Look, why don't you sit down, eat your burger, and I'm sure we can come to a mutually beneficial agreement. Okay?'

His brow creases, probably trying to work out what 'mutually beneficial' means, but a few seconds later he's at the table, stuffing the food into his mouth as though it's the first proper meal he's had for several days. Sadly, I think as I watch him, it probably is.

. . .

I HEAD up to my broom cupboard and find Grace already there.

'How did it go?' she asks, sliding her ubiquitous bag of pastries at me across the desk.

'So far, so good,' I reply, squashing my disappointment at the lack of a bacon sandwich and helping myself to a chocolate croissant. 'You need to arrange for young Clive to be released with a caution, and in return he's going to pass a message on to Shark. I'm pretty sure he'll do it – he's too scared of getting on the wrong side of his boss not to. After that, all we can do is wait.'

Grace goes off to see to the youngster, and I sit tight for the next couple of hours, doing a good impression of a bored stolen-dog investigator, and visiting the staff canteen a couple of times to make sure I'm seen passing the time of day with whoever happens to be taking a break. There's a sheaf of papers on my desk, but luckily nothing urgent enough to warrant my attention. Grace has had the foresight to put the word out that given the high value of the Doberman theft, I've been tasked to deal with it exclusively, while a uniformed constable deals with the rest. On the way down to the car park, I take a stroll past the CID office. Aside from a couple of DCs, heads bent over their desks, the squad room is empty. Sillitoe's team is out doing its job. I just hope their DI is with them and not somewhere she isn't supposed to be – like anywhere near my son-in-law in Weston-super-Mare.

I'VE BEEN BACK HOME LESS than an hour, and I'm rooting in my fridge for lunch, when an explosive bang, loud as a gunshot, reverberates through the house. Before my brain can process the sound, my body reacts. My right leg locks, and I try to grab onto the sink to stop myself falling. At the same time, though, my hands start to twitch, and my fingers won't close, so I end up crashing to the kitchen floor, where I'm stuck for at least a minute, breathing heavily, drenched in sweat and swearing under my breath. I wait for the tremor to die down, and get cautiously back to my feet. There have been no other sounds, so I make my way slowly towards the source of the noise at the back of the house.

The first thing I notice is a large mud splatter – at least, I hope it's mud – on the pane of one of my French windows. Moving carefully, just in case whoever threw the missile is hanging around, I peer through the window. There's what looks like a mud-coated package on the back patio – too irregular to be a brick, and there are glimpses of plastic through the dirt. I pause, considering. The official line of action would be to call in the bomb squad. The rules particularly apply to suspicious packages that turn up in the gardens of serving police officers. On the other hand, not only would an alert waste several hours, cause an evacuation of the whole street and alert every criminal this side of Bristol, the package would be blown up anyway, together with whatever is in it.

'Fuck it,' I mutter to myself, open the French windows, and scoop it up.

The coating of mud was designed, I assume, to make a mark on the window and give me a heads-up to the location of the package. Beneath is a plastic carrier bag containing a handful of pebbles – the source of the noise and the equivalent of ringing the doorbell, but not enough to smash the window. The main content, though, is a small, oblong item wrapped in several sheets of paper – pages carefully selected from a soft porn magazine. Whoever the package is from, they have a sense of humour. I take a deep breath, remove several layers of naked models in provocative poses, and end up holding a burner phone. Things are starting to make sense.

I turn on the phone. A minute or so later it pings. The text message reads:

The Bear Pit. Come on foot. Wait for a call.

The Bear Pit is a warren of underpasses beneath a roundabout in the centre of Bristol. Despite several attempts to turn its central sunken area into a peaceful haven for shoppers and office workers, it has doggedly remained a refuge for the innocent homeless and not so innocent petty criminals and drug dealers of the inner city. As a meeting place for those who don't want to be observed, it's perfect. Shark isn't going to hang around waiting for me, so I wedge a hunk of cheese between two slices of bread, grab my jacket and head off the mile or so into town.

TWENTY MINUTES later I reach the Bear Pit and hover at the entrance to one of the underpasses, chewing on the remains of my sandwich. I haven't seen anyone following me, but that doesn't mean anything – I'm pretty sure Shark has been kept fully informed of my exact movements, probably by a clutch of kids Clive Gingell's age on foot and on bikes. Sure enough, I've only been waiting a few minutes when another text message arrives.

The Moon. Walk past.

The Moon is an 'adult' nightclub tucked down a lane in the old part of the city. It's well out of Shark's territory. Its owner is an even more unpleasant local gang boss by the name of Vincent Perrin – known to his friends, naturally, as 'Reggie', after the eponymous hero of a popular 1970s sitcom.

Reggie Perrin moves in more refined circles than Shark Johnson. He works out of his own commercial premises and pays his taxes on time. While Shark ploughs his profits into gold neck-and-fingerwear, Reggie favours cashmere overcoats and handmade shoes from Crockett and Jones. Under normal circumstances, the two would be giving each other the widest possible berth. That they have set aside their differences, even if only temporarily, is yet more evidence of the seriousness of the situation we're all in. That both are willing to include the police in their deliberations is unprecedented. I follow the instruction and stroll past the main entrance to the club, which at this time of day is firmly locked and protected by a thick steel shutter. A little further down I reach a narrow blind alley leading down to the rear entrances, with just enough room for a body to squeeze past the ranks of rubbish carts and general detritus left by last night's drunks, addicts and pimps. A soft whistle greets me as I come alongside, and I turn into the alley.

I'm met at the club's back door by a subdued Clive Gingell, who in the brief time since his release from West Hill nick has gained a swollen lip and a black eye. 'You all right, son?' I ask as he opens the door and gestures me through.

'Fuck off,' he mutters resentfully as he leads me up the back stairs to the proprietor's office. Perrin is sitting behind his massive leather-topped desk, fully decked out in a grey silk suit and an eye-wateringly bright puce tie clashing with dingy claret décor that looks as if it's been modelled on a 1950s gangster movie. There are two chairs in front of the desk, one of them occupied by Shark, who for once is dressed quite soberly in a military-style greatcoat with buttons that I suspect are probably pure gold to match his neck chains and rings. As I enter, he jerks his head to dismiss Clive, and the boy disappears, closing the door behind him.

Perrin gets to his feet and gestures to the empty chair. 'Inspector Crow,' he says, giving me a wide smile, 'it's good to see you looking so well. Can I get you anything?' He waves a hand at the fully stocked bar lining the back wall of his office.

I take the chair. 'You too, Reggie,' I say affably. 'Thank you, but it's a little early for me.' I turn to Shark. 'And you, Jermaine – still in good health, I see. Your lad looks as if he's been in the wars, though. Run into a door, did he?'

Shark shrugs. 'You know the score, Bird Man. Private enterprise is strictly forbidden, yeah? Got to keep up appearances, y'know? But I've made it up to him, and he knows I'll look after him, you get me?'

I get him and let my expression make my feelings clear. Perrin diverts us from further discussion of Clive Gingell's welfare.

'Your request for a meeting,' he says, 'has come at a most fortuitous time, Inspector.'

'And your interest is what, exactly?' I ask, through gritted teeth, starting to feel more than a little hacked off that despite not being the target of my message, he nevertheless seems to have taken charge of proceedings. Shark, meanwhile, is hunched quietly in his chair, arms folded, waiting to see how things pan out.

Perrin holds up a conciliatory hand. 'My apologies,

Inspector, if I speak out of turn. Mr Johnson here felt a collective response would be of most benefit to all concerned.'

I glance at Shark, who nods his agreement. 'We're all involved here – you, me, Mr Perrin – everyone's getting shit from these fucking Greeks, and the longer it goes on, the worse it's going to get.' He shifts uncomfortably before adding, 'It was a bad business, you know, when ...' He gives me a meaningful look and taps his forehead with a finger. 'It wasn't part of the plan – not the shooter – we got fucked over that night, same as you. They took the merchandise and the cash, left us with one dead cop and you bleeding all over my turf, and fuck all else. I swear, Bird, that fucker's a total psycho – goes everywhere with a gun and this fuck-off bloody dog that's trained to kill. Anyone looks at him the wrong way, he puts them in a cage and sets the dog on them. A mate of mine saw it once, a few years back, up in Liverpool. The poor sod didn't stand a chance, and by the time the dog had finished, there weren't nothing left. And all the time, he said, that mad fucker just stood and watched with a big smile on his face.'

Perrin leans forward, elbows on his desk. 'You asked what my interest is in this business, Inspector. Do you remember Jimmy Nevin? He was my manager here at the Moon until around a year ago.'

'Sure, I remember Jimmy,' I reply, calling up an image of Reggie's formidable long-time minder. An ex-heavyweight boxer with biceps the size of my chest, Nevin had taken up the lucrative position of Perrin's personal minder following retirement from the ring. Like many boxers, Nevin was a gentle giant, and I doubt he'd ever caused serious damage to anyone – he didn't need to. After all, who wants to start an argument with someone who can break your spine with a friendly pat on the back? 'I haven't seen him around for a while. What's he up to these days?'

Perrin shares a glance with Shark and sits back with a bitter smile. 'It's like this, Inspector. A year or so ago, I had a visit from a Greek gentleman. He said his name was Leon Sidaris. He was head of a consortium in Athens and was looking for a partner in this part of the UK to expand his business.'

'Business?' I ask, raising an eyebrow.

Perrin spreads his hands. 'Please, Inspector. I think perhaps we should temporarily set our many differences aside, don't you?'

'Fair enough, Reggie,' I reply, 'as long as you understand that it *is* temporary.'

He nods and continues, 'I won't go into the details of our conversation, but it became clear to me that this Greek was connected to that bad business you were involved in over in Mr Johnson's territory. We didn't know them as Medusa back then, and they seemed to disappear from our part of the world after that. We did hear of Greek-based outfits moving into Glasgow and Liverpool, but that didn't affect us so long as they didn't come back south. When this Sidaris appeared, though, there was no mistaking that his idea of a partnership was what the commercial world might call a "hostile takeover". It was also clear from the conversation that he was representing the groups in the north – it was all one big organisation. I declined his offer, naturally, and at that point he became quite aggressive – not physically, you understand, but the threats were clear. Medusa – as we now know – was going to take over, and our only option was to toe the line. I got Jimmy to throw him out.'

He pours himself a large slug of whisky from a decanter on the desk, downs it in one, and shakes his head. 'I got a text message the next morning from Jimmy's phone, saying he'd gone down with a bug and wouldn't be in for a couple of days. I thought nothing of it. My employees are entitled to sick leave, just like anybody else. When he didn't turn up on the third day, I called him and left a message. By the fourth day, I got worried – he still wasn't picking up – so I decided to pay him a visit, see if there was anything I could do.'

'You went yourself?' I interrupt. 'That's a bit unusual, isn't it?'

Perrin bristles. 'You have to understand, Inspector Crow. Jimmy and I, we go back a long way. He was like a brother to me, so yes, I did go round to make sure he was all right, had everything he needed.'

'Was? He *was* like a brother to you?'

He pours himself another whisky. 'Like I said, I went round to his house. There was no answer when I knocked, so I tried his phone again. I could hear it ringing inside. I had my driver with me, and there was an upstairs window open, so he climbed up, got in and opened the door. The place was empty – at least, we thought it was. Jimmy's phone was on the kitchen table, and there was a plate with food still on it, dry, as if it had been there several days – there was even a half-drunk cup of coffee. But no sign of Jimmy. Then we went into the lounge and saw a suitcase in the middle of the carpet. I opened it.' Perrin takes a handkerchief out of his top pocket and dabs a sheen of sweat from his forehead. His hand is shaking. 'Jesus fucking Christ – I've never seen anything like it, Inspector, and in my life I've seen a lot, believe me.'

'I believe you,' I say, and after a suitable pause, 'Are you sure it was Jimmy?'

He nods slowly, and I can tell he's struggling to keep his voice even as he says, 'He had a ring – a platinum signet he had made when he won his first big fight. They put it on top of what was left of him. It was Jimmy all right.'

'So someone killed him, cut up the corpse and put it in a suitcase for you to find, yes?'

The grin he gives me is almost ghoulish. 'Oh, no, Inspector Crow. He wasn't cut up. He was ripped apart. We saw the teeth marks in what was left of him – the bits that hadn't been eaten. I wouldn't play ball, so Sidaris called in his trusted executioner and literally set the dogs on Jimmy. Since then, we've all been sent the same message. If we don't stand aside and let Medusa take over, and if we don't do exactly what they want, they'll simply chew us up the same way that dog chewed Jimmy. That's all we are to them, Inspector – dog meat.'

17

There's no point asking why the murder of Jimmy Nevin wasn't reported to the police. Given the company I'm keeping, failure to report a death and the illegal disposing of a body hardly count as offences.

'I'm sorry,' I say, 'about Jimmy. He was a good man.' I don't add, *for a paid thug*.

'He ain't the only one,' Shark puts in, pre-empting my next question. 'I've lost two of my boys – haven't found the bodies yet, but wherever they are, they ain't fucking walking around, that's for sure. That outfit, they don't call themselves Medusa for nothing – look 'em in the eye and next thing you know, you're wasted.'

'It's the same all over the city,' Perrin says. 'We all decided, after that first business on Cabot Rise, we weren't going to lie down, let them take our livelihoods. Everyone has lost at least one of their people. A few of the smaller outfits have bent the knee, the ones out of town, and I'll tell you the truth, Inspector, it's got to a point we don't know who we can trust anymore.'

I just about manage to keep a straight face at that. If the situation weren't so serious, it would be ludicrous. 'You and me both, Reggie,' I reply, sobering up sharply at the thought of Joe Bailey's brain sprayed all over my shirt, and young DS Vicky Brent, the earth still fresh over her coffin.

Perrin, guessing my thoughts, nods in acknowledgement. 'We've got a common enemy, Inspector Crow. Much as it pains all of us, I think the only way forward is to join forces' – his mouth gives a momentary twitch at the unintended pun – 'and persuade Medusa that it would be inappropriate to try to establish themselves here.' He gives Shark a hard look before continuing, 'We all understand that our organisations have different approaches, different modi operandi ...'

Shark jerks up in his seat, scowling at the reminder of Perrin's superior level of education. 'Fuck's sake ...'

'As I was saying,' Perrin goes on, silencing Shark with a glare, 'we all want the same thing, and at this moment, I believe we have something you've been looking for – at least, Mr Johnson here does.'

'I can't make any deals, Reggie. You know that.'

'We're not asking you to,' he says quickly, and looks away. If I didn't know him better, I'd think he was embarrassed. He turns to Shark. 'Mr Johnson, perhaps you would be good enough to explain the situation to the Inspector?'

Shark is still glowering, but nods and takes up the story. 'That beer my boy nicked this morning – I told him to do it, and I told him to get caught. I figured you'd get to him before anyone else. You might have had part of your brain shot off, Bird, but you're still twice as quick as most of the others.'

'You were taking a hell of a risk,' I comment. 'What if someone else had got there first?' I can't help thinking of

Sillitoe, who knows Shark and his gang almost as well as I do.

He shrugs. 'He had his instructions. Nothing you need to know about. The point is, you're here, right? And we can't risk anything in writing. I told the kid to make sure you were up for a meet, and if the answer was yes, to deliver the phone. You'll need to leave that here before you go, yeah? Not that I don't trust you, Bird, or my boy, but the kid's been carrying it around, and you can never quite be sure where he's been and who might have taken a look in his pockets while he was taking a leak, you get me? '

'Of course,' I say, yank it out of my pocket and throw it onto Perrin's desk. 'So how about we cut to the chase, Jermaine? You've got something to tell me that's so important you've gone to all this trouble to get me here. I've got plenty of stuff to get through today, so I suggest you get the fuck on with it.' I glance at Perrin. 'Apologies for the bad language, Reggie.'

Shark bares his teeth briefly, but quickly translates the snarl into a faint smile. 'Sure. You're after the girl, right? The one who left you the message. I might be able to help.'

'How? You know who she is – where she is?'

He nods. 'I can't tell you where. She moves around, and she's careful. She belongs to the bastard – has done the last five years or so. They call her his vet – she looks after his dogs, treats them when they're sick, takes 'em for walks when he's not around. Thing is, Bird, she wants out. She's had enough, but if he even gets a sniff she might walk away, he'll feed her to the dogs just like anyone else.'

'If she's so careful, how do you get in contact with her?' I ask.

He grins. 'Got an arrangement with my boy. There's a

route she takes, walking, down by the New Cut in town. He goes over there every day, same time, under the flyover where all the kids go with their skateboards. Sometimes she's there, sometimes not. She's got a minder who follows her everywhere. When she's walking off road, he uses one of those electric scooters, if you can believe that – looks a right dick, but those things move fast. He's looking for cops and knife men, not kids, so it's easy for Clive to get close. Listen, Bird Man – she's not stupid, and she's got enough information to bury Alastor, or whatever his real name is, and his fucking dogs. But she knows Medusa's got a tame cop over at West Hill, and she's scared shitless. I convinced her you're straight, so she's prepared to trust you, and the only way to get what you need is for you to make sure she gets the right protection. You get what I'm saying?'

Suddenly, I'm sitting up in my seat, my mind running through the possibilities faster than one of Larson's computer programs. 'You get her to me,' I say, 'and I'll make sure she's safe.' It's a promise I'm not sure I can keep, and seeing Shark's expression, it's clear he's not buying it either.

Nevertheless, he nods. 'I'll need to convince her,' he says. 'She won't be safe in a cell – you know that as well as I do, and anybody sees her round your nick, she'll be at the bottom of the Cut before you've had time to piss.'

'And you're sure you don't know where she is?'

'Safer for all of us if none of us do,' he answers. 'And that goes for your lot too. There are snitches round every corner these days, and we're all watching our backs. You got to ask yourself, Bird, who knows what you're doing, and are they reliable?'

'Don't worry about me,' I reply. 'You look after yours, and I'll take care of mine.'

'I'm sure,' Perrin butts in, 'that Inspector Crow has matters well in hand in that direction. As have we, Inspector,' he adds, giving me a look that makes it clear his approach to the problem is something I shouldn't ask about.

'Fair enough. You'll have to give me some time to make arrangements – a day should do it. How will I let you know?'

In response, Shark digs into his pocket and brings out a second burner. 'It's got my boy's number on it,' he says. 'Text him when you've worked it out, and he'll find you.'

I take the phone and put it in my pocket. 'There are a couple of other questions you might be able to help me with – in the spirit of cooperation?'

Shark opens his mouth to object, but Perrin silences him with a gesture. 'If we can, Inspector. Ask away.'

'Kelvin Draper and his wife – they weren't doing any work for you as far as I know. Kelvin wasn't a threat to anybody, so who did he piss off, and why?'

Shark's eyebrows come together in a thunderous frown. 'Are you for real?' he growls, and I see his fists clench, but he manages, with an effort, to keep them on his knees. 'He was done for the minute you went sniffing around down at the centre – you and that other bitch, the one who got your job. Me and Kelvin, we went way back, grew up together – went our separate paths, y'know, but he was a brother all the same, and we looked out for each other.'

'I'm sorry,' I say, with genuine feeling. 'Whether you believe it or not, I liked him too, and I wouldn't knowingly have seen him come to harm, even though I nicked him once or twice.'

The tension lasts another couple of beats; then Shark lets out a long breath and gives me a nod. 'Yeah. Just doing your job, right? Maybe they would have shut him up anyway.

Kelvin came to see me, a couple of days before the bastards got him. One of them was over at the centre, got him talking, about the animals, said he was a dog lover and had a mate who'd bought a Doberman somewhere round here. He wanted to know where, as he was thinking of getting one himself. You know what Kelvin was like – talk to anyone about anything, stupid prat, so of course he told him. He was worried afterwards, though, and came over to see me. Said that thinking back, something wasn't quite right; the guy didn't look like a dog lover, more like he might be connected to the Greeks. Things sounded a bit off to me, so I warned him to keep his mouth shut and got one of my lads to keep an eye, just in case, right?'

He sighs and shakes his head. Perrin, the picture of sympathy, pours him a generous tot of whisky from a decanter on the desk and pushes it across to him. He takes a slug and goes on. 'That night, the dogs were stolen, and you turned up on Kelvin's doorstep hours later, asking about the theft. As soon as you'd gone, Kelvin rang to tell me your lot were sniffing around, and that's when the other one turned up – Polly the fucking parrot. She probably heard the conversation. A few hours after that, Kelvin and his family were wasted. So you tell me, Bird – somebody squawked, and my money's on pretty fucking Polly, and either you're in on it, or she's tailing you, clocking your every move. You're the dog guy, right? So maybe she's worried you might find out things you shouldn't. Mr Perrin here thinks we can trust you. I'm still making my mind up.'

'You can trust me, Jermaine,' I assure him. 'And as for Inspector Sillitoe, you don't need to worry about her for the moment.' I don't add that I'm getting more worried by the minute. 'So, you think this Alastor character did for Kelvin and his wife?'

He grunts. 'True enough – but not directly. He ordered it – might have watched, but I doubt it. Not his style. There's another guy, one of his minders, meaner than the one who's keeping an eye on the girl. He's the one who went to see Kelvin. I don't know his name, but he's almost as much of a bastard as his boss. I reckon they were going to get rid of anyone who could connect them with the raid.' He pauses and then adds, 'Y'know, I think Alastor's overstepped himself. He's obsessed with those bloody dogs. It's my guess this was a private enterprise, and if his bosses get wind, they won't be too pleased, so he's trying to make the problem go away.'

'If that's true,' I say, 'he's made a big mistake. Thank you, Jermaine. I give you my word I'll do whatever I can to bring the killers of the Drapers to book. If one of ours is to blame, I'll get them, trust me.' This time, I really mean it, and it must show, because he relaxes a little and acknowledges it with a nod. At the same time a less reassuring thought hits me. Perhaps, given Shark's assessment of Alastor's attitude towards his dogs, being West Hill's official dog catcher could be a distinct disadvantage.

'You have another question?' Perrin asks.

'Eddie Hall. What's his story?'

Shark laughs out loud. 'Eddie? He's a fucking dickhead, that's his story!'

'I think,' Perrin puts in, 'that Inspector Crow is referring to Eddie's involvement with Medusa.'

'Involvement?' Shark's lip curls in a contemptuous smile. 'Thinks he's a big man now, the stupid little prick. Reckons he's untouchable, Alastor's right-hand man. I'll tell you what he is – he's a dead man walking, and the fucking idiot doesn't even realise it. He's the fall guy, does all the clearing up, all the risky stuff, and thinks he's that bastard's best friend – probably cleans his bathroom and offers to suck him off at night too. He can't see that he's only there to take the rap if anything goes tits up. Thing is, he's a total liability, and the first major cockup, he'll be in the cage getting his balls ripped off before he knows what's hit him.'

'I agree, he's not bright, and he's unreliable, so why take the chance? If I were Alastor, he wouldn't be my first choice.'

'That's easy,' Perrin says. 'Two things – money and power. The kid's a fool, but he's got one big advantage – that is to say, an advantage to the Greeks – not so much for him, the poor sod. His daddy is very rich, and he's got political sway. It's my bet they'll use little Eddie to gain traction with the Honourable Gerard, financially, politically, however they can. The more dirt they have on Eddie, the more likely it is that Gerard will knuckle under when they come in waving the big stick. Unfortunately, once they've got control of the Hall-Warner real estate and contacts, the son and heir will likely have served his purpose.' He shrugs. 'If I were them, that's what I'd do.'

'Except the kid won't last that long,' Shark puts in. 'He'll mess up, and they'll be sending him back to the stately home a bit at a time.'

I can't deny that their analysis is probably accurate. I suppose it should have occurred to me that an organisation like Medusa would aim to get their people as high up the food chain as possible, be it the resident criminal gangs, the police, or local government. I'm not, I remind myself, dealing with small-time crooks like Johnson and Perrin. This is an outfit that spans continents and probably counts its profits in billions of dollars – and thousands of bodies.

I get to my feet. 'Thanks for the information. I'll be in touch as soon as I've arranged something for the girl. In the meantime, if you come across anything I should know ...'

Perrin gets to his feet and holds out a hand. 'It was good of you to come, Inspector. I hope we can all meet again in happier times.'

I give him the best smile I can manage in the circumstances. 'Believe me, Reggie, if we get through this, I sincerely hope the next time we meet will be when I'm giving evidence against you in court. No offence, of course.'

He grins widely. 'None taken, Inspector Crow. We all have our own paths to tread, and I wish you good luck in your efforts.' The grin disappears, and he leans forward, serious now. 'Listen, Inspector, I meant what I said, about assisting where I can. I can give you my personal guarantee that while this matter is ongoing, my employees will do their best to cause as little disruption as possible.'

'Much appreciated, Reggie,' I say, and turn to Shark. 'Does that go for you, too?'

He nods an acknowledgement. 'That's fair.'

I reach the door and have another thought. 'There is just one more thing. Your boy, Jermaine – Clive Gingell ...'

'What about him?' Shark's eyes narrow in suspicion.

'Two things. First, I don't want to see another mark on him. He runs into any more doors, and I'll be knocking on yours – with a bloody great ram. You understand me?'

He shrugs. 'I can't be responsible for other people, but I'll keep an eye. What's your interest anyway?'

'He's a bright kid. It's my guess he could make something of himself if he had the chance. Which brings me to the second thing. He thinks the sun shines out of your arse. That means he'd shove his head in an oven if you told him to, right?'

I get a nod. 'So?'

'So, you tell him to get the fuck into school – school, college, university, whatever. Use whatever reason you like. If it comes from you, he'll listen. This is the deal – I'll be taking a lot of risks. If they don't pay off, chances are I won't be around to check on him, and maybe neither will you. If we get to the other side, and we're both still standing, you do this for me. Agreed?'

'And me? I do this for you, what do I get out of it?'

'A warm glow. The feeling that for once in your life, you did something good. Didn't you ever wonder what that was like? And like you said about Kelvin – he was on a different path, but he was still a brother. Young Clive is going to grow up, faster than you think, and he's either going to be one of your grunts – worthless cannon fodder on the street, or maybe he could be a doctor, a lawyer – hell, anything. But he'll still be a brother. You understand?'

There's a long silence while Shark thinks it over. Then he pushes himself upright.

'If we're both still standing,' he says, spits into his palm, and holds it out. I grasp his hand, and the bargain is sealed.

Outside, Clive is waiting to make sure I'm safely escorted from the premises. 'Take care of yourself, son,' I say as I walk out into the alley.

'Fuck you,' he replies.

18

Back out on the street, my first act is to call Grace and tell her to set up a meeting with the chief constable as a matter of urgency. Thankfully, she catches my tone and doesn't ask any questions.

'Get straight over to headquarters,' she tells me. 'I'll make sure he's available, even if I have to drag him out of the executive toilet myself.'

I make for the cab rank at the bus station, and as soon as I'm settled in the back seat, I check in with my son-in-law.

'I've stayed on, to give Sergeant Saint a break,' he explains, when I ask him why the hell he's still in Weston and not back at home getting on with other things. 'He was up most of the night, keeping an eye out for any activity, but nothing so far. I went through the recordings, just to be sure, and I've got my laptop with me, so I'm not wasting my time.'

The last point is delivered with some irritation, which I realise is probably justified, at least from his point of view. From mine, having the father of my grandchildren within a mile of a gun-and-dog-toting psychopath is completely unacceptable. I remind myself that despite my misgivings, he is an adult after all, even if he's a naïve one, and if he were one of my Sinkhole cadets, I wouldn't have any qualms about giving him experience at the sharp end of policing. He's also made a good point – George, despite appearances, is dedicated to his job and probably hasn't slept all night.

'Sorry, son,' I say, gritting my teeth. 'Just be very careful, okay? And don't forget to talk to Rosie. We can meet up at home later and swap notes.'

I manage to get his agreement to be back in Bristol by evening, and focus my attention on the problem at hand – how the hell we're going to snatch a ruthless assassin's dog-sitter from under his nose without unleashing a bloodbath on West Hill.

WHEN I finally manage to get a word out without descending into the kind of inappropriate language that would normally end in disciplinary proceedings, it is to say, 'No! Absolutely not – if you think I'll let this happen, you've lost your bloody minds!'

I'm sitting on the wrong side of the second desk I've encountered since lunch, and the person in its driving seat, on this occasion Chief Constable Gosford, simply raises an eyebrow and comments, 'I would remind you, Inspector Crow, that as the lowest-ranking officer in the room, you are not in a position to allow or disallow any course of action we decide to take.' He pauses and then carries on in a softer tone. 'I do understand your concerns, Inspector, and I sympathise with your position, but given our options, I can't see any alternative. If you have a suggestion, I'm perfectly willing to consider it.'

I look across at Grace, who gives me a helpless shrug. 'I'm sorry, Al. I can't see how else this is going to work.'

'Jesus fucking Christ,' is my automatic response, and I immediately hold up a hand to Gosford. 'Sorry, sir. But he's a civilian, not a frontline officer. He hasn't got a clue what the risks are, and if the wheels come off, he could end up getting shot or worse. What am I supposed to say to my daughter if that happens? She's about to have a baby, for God's sake!'

'It's our job to make sure it doesn't happen,' Gosford says, trotting out the well-worn phrase as if he's discussing which club to use on the fairway of Long Ashton golf course. 'If we can get a message to this woman and time it right, both she and Larson will be safely tucked away before anyone realises she's gone.'

'And when they do, and all hell breaks loose?' I'm seriously starting to question the wisdom of my arrangement with Perrin and Shark Johnson. 'If they get spooked now, they could swap location, disappear overnight, and we'll lose our chance to put the whole lot of them away. Then we'll all end up looking over our shoulders for the foreseeable future. If I read that psychopath right, he's not the type to shrug his shoulders and let things go.'

'If things go according to plan, they won't connect her disappearance to us,' Grace says. 'Hopefully, right now, they don't know we're aware that one of our officers is working for them. We can put out a story and let whoever it is take the message back that we aren't involved. If we're lucky and keep our eyes open, we might catch them at it, and that will solve another problem.'

Grace's analysis has thrown up two of my least favourite phrases when it comes to police work – 'according to plan', and 'if we're lucky'. I scrabble for an alternative proposition, but come up empty-handed. 'Bloody sod it!' is the most helpful comment I can think of. There's a tense silence, during which I think of one final objection. 'Like I said, he's a civilian. That means you can't make him do anything he doesn't want to do. It will be his decision.' I meet the chief constable's eye and add, 'It also means that you make him aware of all the risks – his decision has to be an informed one. I don't want my son-in-law walking blindly into a situation that might end up with him getting his head blown off.'

Gosford gives me a tight grin. 'A fair point, Inspector. I think I'm quite confident Mr Larson will be given all the information he needs. After all, Inspector Crow, you will be the one giving it.' He gets up and straightens his jacket. 'I must go – interview about knife crime with *Western Eye* in half an hour, and it's going out live, so I ought to get their make-up girl to give me the once-over. Oh, by the way, Inspector,' he adds, with what seems to me a perverse satisfaction, 'I'm sure DCI Helston has explained the importance of cooperating with the new mental health initiatives that are currently being trialled in all inner-city stations. According to my record, your last meeting with your clinical therapist was just over six months ago. I am very aware of your reluctance to engage with psychological services, but I remind you that it is a condition of your return to work, and that as a senior officer, it is your duty to set an example. Therefore I expect the situation to be rectified within the next fourteen days.' With that, he sweeps out, leaving me and Grace staring at each other in exasperation.

'Make-up girl?' I shake my head. 'For fuck's sake! What bloody universe is he living in?'

Grace's mouth twitches into a smile. 'He'll have a bit of a shock when he gets down there. The "make-up girl" is most definitely male – ex-army with some very impressive tattoos. Last time I went over to do a *Crimeline* appeal, he asked me out to dinner.'

'Did you go?' I ask.

Her smile widens. 'None of your business, Inspector.'

It's just after five by the time Grace drops me back home on her way to West Hill, with a promise to return later in the evening to help me break the news to Larson of our plans for his immediate future and, assuming he agrees, fill out the details. I make myself busy in the kitchen, mulling over all the things that could possibly go wrong, and how I would ever be able to look Rosie and Chrissie in the eye again if any of them did. When Larson finally gets back an hour and a half later, my brain is about as stewed as the casserole I've reheated in the oven.

I manage to sit through my son-in-law's report reasonably calmly. Nothing has been picked up by the cameras in Weston. Of course, that doesn't mean 'nothing' in the literal sense. We only have surveillance set up on the back garden and shed. Anyone coming into the bungalow from the front might easily be missed. Grace has already checked on the possibility of using CCTV from one of the shops opposite. The only system is on the minimarket, and unfortunately for us, the images don't extend to the other side of the road. Nevertheless, George has arranged for Larson to check it regularly, just in case.

'Rosie's fine,' Larson informs me, pushing back his half-empty plate. 'I dropped in on my way back. Ben got a gold star in his computer programming class.' I almost see his chest swell with pride.

'Computer class?' I stare at him, remembering my own schooldays and the nightmare of daily recitation of times tables. 'He's only six! They do computer programming at that age?'

He laughs. 'Of course – there are special teaching methods these days. After all, technology is supposed to be the future ...' He hesitates and then says quietly, 'Although sometimes, you know, I'm not sure whether it's a good thing – with all that's going on in the world ...'

'But you're a geek,' I remind him. 'Isn't nerdy stuff your reason for living? I would have thought Ben following in your footsteps was pretty high on your wish list.'

He gives me a frank look. 'Would having Rosie join the police force be high on yours?'

He's got a point. 'No,' I admit. 'I suppose not.'

'Have you ever read E M Forster's short story – *The Machine Stops*?'

I shake my head. 'I didn't really have time for literature – too busy catching villains to catch up on my reading.'

He smiles. 'It was way ahead of its time – a cautionary tale about the fate of the human race if it places too much reliance on computers. I read it as a teenager, but didn't really pick up on the message until Rosie was expecting Ben. I started off as a games programmer, but when I met Rosie, I was getting offered work programming smart home applications, and that's when it hit me that by the time Ben is my age, we could be really close to a world where we can run our entire lives without getting out of our chairs, and never actually go outside and meet another human being. I love computers, but it's not the life I want for my children.' He pauses, frowning, and then says, 'The effect on our lifestyles isn't the only thing. The more we rely on apps to run everything, the more opportunities criminals have to break in and help themselves to whatever they like without ever taking the risk of coming round to your house and climbing through the window. Every piece of software I design has to be as secure as possible, so I need to be able to test it in scenarios that are as close to the real world as I can get.'

'In other words,' I say, 'you have to become an expert hacker in order to stop the real criminals.' It's the first time he's really explained to me how, precisely, he does provide for my daughter, and I have to admit I'm starting to understand that perhaps I've been just a little too dismissive of his skills.

'Exactly,' he replies. 'I get requests from some fairly big organisations now and then, especially when they want to make use of bespoke software and aren't sure about security. Working for the police is different, though – I'm not working in a simulated environment, closing loopholes that might lead to crime. I'm back in the real world, helping to catch real criminals, and that makes me feel as if I'm using whatever talent I have to really do something useful – make the world a better place for Ben and the baby to grow up in.' He shrugs. 'You probably think that's stupid or at least naïve.'

He looks away, retrieves his plate and focuses on pushing the remains of his dinner round it. I watch him for a moment or two, thinking of the bloody great spoke Grace and I are about to shove into the smoothly running wheel of his career aspirations. What's worrying me more than anything is that whatever I do to try to put him off, he's going to grasp the poisoned chalice with both hands, and once he gets a taste for it, he's not going to want to let it go.

'No, son,' I say finally, 'I don't think it's stupid. Bloody naïve, yes – but not stupid.'

19

Grace arrives on cue, just as the kettle boils, and we convene in my lounge with coffee and slices of Joyce's Victoria sponge. For Larson's benefit, I explain the essentials of my meeting with Shark Johnson and Reggie Perrin. I leave it to Grace to tell him what we have in mind.

'We know that the woman's regular walk takes her across the river to the south end of the harbour, by the boatyard. There's a pub, the Newfoundland, right on the waterfront. Do you know it?'

Larson nods. 'Yes, of course. It's a good place – pretty crowded though, when there's a match on at the City ground.'

'That's what we're counting on,' Grace says. 'It's on her normal route, it has a large sitting area out the front, and the back leads out into a yard sealed off by electric gates. The gates exit onto a road leading back into town. It's also the main route for football supporters heading for Ashton Gate. The thing is, the road behind the pub is closed off for roadworks at the moment, except for resident access. That means the football crowd will be funnelled down the roads on either side.'

I can see from Larson's expression that he's up to speed. 'So all we need is a football match?'

'Precisely.' Grace grins. 'And we're in luck, if we can get it arranged in time. Bristol City are playing Cardiff the day after tomorrow, and it's a late kickoff. It starts at five, and it's one of the big local grudge matches of the season. There will be uniforms everywhere, all along the route – vans, horses, dogs – the lot. There are going to be upwards of twenty thousand feuding fans milling around from around three onwards, and the Newfoundland will be stacked with drinkers, inside and out. Our target quite often stops off there for a refresher, and the timing fits perfectly with her normal routine, so the minder will be used to her dropping in for a G&T or whatever. If she can get there just before the main influx of fans, we've got a chance of getting her away before the minder realises she's gone.'

'How, exactly?' Larson asks.

'You've still got that awful sports car of yours, haven't you?' I say.

'If you mean my classic MG, yes of course. It's been under a tarpaulin in the garage over the winter, but I fire it up once a week so that it's ready to go as soon as the weather's good enough.'

'Perfect,' Grace says. 'The plan is to get her sitting out with her drink just before three. She waits until the place fills up – it shouldn't take more than half an hour or so. Once the pub is heaving, she leaves her glass and jacket on the bench to make it look as if she's coming back, and goes inside to use the loo. Whoever's watching won't be surprised if she takes longer than usual. By the time he decides to go in to find her, she'll have gone out the back way, where you, Mr Larson, will be waiting in your MG. The landlord will give you the remote for the gates, and you'll be out onto the empty street. When you get to the roadblock at the end, the police will assume you're a resident and let you past the barrier. Actually, if I can, I'll try to be there as well – I can use the pretext of checking on crowd management.'

He nods. 'That seems straightforward enough. What do I do once I'm past the barrier?'

'That's where we think we've surpassed ourselves,' she says, grinning, and turns to me. 'The chief constable does have his uses, believe it or not. He's got a property developer friend who owns half a dozen waterfront apartments on Redcliffe Wharf. Three of them are vacant – they've just been renovated, and the tenants haven't moved in yet. Gosford mentioned his niece was looking for somewhere to stay for a few days, and after a bit of backscratching, the guy was happy to offer one of his empty flats – the penthouse, no less – for a month, at half the normal rent.'

'Christ!' I comment. 'How did he manage that?'

'Put it this way,' she replies with a laugh. 'Maybe we should both take up golf.' Serious again, she goes on. 'The beauty of it is, the block has a secure underground car park. Nobody can see who goes in or out on foot. The plan is that you, Mr Larson, head straight over there – you'll only be on the road a few minutes – you'll have an entry key for the car park, and as soon as you're in, your car will be next to impossible to find. You can quite safely leave it there until the fuss has died down.'

'And then what?' he asks. 'Once I've got her into the

apartment, do I just leave her and hope she doesn't wander off?'

Grace shakes her head. 'No. I want you to stay with her. Keep her company, make sure she has anything she needs, within reason, and make sure she doesn't go outside. When we're confident nobody has followed, we'll get in touch, and one of us will come round to talk to her. Until then, your job will be to keep her happy and report anything she says to us.'

'Stay with her?' For the first time, he looks distinctly nervous. 'How long for? I mean, you want me to sleep there?'

I can't help but laugh. 'Welcome to the world of police work, son,' I say when I've got my breath back. 'Are you trying to tell me that you're about to put your life on the line getting the woman away from a dangerous gunman, and all you're worried about is whether or not she tries to climb into your bed in the middle of the night?' He bristles at once, so I hold up a placating hand. 'I don't think you need to be concerned. No matter how calm she appears to be, she's crossing a dangerous line, and if I were her, I'd be scared out of my wits. You won't be there to relax, son. Until we can work out a next move, you're her security blanket, and you're there to protect her – at any cost. I want you to bear that in mind and think carefully before you agree to this. If you've got any doubt at all, just say no, and we'll think of another way – nobody will think any the worse of you.'

He looks me in the eye. 'If there was another way, you wouldn't be asking me, would you?'

'No,' I reply. 'We wouldn't.'

'Then there's no discussion.' He shrugs. 'If we want to get her away from them, and she can help us get these monsters off the street, I don't have a choice. Count me in.'

Grace exhales audibly. 'Thank you, John.' She turns to

me. 'You'd better get in touch with your contact right away. If we're going to do this, we need the information from their side as soon as possible.'

'I'm on it, Grace.' I retreat to the kitchen to compose a text message, and on the way out say to my son-in-law, 'You'd better pack some essentials, then go off and spend some time with Rosie and Ben. You may not see them for a few days. Don't stay too late, though. If this kicks off, you probably won't get much sleep, and you'll need to be alert.'

His exasperated sigh follows me into the hallway. I decide that short and simple is best, so send a text to the number on the burner.

Need to speak. Now.

I pour myself a whisky and head out into the garden to think.

I don't have to wait long. I've been mulling things over for about twenty minutes when there's a rustle in the back lane, followed by the appearance of a small, shadowy figure on top of the fence. Clive lands on my lawn with a soft thud. He trots over to join me at the table.

'How's it going, Clive?' I ask.

'Yeah. Suppose.' He hesitates, then adds, 'Thanks.'

'Thanks? Did you fall off your bike and land on your head?'

He scowls. 'Shark told me I had to be respectful and stop fucking swearing, but if you're just going to take the piss ...'

'Okay. Sorry, Clive. You hungry?'

He shrugs.

'Wait there.' I go inside, grab one of the pasties George sent to the hospital, still just about edible, and a chunk of cake, and take them out to him. I explain our plan to him as he eats. 'Do you think Shark can get the message to her in time? The Newfoundland, three o'clock on Saturday?'

He nods. 'I reckon.' He pulls out one of his many burners and dials. There's a short conversation; he hangs up and says, 'Shark says leave it to him. She'll be there. You'd better be ready, though. He says we only get one chance.'

'Don't worry – we'll be ready.'

I watch him go, melting silently into the darkness with the skill of a seasoned housebreaker. When I get back to the lounge, Grace is waiting alone.

'Are you thinking of opening a café when you finally retire?' she asks, smiling. 'Maybe there's a side of you I don't know anything about.'

'The kid was hungry,' I protest. 'It was either that or arrest him for attempted breaking and entering. What was I supposed to do?' I rapidly change the subject. 'It's all agreed. Shark's going to get her to the pub at the right time. Then it's up to us.'

'Good.' She stands up. 'I'd better get started on the details and give the chief constable a heads up.'

I'm seeing her to the door when my phone rings. 'Thought you'd better know,' George says. 'There's been some activity over here. You might want to take a look.'

I touch Grace's arm, and she stops in the hallway, coat half-on. 'You got any details, George?'

'Best you see for yourself. The time stamp is 6.43pm. There's a lull around 7.15, but keep watching.'

'Okay. Thanks, George. I've got the DCI here, so we'll check it out and get back to you. Meanwhile, keep your eyes peeled, okay?'

'No problem, Al. I've got a rogan josh with my name on

it, and Mr Khan has lent me a TV. There's a new David Attenborough documentary on tonight.'

'David Attenborough? Is there no limit to your hidden depths, George?'

I hear him chortle to himself as he hangs up.

It's just as well Grace is on hand, as Larson's array of computer equipment is a bit out of my league. However, it appears George is not the only one with hidden depths. The DCI rolls up her sleeves and makes a beeline for one of the monitors, which is displaying the live feed from the surveillance camera. After a minute or so of rattling at the keyboard and a few mouse clicks, the image changes to a rerun of the day's capture. She forwards the recording to just before the time George has given us, and we both settle to watch.

We don't have to wait long. The first person to appear is Edwin Hall-Warner, striding confidently down the garden. He doesn't go straight to the shed, though. There's a dilapidated bench seat halfway down the garden, and he makes himself comfortable on it and lights up – not a cigarette, I decide, judging by the size – a joint, I have no doubt. I recall Shark's comments on young Eddie's probable fate as I watch him – relaxed, cocky, not a care in the world, getting stoned as he blindly totters closer to the cliff edge that his new friends are going to push him off before too long. One telling fact is that he clearly hasn't been entrusted with a key to the shed. He's the hired help and no more. After a few minutes the back door to the bungalow opens again, and the old lady comes out with a tray – bringing him tea and biscuits.

'Jesus bloody Christ!' I hiss under my breath, and Grace puts a hand on my arm, silent and tight-lipped.

The woman disappears back inside, and we wait another

ten minutes before the door opens again. This time, it's a man – the same individual Larson and I saw with Hall-Warner on our first visit to the bungalow. I also now know, from my meeting earlier in the day, that he's the murderer of Kelvin Draper and his pregnant wife, and perhaps of DS Brent as well. Sadly, at this moment, we can't prove it, and even if we could, bringing him in would kill our chances of getting hold of the main villain of the piece, his boss, Alastor. At least the image we have of him now is clear enough to perhaps get an identification.

I feel Grace tense beside me. Alastor's thug is clearly unhappy as he makes a beeline for Hall-Warner, grabs the joint out of his hand, and hauls him to his feet by the lapels. There's a great deal of gesticulating and shouting, ending with a slap in the face that sends Eddie reeling halfway across the garden. The boy recovers himself and falls into line, dabbing at his face with a handkerchief while his controller opens the shed, and they both go inside.

'I don't see a key,' Grace comments. 'That probably means they have quite a sophisticated entry system. Even without the CCTV they've set up, we'd probably have to take the whole thing apart to get inside. Can you make a note to ask John what the possibilities are?'

I nod, and we keep watching. They are in the shed for no more than a couple of minutes and emerge empty-handed except for a small rucksack that the thug had brought with him. Whatever they came for must be small enough to fit inside. The shed is secured, and they leave together, back into the bungalow and, presumably, out the front door.

'What do you think?' I ask Grace. 'Heroin or cocaine? That rucksack was big enough to carry a good few thousand quid's worth.'

'That's my bet,' she replies. 'Christ – they could have a fortune stashed away in there. You need to keep in touch with your contacts, Al, see if they can tip you off about any new supplies on the streets, and if so, where. We might be able to stop at least some of it without them realising we're watching.'

'I can try,' I say, but like my DCI, I don't hold out much hope.

We settle back in silence. *Keep watching*, George had said. For ten minutes, there is no movement. Then the back door opens again, and the old lady comes out, accompanied by another figure. For a moment, we are both frozen, too stunned to breathe. Then Grace wipes a hand across her face and whispers, 'Jesus fucking Christ!'

Polly Sillitoe, framed by the light in the back doorway, chats for a moment with the woman, who goes back inside, leaving Polly alone in the garden. We both watch, horrified, as she makes her way slowly towards the shed, first in the dark, and then by the light of the torch on her phone. She seems to be searching for something. At the bench, she crouches, picks something up, shoves it in her pocket, and continues on.

'What the fuck is that all about?' Grace says, giving me a puzzled glance.

I shrug. 'Maybe she dropped something last time and went back to retrieve it?'

She shakes her head, but doesn't reply.

For at least a minute Sillitoe is hidden by the bulk of the shed, making it impossible to see whether or not she goes inside. Then she emerges from the blind spot, carries on to the end of the garden, and without hesitation lifts up the section of fence that has been clipped away from the boundary post, and ducks through onto the lane. Once there she stops, turns off the torch, but doesn't move. It takes me a moment to realise that she's looking up. Her gaze is fixed on the tiny loft window in the building opposite, behind which video cameras are capturing her every move, and George is halfway through his rogan josh. I can't be sure, but as she turns away and heads down to the main road, I think I see her smile.

20

I wake expecting to spend much of the day in a state of helpless frustration. There's no sign of Larson, and I'm on my second coffee when he finally comes through the front door carrying a box filled with foil parcels, which he unloads on the worktop.

'Joyce is convinced we're starving to death over here,' he says with a shrug. 'I guess it's her way of making herself feel useful.'

I smile. 'It's always been her first resort in times of stress – a hell of a lot cheaper than counselling, and everyone else benefits. I don't suppose there's anything in there resembling breakfast?'

In response, he pulls out a large plastic container, removes the lid, and the scent of warm bacon fills the kitchen like a comforting hug. I send my silent and heartfelt thanks to my ex-mother-in-law, and we both settle down to get the most out of the unexpected bounty that's landed on the table.

While we're eating, I fill Larson in on the depressing contents of the video recording.

'Do you think she's onto what we're doing?' he asks. 'If she is, Sergeant Saint might be compromised, so maybe we should rely on remote monitoring instead?'

'Pull George out, do you mean? Son, you're on a hiding to nothing. He hasn't had so much fun for at least five years. Don't worry, he can look after himself, and if she has clocked our surveillance, we need someone on the ground to raise the alarm before they destroy Mr Khan's B&B business – or more likely, turn it into a tourist attraction – posthumously, of course.'

'Are you always this cynical?' he asks.

'When it comes to organised crime, you can bloody bet on it,' I answer. 'Take it from me, son. They don't take prisoners. You may not know it, but I do, and so does George. Don't worry about him. He's as savvy as they come, and he'll know the right time to bow out. Somehow, though, I don't think she's aware we're watching. If she was, she wouldn't have put in an appearance, or at least she wouldn't have stood there, all but waving at the camera on her way out.'

He doesn't reply, but seems to shrink into himself for a minute and then says, almost in a whisper, 'You said, when Rosie got out of prison, that I could call you Al.'

'Yes,' I say, wondering where this is leading. 'I did.'

'Al,' he says, 'I'm scared. Not for me – for Rosie and Ben and the little one. If anything happens to me ...'

My mind goes back to the days when Chrissie would say to me, 'What will we do, Al, if anything happens to you? If one of these days you don't come home, and Rosie's last memory is of a body bag and a funeral for her dead father?'

It was the start of the long road to divorce.

'Listen, John,' I say, trying to sound reassuring, 'I can't pretend there aren't any risks. Police work means putting yourself on the line now and then, whatever role you've signed up for. But I can promise you, we'll be watching every step of the way, and if everyone does their job, you and this Becks, or whatever her name is, will be safely tucked up before anyone realises she's gone.'

'I know.' He gives me a weak grin. 'It still doesn't stop me feeling like a fireman running into a burning building to rescue someone's cat.'

He slides his chair back. 'I have to go and check out the car, but if you haven't got any plans, there's something you could keep an eye on for me.'

I follow him up to his room and its array of monitors. One is relaying the live feed from Weston, and he shows me how to bring up the recording.

'If George rings through with anything of interest, you can watch it from here.' He gives me a sheet of paper. 'I've written the steps down, just in case.'

'You mean, in case I delete the whole lot by mistake?'

He shuffles awkwardly.

'Don't worry, son,' I say, laughing. 'I know my limits!'

He goes over to a second monitor. 'I'm going to set up a facial-recognition search,' he explains, and brings up a still image of Hall-Warner and his unidentified companion, taken from last night's surveillance footage. He zones in on the second man, taps a few keys, and the image begins to change, becoming clearer with each pass through the software he's using. After a minute or so, the computer beeps, and a final picture shows a clear, unsmiling face that looks as if it's been carved from a block of granite. It's the face of a man who thinks nothing of beating a defenceless pregnant woman to death before calmly strolling off to have breakfast.

'Nasty piece of work,' I comment, and Larson and I exchange a look.

'It's a good, clear image, full face. If he's on any database, anywhere, we should be able to identify him.' He hits a few more keys and stands back. 'The program is running. I don't know how long it will take, but if there's a positive ID, it will display on the screen with an alert. We just need to cross our fingers it comes up with something.'

'It hasn't worked for his boss,' I say. 'We still don't know who Alastor really is.'

'No,' he agrees. 'And that's a worry. It may mean he travels illegally – smuggled in and out, but that would be very risky.'

I shake my head. 'That might work in some countries, but this bastard seems to turn up in some pretty dangerous places, if the movements of his dog are anything to go by. It's far more likely the organisation has contacts in high places just about everywhere, and he's allowed to slip through wherever he goes. The records can always be altered later if enough money changes hands – that, or pressure is brought to bear. What we're dealing with is an outfit that probably has more money and influence than all the big computer companies put together. Even if we chase them off our patch, we're like a flea on a dog's back – an irritation, no more.'

'In other words,' he says, 'we're going to all this trouble, putting ourselves at risk, for something they probably won't even notice in the grand scheme of things. Whatever we do, it won't make any difference.'

'To them, probably not a lot, but to us, a great deal. Drugs, guns, people – we'll never stop the trafficking altogether, but we can try to slow it down, make it harder for organised crime to get a foothold on our own little patch of ground. Every little success makes the streets safer, even if it's only for a short while. Mind you, if we can get our hands on their hired assassin, take him out of the picture, it will at least be the equivalent of shooting them in the foot, and I'll be satisfied with that, for now.'

There's a third screen crammed into my tiny spare room, showing a map of the local area and several flashing dots in different colours. 'Bit early for the Christmas decorations,' I comment. 'What is it doing?'

He gives me an apprehensive look. 'It's just a precaution, really – a little extra monitoring, just in case.'

'In case of what?'

And before he can stop me, I reach for the mouse and click on the little magnifying glass at the top of the screen until the map zooms in to show the streets clearly. Bang in the middle of the screen – in the middle of my house – are two little flashing dots, one yellow, one blue. I turn to my son-in-law, who is staring out the window, a pained look on his face.

'You're tracking me? Jesus Christ! I hope you've got the proper authorisation, son. Otherwise, you'll be in one hell of a lot of trouble. Illegal snooping does happen to be a criminal offence.'

'I'm tracking all of us,' he replies. 'You, me, Sergeant Saint, DCI Helston and DI Sillitoe. And yes, I have direct permission from the chief constable. He felt it was a sensible precaution given tomorrow's operation, in case any of us got into difficulty. Plus, I can see where DI Sillitoe is relative to any one of us at any time. The patterns will show if she's following or keeping a watch on us. If there's any indication she knows our movements in advance, we'll be alerted to it.'

I have to admit it makes sense, even though the idea is making me far from comfortable. 'So what am I? Blue or yellow?'

'You're blue. I'm yellow.' He scrolls back out until we can see all five dots. 'The DCI is green – she's at West Hill station. So is Sillitoe – she's the red dot. Sergeant Saint, the purple marker, is on the move. Looks like he's on his way to the caravan he's supposed to have rented in Brean Down. He puts in an appearance there at least once a day, usually in the morning when there's the least chance of anything kicking off at the bungalow. If there's any unusual activity from any of us, it will be picked up very quickly.'

'It won't be if nobody's looking at the screen,' I point out. 'One of your twinkly little dots could be floating in the middle of the Bristol Channel or halfway down the gap between the suspension bridge and the River Avon before anybody notices.'

'That's true,' he admits. 'I do have an alert set up for Sillitoe. If she goes near certain places, for example the bungalow, I'll know. For the others, though, it means we can pinpoint your location, or at least the location of your phone if you don't turn up where and when you are expected, or if you don't check in when you normally would.'

'So you trace the signal,' I can't help saying, still feeling a bit ruffled, 'and find the phone dumped in a bin or at the side of the road. Criminals aren't stupid, son – especially these criminals. They know all about phone traces, and it's the first thing they'll think of. Then what do you do?'

He shrugs. 'If that happens, at least we'll know you're in trouble.'

21

I wake up on Saturday morning with a headache and a slight tremor in my right hand, both probably brought on by spending the best part of Friday staring at Larson's computer screens and clicking the replay button on the video feed from Weston-super-Mare. I give them all another quick check before going downstairs. Just like yesterday, nothing has changed. The garden of the bungalow is still deserted, and there have been no alerts from George. The red blip that is Polly Sillitoe's mobile hasn't moved from her home address for the last twelve hours, and the third monitor is still scrolling fruitlessly through every valid driving licence, identity card and passport photograph in the world's copious databases.

Larson, as usual, is already up and about, shrugging into a very expensive, and to my mind pretentious, aviator jacket.

'Is this what you call keeping a low profile?' I ask him. 'This is serious stuff, son, not a fancy dress party.'

'You think I don't know that?'

He turns to face me, and although he's doing his best to

hide it, the spring in him is wound so tight I feel a sudden urge to backpedal out of arm's reach.

'Sorry,' I say. 'It's fine. It's all going to be fine.'

As I'm speaking, I notice a flash of orange poking out from his jacket pocket, and recognise the dreadful scarf he bought over in Weston. He follows my gaze and pulls it out, holds it up with a frown. Then, suddenly, the tension seems to dissolve, and he starts to laugh.

'At least,' he says, grinning, 'I've found a use for this bloody thing.'

'You're going to polish your car with it?' I suggest.

He shakes his head. 'You may think this is a stupid idea, but aren't I using my MG because anyone watching isn't likely to be looking for it?' When I nod, he goes on. 'So I thought that if they were likely to miss an open-top sports car, they would be even more likely to ignore a sports car with a couple of poseurs in ridiculous clothes and aviators.'

He whips said sunglasses out of his pocket and puts them on to demonstrate. He's got a point – he's hardly recognisable, and in scarf and glasses that will apply to the woman, too. It's ludicrous, but in fact, it actually works.

'It is a stupid idea, son,' I tell him. 'But it's so stupid it might even pay off.' I have another thought. 'What does Rosie think of it – your car, I mean?'

'She loves it. We used to go all over the place in it in summer before Ben was born.' He smiles, reminiscing. 'It's trickier now, of course, but we still manage to go for the odd drive. She'd never forgive me if I got rid of it.' He sighs and shakes himself back into the present. 'I've borrowed her jacket and shades for today, for our guest. We'll just have to hope it doesn't rain.'

We're interrupted by a loud ping from the new burner

phone Shark gave me. The message is just two words: *All good*. I give Larson a nod. 'We're on.'

He takes a deep breath. 'Okay. I'd better go and get the car over to the pub, then, and pick up the remotes for the gates.' He hesitates. 'I suppose I won't see you again until it's all over.'

'No, I suppose you won't.' Some sentiment I don't quite understand makes me stick out my hand. 'Good luck, son.'

He takes it. 'Thanks.' He pauses again and then adds, 'You know, truth be told, I'm fucking terrified!'

With that, he heads out the door and disappears down the street, a man on a mission.

'You and me both,' I murmur to myself, and retreat to the kitchen to make coffee and check in with Grace.

I ARRIVE at the harbour just after two thirty. It's already busy, steady streams of supporters flowing across the bridges, heading for the City ground. The benches outside the Newfoundland are rapidly filling with home fans intent on swilling down as much beer as possible to avoid the higher prices at the bars in the stadium. For a moment I worry that our plan might fail simply because, when the target arrives, there will be nowhere for her to sit. Then I notice a group of three lads, decked out in red and white scarves, taking up seats at a bench close to the pub entrance. One of them is Clive Gingell. That's pretty smart, I think to myself. One thing about young Clive – he knows how to use his initiative.

Football fans aren't the only ones cluttering up the streets along the route. As I make my way round to the rear of the pub, I count three police vans and two patrol cars, and when I turn the corner to the blocked-off road, a gaggle of uniforms is loitering in the street, clutching paper coffee cups, together with two mounted officers on standby in case anything serious kicks off away from the pitch. I go up to the barrier, and at once one of the stockier PCs strides towards me, practising his 'don't try it on, son,' face. When he gets closer, though, he does a double take and relaxes.

'Inspector Crow, isn't it?' he says, breaking into a smile. 'We don't often see you in this neck of the woods. Is there something I can do for you, sir?'

I gird myself up and return the smile. 'We all have to slum it now and again, Constable,' I reply, and get a satisfying chuckle in return.

'You'd be surprised what goes on round here sometimes, sir – makes West Hill look like Shangri-La! Are you looking for someone in particular?'

'DCI Helston asked me to meet her here. You got any idea where she is at the moment?'

He nods. 'Just at the end of the street, sir, last I saw a minute ago. In fact,' he says, pointing, 'there she is, getting herself a coffee, by the look of it.'

He steps aside to let me through, and I head on up the street, glancing into the pub's rear yard as I go. Larson's MG is where it should be, but there's no sign of him. Hopefully, he's in the rear lobby of the Newfoundland, waiting for his target to appear. I carry on past the second barrier and catch up with Grace at a mobile coffee van making a killing from police and football supporters alike.

'Add a black, three sugars,' she says to the man at the counter. He gives her a glare and turns back to his machine, clearly annoyed at having the local constabulary putting off a potentially more lucrative trade from the football fans. 'Seems to be going according to plan so far,' she comments as we take our drinks and head for a quiet corner away from the milling crowd.

'She's not here yet,' I point out. 'This could all be a wind-up, or worse, she could be acting as bait to winkle out anyone they think is on their tail. They could have people watching us at this moment, Grace.'

'Or,' she says, grimacing into her paper cup, 'they've got wind of what she's planning and she's dead already. God, this coffee is bloody awful!'

I look at my watch. It's just after two fifty. 'I'm going back out front,' I tell her. 'Someone needs to keep an eye on Shark Johnson's lads, if nothing else.'

She puts a hand on my arm. 'Be careful, Al. Keep your head down – literally.'

I nod and head off back to the front of the Newfoundland. The crowds are even thicker now, making it fairly easy to melt into the background on the opposite side of the road without losing sight of the pub benches. Clive and his mates are still installed near the door, clutching pint glasses of what I sincerely hope, for the landlord's sake, is lemonade. The minutes tick by; three o'clock comes and goes, and there's no sign of the woman I know as 'Becks'. The boys haven't moved, and I'm starting to get buffeted by the army of fans on the pavements. I make a decision, ditch the paper cup of foul coffee, cross to the pub, and elbow my way inside.

I spot a gap at a dim corner of the bar and wedge myself into it, hoping I'm not making a terrible mistake. From my position I have a good view of the entire room and the main door, but hopefully I can't easily be seen lurking in the shadows.

'What can I get you?' The barman leans across, elbows on the bar as if he's about to challenge me to an arm-wrestling contest. I hand over a tenner and ask for a half of real ale to keep up appearances. He sighs. 'You'll have to wait for change.'

He goes off to see to my beer, leaving me to stare anxiously at the old, smoke-stained clock hanging precariously above the optics behind the bar. As I watch, the minute hand clicks round to three twenty-one. Things aren't looking good. In another fifteen minutes or so, the mob will start to thin as the fans move further towards the stadium, and any chance of getting her away from her minder cleanly will be gone. The barman puts a glass down in front of me, together with a five-pound note, and I'm about to give in to the urge to cut my losses, leave the beer and the rest of my change and rejoin the crowd outside, when two people come into the pub – a man and a woman. *The* woman.

I grab my drink and shrink back against the rear wall, next to the short passage leading to the toilets – and the rear exit. The pair jostle their way to the bar, and he waves a card to attract the barman. There's no doubt he's the minder, and one nobody is likely to want to meddle with – broad shouldered, muscular and with the sort of flat expression that I've seen once or twice before on the faces of cold-blooded killers. I watch as he orders, without any consultation, a gin and tonic for her, plain tap water for himself. He's a man who takes his job seriously. Next to him, she keeps her eyes down, her body rigid, a woman in fear of her life.

The drinks arrive, and she clutches her gin glass like a comforter, taking the occasional sip. He doesn't touch the water, but simply leans against the bar, eyes never still, keeping watch. It occurs to me, perhaps too late, that we should have taken the effect on a professional bodyguard of having to negotiate a large crowd into account. It would make a man like this more vigilant, not less.

'Damn it!' I mutter to myself, and at the same time, I see her tap his arm and say something. He shakes his head. She persists, and in the end he shrugs, and she begins to move away. He reaches out, grabs her arm, and says something – a warning, from his expression. She nods and begins to weave her way through the bodies, coming in my direction. I quickly lean on the bar, one hand obscuring my face, the other signalling to the barman. I feel the minder's gaze sweep over me, focusing on the woman. She comes alongside and glances at me. Her eyes widen with recognition, but she makes no other reaction and without breaking stride moves past and through the door to the women's toilet.

At almost the same moment there's an eruption of noise outside. The minder's head jerks towards the door, body tense, one hand reaching into his jacket in a reflex action. A second later, Clive, surrounded by three or four other kids, appears in the doorway whooping and revving the guy's expensive-looking electric scooter. He gives the man a two-finger salute and reverses the thing out, scooting round the benches and upending beer glasses as he goes. I see the minder blink in disbelief, and then, in a sudden eruption of fury, he launches himself towards the door and out into the mayhem. Predictably, the crowd inside the pub collectively makes a mad dash for the doorway to see the fun, and the minder is blocked outside.

I slip across to the toilet, open the door a crack and whisper, 'Move. Now!'

She doesn't need to be told twice. I shield the door with my body; she slips out and disappears out the rear exit. I turn back to the now deserted bar and my half-finished beer to find the barman staring at me. I raise my eyebrows. His mouth twitches into a smile, and he hands me a second fiver.

'On the house,' he says quietly, and moves off to start collecting glasses.

I manage to push my way out of the pub just in time to see Shark's boys heave the scooter off the end of the harbour ferry landing stage. It hits the water with a loud splash, and the kids scatter. Within seconds, there's no trace of them. For a moment the minder is frozen, but then he realises his mistake and turns back to the pub. As if on cue, his path is blocked by two PCs. As I round the corner, heading back to the coffee van where Grace is waiting, I hear one of them clear his throat and say calmly, 'Was that your scooter, sir?'

22

Despite the circumstances, it takes Grace quite a while to stop laughing.

'It's priceless,' she says, between chuckles. 'It must be the first time in history that a hired thug has been arrested for illegal use of an electric scooter! I can't imagine what his bosses are going to say, especially when they find out his wheels were more important to him than the person he was supposed to be minding.'

'I have a feeling,' I reply, not without humour, 'that they'll be asking him to dredge it off the bottom of the harbour – wearing a concrete diving suit.'

'What about Shark's kids?' she asks. 'Our lot didn't go after them, did they?'

I shake my head. 'Even the most rookie PC knows when they're on a hiding to nothing. They were gone before the scooter hit the water. You know, Grace, they did a fantastic job, Clive in particular. He'd make one hell of a detective if he ever decided to work on the right side of the law.'

'I know you've got a soft spot for him,' she says, 'but don't hold your breath.'

We're in Grace's office, and it's just coming up to 7pm. Larson has reported in a couple of times since their arrival at the penthouse. Everything, he said, went smoothly, and by the sound of it, they were tucked away safely within minutes of the flight from the Newfoundland. Grace has made sure that the fridge in the flat is stocked, together with tea, coffee and a small selection of alcoholic drinks. We've arranged for me to arrive there around eight, using the service entrance at the back and delivering a change of clothes for 'call me Becks'.

I shrug. 'Just taking the horse to water, Grace. Everyone's a bloody philanthropist these days – I have to do my bit.'

'And it's got nothing to do with the fact you're about to become a grandfather again?' she comments. 'I've heard people can get a bit sentimental when they're expecting.'

I raise an eyebrow. 'And you're an expert on family psychology?'

For as long as I've known her, which is longer than most, Grace has been a woman without a history. No dog, cat, hamster or lover – male or female – that anyone has ever uncovered. She has always been a shining example of a blank slate as far as her personal life is concerned.

She gives me a mischievous grin and taps her nose. 'Need to know, Inspector – need to know.'

One day, I decide, I will definitely need to know.

She changes the subject. 'Are there any updates on DI Sillitoe? Apparently she messaged this morning saying she wasn't feeling too good and wouldn't be in today. Is John still monitoring her mobile?'

I yank out my phone. 'He's given me a link to the location feed.' I fumble for a minute and manage to bring up the screen. 'She's still at home,' I tell her. 'Looks like it's legitimate.'

'I'll wait until morning, then send someone to check. Hell, I'll go myself if she doesn't turn up for work. You never know, she might actually be ill.'

'You never know,' I agree, hoping Grace is right. In my bones, though, I'm pretty sure she isn't.

I HOLE up in the station canteen for another half an hour, then leave by the back exit and jump on the next bus into town. I get to the rear of the apartment block just after eight, clutching a brown paper parcel containing a change of clothes for our guest, and let myself in using the code I've been given for the service entrance. Unlike most of the blocks of flats in West Hill, the lifts in this piece of prime real estate are all working. I ride up to the penthouse, and a relieved Larson lets me in.

'Everything okay?' I ask.

He nods. 'Fine. Glad to see you. She hasn't said much. I offered to make some food, but she said she wasn't hungry – had a shower and a couple of large gins though.' He gives me an awkward grin. 'I think she's waiting for a proper policeman.'

I pat his shoulder. 'Well, there's one here now.'

I go through to the cavernous lounge, where she's wrapped in a bathrobe and curled in the corner of a massive sofa, looking out the window and nursing a gin glass. I pause in the doorway, taking the chance to study her properly for the first time. She's older than I first thought, perhaps in her mid-forties, with the beginnings of crow's feet round the eyes, worry lines on the forehead. Nevertheless, her hair, long and deep blonde, looks entirely natural, with no sign of grey. Despite the voluminous bathrobe, it's clear she's well toned, muscular – a woman who works out regularly.

She turns her head, and when she sees me, she stands and moves forward, holding out a hand.

'It's good to see you again, Inspector Crow. I suppose I should thank you for your assistance this afternoon.'

I take her hand – small, but dry and firm, although I think I detect a slight tremor as she pulls it away. 'No thanks necessary,' I say. 'But I think you have me at a disadvantage. I assume your name is not Rebecca Gripton, or any of the other aliases we've managed to come across in our investigations so far.'

She smiles, making the tiny lines at the corners of her eyes crinkle. 'You assume correctly. My name is Jennifer Teresi.' The smile fades. 'Inspector, you know as well as I do that any information I give you may, if we are not very careful, be heard by the wrong ears. Is there someone you can contact at your police station whom you can trust completely?'

'You can trust me,' I say. 'Completely. You can also trust Mr Larson, who brought you here.'

'I'm sure I can,' she replies. 'But I need to provide you with evidence of my identity, yes?'

I nod. 'That's true. You can also trust my superior officer, DCI Helston.'

'Then please contact DCI Helston and ask her to call Police Colonel Hector Dukas of the Athens police. Tell her she must not give her reasons to anyone except Dukas. That's very important. He will explain everything, and then I will talk to you.' She points to the package I still have under my arm. 'You have some fresh clothes for me?'

'Yes. Just a jogging outfit, I'm afraid. It's the best we could do at short notice.'

'Perfect.' She smiles again. 'While you are contacting your DCI, I'll go and change.'

She takes the parcel and disappears into one of the bedrooms. I get out my mobile and call Grace.

AN HOUR LATER, the three of us are sitting around a coffee table with glasses of very decent whisky and biscuits, having polished off bowls of pasta, courtesy of Larson's skills in the kitchen. Teresi has changed into jogging pants and T-shirt, an outfit that seems to accentuate the honed biceps, bearing out my initial impression of someone who takes her time in the gym very seriously. Given the information that has come through from Grace, it's not surprising.

Major Jennifer Teresi of the Athens police department sips her Scotch and sits back with a contented sigh. 'Thank you.' She gives Larson a nod. 'That was just what I needed.' She turns to me. 'I trust you have been able to validate my credentials, Inspector Crow?'

'We have, Major,' I reply.

'Jenny, please,' she says, treating me to a smile that lights up her face and makes her look ten years younger.

I suddenly feel a little awkward. 'That doesn't sound very Greek,' I say, which is the least intrusive comment I can think of at short notice. Her English is perfect, without any trace of an accent.

She laughs. 'It isn't. My mother was English. According to the tales my parents told me, she went on the hippy trail in the late 1960s, ended up in Greece and met my father – he was the local policeman – when he raided the commune she was living in. He said he had two choices – arrest her or marry her. It was love at first sight. My mother accepted his proposal, and they settled near Corinth.'

'And you followed in your father's footsteps,' Larson chips in.

'Eventually,' she replies, turning the smile on him. 'I went to university to study veterinary medicine, and when I graduated, I joined the army as a vet. I became a police officer when I left the army eight years later. It was the beginning of a long road that led me here.'

Suddenly, I can see it all in my mind's eye. A cold-blooded killer obsessed with his dogs, and an undercover cop who just happens to be a vet – the perfect way in. I can't begin to imagine what the last few years have been like for this woman, spending every minute of every day in the company of the worst kind of criminals, living with the threat of discovery at any moment. Whatever else she has, she's certainly got some guts.

'So how *did* you get here?' I ask. 'You've been taking one hell of a risk. I mean, why take on such a dangerous assignment? I don't know much about the Greek police, but here, the officers who work with the dogs and horses are usually trained to be high visibility, not used in undercover operations like this.'

This time she doesn't smile. 'I could ask you the same question, Inspector. I don't know exactly how much you know about the man you call Alastor ...'

'I know that three years ago he killed my sergeant and almost killed me,' I say, 'and just a few weeks ago he tortured and murdered another of our officers. I'm guessing that's just the tip of a very large iceberg.'

She nods. 'Yes, I know all about Sergeant Brent. There

was nothing I could do. I'm very sorry.' She sighs and then goes on. 'I knew about the raid in which you were shot, too. I think you were very lucky to survive. I have to tell you that he hasn't forgotten. You are unfinished business as far as he's concerned, and he doesn't like loose ends. I'm not saying he would go out of his way to find you, but if you happen to cross his path, he will kill you, just for completeness. It's the way his mind works.'

Larson shoots me an alarmed look, and I try to reassure him with a wave of the hand. 'Don't worry,' I say. 'I've been threatened by some very ugly characters in my time, and I've had some close shaves. Believe me, I've learned to keep my eyes open.'

Teresi makes a doubtful noise in her throat. 'And you must believe me, Inspector, when I tell you that once this man has decided to go after you, it won't matter whether your eyes are open or shut. For both of us, the situation is very serious. However careful we are, it might not be enough.'

'So,' I say, 'maybe it's time you answered some of my questions. Who is he? I mean, who is he really? And how did you get to be his mule, lugging his dogs around after him wherever he goes? It's not the kind of job I would want to volunteer for.'

Her smile this time is grim. 'Neither did I, but I really didn't have a choice. His name – his given name – is Darius Kyriaku. He grew up on the streets of Athens, a young thug running drugs, mostly, and occasionally guns, for one of the local gangs. You know the sort.'

I nod, thinking of Clive Gingell and all those like him running through the streets of West Hill.

'There was something different about him, though,' she

goes on. 'It was the sort of difference that was noticed when Medusa, as it came to be called, started to muscle in on the drug and arms trade in the big cities. The organisation was in its infancy then, back in the mid-eighties. They had a direct smuggling route out of Afghanistan and set about throttling supply to the other outlets, first in Greece, then elsewhere. By the mid-nineties they more or less had a stranglehold on all the supply lines of heroin, arms, and people desperate to flee the conflicts in the Middle East. The clever thing is, rather than start turf wars in any territory they wanted to take over, they would simply move in and either pressure the minor players or get rid of them in one large move. All they had to do then was follow up by offering lucrative deals to any gang members still alive. Loyalty is a fragile thing when it comes to crime. In Athens, for example, nine gang bosses were wiped out and their organisations absorbed by Medusa in a single day. The ones who were left capitulated immediately. As you know, they are still expanding today, gaining footholds in Europe, even in Russia and South America.'

She pauses and takes a large sip of her whisky, as if she needs to work herself up to the next part of her story. It's not just the pressure she's been under, or the fear of pursuit. For her, this hasn't just been an assignment – it's much more personal.

She takes a breath and continues, 'In 1991, Medusa had more or less taken over in Athens. They had eradicated most of the local crime bosses and had members of their organisation in positions of influence in politics, the judiciary and local commerce. There was just one person left in their way, an inner-city drugs baron who refused to toe the line. His name isn't important. What is of note is that he was Darius

Kyriaku's adoptive father. He took Darius in when the boy was only six years old, abandoned and living on the street, stealing food to survive. He raised him, educated him, and not just in crime – he sent him to school, and it turned out his new son was very bright. Darius wanted to continue his education, go to university, but the father refused. It was payback time, and the boy was expected to shadow his father, become a student of advanced thuggery instead. Not that he needed lessons in those particular skills, even then.

'Darius appeared to defer to his father's wishes, bided his time. Nineteen-ninety-one was his sixteenth birthday, and his father gave him a puppy – a Doberman. He became obsessed with it – he's owned them ever since. He raised it and trained it to kill on command. Then he went to Medusa and made a deal with them. He would get rid of their last remaining obstacle, and in return they would allow him to finish his education. Then he would work for them, become their resident assassin, for a salary that would allow him to pursue his other interests – his dogs and fine art. I think that at first they must have thought it was either a joke or some kind of complicated plot. Somehow, though, he convinced them to give him a chance, and they agreed. The next day, he walked into his father's study, let loose the Doberman and watched the dog rip him to pieces. He went back to Medusa, and they honoured the agreement. They sent him to study art at Humbolt University in Berlin, and when he graduated, he became their international fixer. That's been his job ever since.'

'Jesus Christ!' My mind goes back to the deal I made with Shark Johnson, to educate young Clive, and I wonder whether Grace is right – it won't make any difference. If anything, my meddling might make things worse. I take a swallow of my own Scotch and ask, 'What is it, Major Teresi, that you're not telling us?'

She stares into her drink for a long moment and then says, 'The killing of the last gang boss in Athens made big news. Neither Kyriaku nor Medusa made any effort to cover it up. The whole idea was to send a very public message to criminals and the authorities alike. A murder hunt started, and my father, a colonel at the time, was put in charge of it. It didn't take him long to work out who was responsible. One night he received an anonymous call giving the whereabouts of Darius Kyriaku, at a nightclub in the centre of Athens. I remember the call – I was on my final leave from the army before shipping out to Cyprus. My father went out to investigate. It was a set-up of course. Medusa had several policemen in their pockets, although we didn't realise it at the time, and my father was lured into a deserted side street. Kyriaku shot him in the head and dumped his body outside the police station. The murder hunt was scaled down – orders from above – and Kyriaku disappeared.'

'But surely,' I protest, 'he's still wanted on a murder charge. There are extradition agreements. If we report his location, he can be arrested.'

'Yes, he can.' She grimaces. 'And he would be released within hours. There is no solid evidence to link him to anything. You can't identify him as the man who shot you. It's my bet he's never turned up in any of your surveillance footage at that old lady's home in Weston-super-Mare. All you have is a dubious picture of a man in a car, with no solid identification. Am I right?'

I have to nod. 'You're right. And I suppose the same is true in the case of your father's murder. But what about the gang boss – the man he knew as a father?'

She shakes her head. 'He didn't actually kill him – the dog did. Given the extent of Medusa's hold on the legal system, he'd never get anywhere near a cell. It would be instantly written off as a tragic accident.'

We all sit in silence. She's right – even if we chased him down and arrested him, there would be no evidence, and all we'd be doing is giving Medusa a heads up, and giving the rest of them twenty-four hours to disappear into the woodwork. After that, Kyriaku would be back on the street, and the reprisals would start soon after. Without speaking, Larson goes into the kitchen and makes coffee. When he returns with the tray, Teresi goes on with her story.

'After my father's death, I knew I couldn't sit back and do nothing. I became determined to bring his killers down if I could. So I left the army, hoping to join the police. Colonel Dukas was my father's closest friend as well as his boss. I've known him since I was born – I still call him "Uncle Hector". He also wanted to see Darius Kyriaku brought down. There was already talk of an undercover operation, but infiltrating an organisation like Medusa is almost impossible. They have too many spies, and no one has ever gotten close. Uncle Hector arranged for me to be interviewed in secret, and I was enrolled into the police service ten years ago. I was given a false identity right at the start and prepared exclusively for this assignment. Of course, my army training was invaluable. The cover story was that I had resigned from the army to avoid a dishonourable discharge, having been caught dealing drugs. It was a risk, but I had two big advantages. I was the kind of woman Kyriaku finds attractive, and I was a qualified vet specialising in working dogs.

'I won't go into the details. It's enough to say that it took a year to track him down and another two to gain his confidence. He needed an expert to care for his beasts, and' – she hesitates – 'put it this way, I was able to perform more than one service.'

Larson's look is one of complete horror, and he almost spills the coffee that is halfway to his lips. I glare at him, and he coughs and closes his mouth.

'I understand,' I say. 'So for the last few years, you have been following him all over the world, making sure his dogs are well cared for and available when he needs them. But why choose now to jump ship? And why keep it up for so long?'

She gives a bitter laugh. 'As always,' she answers, 'it's a question of evidence. That, and a safe way out. Neither has been easy – up to now, impossible. But his obsession has led him to make a mistake. You know those Dobermans he arranged to have stolen are valuable, but I doubt you realise their value to him personally. He has a favourite animal, one he takes with him wherever he goes. It's a seven-year-old male, Charon – funny, don't you think, that he named it after the ferryman to Hades? He has been searching for a suitable mate for it, to continue the bloodline. Imagine his excitement when he discovered Charon's full sister here in Bristol, and not only that, a newborn litter of her puppies. Medusa have had people here for a while, as you must know, and he managed to persuade his masters that his presence was needed following the attempted infiltration by your officer. The real reason, though, was always to get his hands on the dogs. My job was to make sure they were healthy, and perform surgery on the adults to remove their microchips and add new ones, to fake their identities.'

'Do you know where the dogs are now?'

She nods. 'He's keeping them in an abandoned warehouse just outside Weston-super-Mare. It's too dangerous to approach. It's also his killing ground, and it's heavily guarded, day and night. Only the very senior members of the group know the exact location. Everyone else is taken in the back of vans so they can't see where they are going. I was never allowed to attend, and never got the opportunity to search for it.'

Again, she hesitates before saying, 'The thing is, one of Medusa's golden rules is no private enterprise. Nobody, not even Kyriaku, makes any move that will endanger the organisation. It's an automatic death sentence. When he took those animals, he effectively signed his own death warrant. Inspector, Darius Kyriaku has always been an evil, dangerous psychopath, but this obsession has, I think, driven him over the edge. He thinks himself invincible, above every kind of law. When I saw what was happening, I knew it was my chance.'

'And so you informed on him – to Medusa?'

She nods. 'And within days, the watch on my movements suddenly increased. He assigned a new "guardian" to follow me wherever I went – for my own protection, he said. He knows it was me, and he was, in his own way, telling me so. It was time to jump ship. I thought my best chance was to get a message to one of the resisting gang leaders and find out from them who I could trust in the police. Coming directly to you was more of a risk – I didn't know who I could trust.'

I offer up brief thanks to Shark Johnson. 'You chose the right person,' I tell her. 'So what happens now?'

'We get the bastard who killed my father,' she answers, without a pause. 'And we try to stay alive.'

23

I finally tumble into the usual recurring nightmare that I've laughingly called sleep for the last few years at around 4am. The hours between arriving home, close to midnight, and dozing off, exhausted, have been spent swerving between worry and self-recrimination. Worry, mainly about Larson and what I would say to Rosie and Chrissie if anything were to happen to him – not an unjustified concern – and recrimination on account of my not asking Teresi the most important question: does she have any idea who is passing information from West Hill to Medusa? Thinking about it, I can't believe she knows nothing, given her close association with the man now known as Darius Kyriaku. Not even a bastard like him could possibly have such an intimate relationship and let nothing slip. At least, I hope to God she's managed to pick up something, because if not, madman or not, he's a hell of a lot cleverer than every other criminal I've ever come across.

I feel as if I've hardly closed my eyes when I'm rudely awakened by the insistent trill of my house phone. I force myself upright and reach for the handset I stupidly keep on my bedside table.

'Al, get over to Sillitoe's place now. I need you.'

That's it. The line goes dead before I get the chance to answer. Grace's tone, though, is one I don't hear often. If I didn't know her better, I'd say she was distinctly flustered – and that isn't good.

HALF AN HOUR later I pull up outside the entrance to a neat block of apartments just south of the river. Polly Sillitoe's one-bedroom flat, on the second floor with views of the river and Bristol's famous suspension bridge, probably costs more in rent than most people's average annual income, including, I think suspiciously, a police officer's salary. I buzz myself in using the 'trades entrance' button and find Grace staring out the flat's floor-to-ceiling window. I can tell from the stiffness of her back that she's not admiring the view.

'On the coffee table,' she says, without turning round.

I look. And there it is, sitting on top of a pile of magazines – Polly's mobile phone.

'Shit!' I mutter, and join my boss at the window.

'Last anyone saw of her was around lunchtime the day before yesterday,' she says, her voice so quiet I have to strain to hear. It's as if she can hardly bring herself to say what we're both thinking. 'She could have been God knows where for the last forty-eight hours.'

There are two possibilities, and both are unbearable. Either she found out about our investigations and cut her losses, or ... I clamp my mouth shut before I say something I'll regret.

'Get over to Redcliffe,' Grace says, grabbing hold of

herself and taking charge again. 'This Teresi woman must know something – anything we can use, Al. But be bloody careful. If Sillitoe *is* bent, and she knows we've got Teresi ...'

'Don't worry,' I tell her. 'I'll be careful.'

'Make sure you are. Regardless of whether or not she's the informant, we have to assume she's with them, and they know – or will soon know – what we're doing. I'm calling her in as missing and starting a search, so the chances are we don't have much time. As for Teresi's location, the chances are it's still secure – if Polly had somehow got hold of it and passed it on, I'm pretty sure the gang would have made an attempt to get her back by now. Even so, I'm going to get one of the uniform patrol cars down there, tell them there's been a report of drug dealing in the basement or something.'

On the way back down to the car, I give George a call.

'Nothing,' he says. 'And before you ask, I've been keeping my eyes open and checking the tapes just in case.'

'I don't doubt it, George,' I assure him. 'Just tell me precisely what you mean by "nothing".'

'Exactly that, Al. No visitors, not even the old lady pottering in the garden. It's as if they've either cleared out the shed, or found something better to do. That, or ...'

'Or someone's blown the whistle on us,' I finish for him. 'Damn and bugger it. Keep your eyes open, George, and don't go out unless you have to. If anything strikes you as suspicious, however small, I need to know right away, okay?'

George chuckles. 'Don't worry, Al. There's a vase on my bedside table that would make a pretty good offensive weapon, and Mr Khan is a fair cook. I'll be fine. It's you who should be taking care of yourself. Just mind how you go and try not to get shot again. I don't think I could stand another week in a hospital corridor – the coffee's terrible.'

'I'll do my best, George,' I say, and ring off. I make another call, to Larson, telling him to give our Greek guest a heads up, and hitch a ride to Redcliffe in the back of an unmarked police transit van with a distinct feeling of foreboding.

TERESI SHAKES HER HEAD, brows knitted, trying to think back through her time with Kyriaku. 'I'm sorry, Inspector,' she says eventually. 'All I can tell you is that I was present on two or three occasions when Darius took calls from his spies. Not only in the police force, you understand – Medusa has informants in many places. It is one of the reasons he recruited that idiot boy, Eddie Hall. His father is an influential politician, and Darius was hoping to gain information on government employees that might be useful to him.' Her lips curl in a bitter smile. 'I think he was disappointed on that score. The kid has become a liability to him, and I think his time is very short, although he hasn't got enough sense to realise it.'

She glances up, sees my expression and sighs. 'I know. Right now you only want to know about one spy in particular. Now and then I was able to catch the voice on the line, but Darius would always leave the room, or tell me to leave, before any serious conversation took place. All I can say is that whoever he is, he has access to a lot of information, personal and official. Do you think I would have gone to so much trouble to contact you in the way I did if I had known who your traitor is?'

She has a point. 'No, I suppose not,' I say, and then something strikes me. 'You said, "whoever he is". Are you saying that all of Kyriaku's contacts are male? No women?'

She gives a humourless laugh. 'Oh yes, Inspector Crow.

That's one thing I can be quite sure of. You see, Darius has a very low opinion of women. He would never involve them in his business, not even as informants. To him they are weak, untrustworthy, and exist only to perform menial tasks – and for sex of course. Whoever it is passing on your secrets, it is not a woman.'

'And yet he employed you,' I counter, 'to do what, if your previous statements are correct, is one of the jobs closest to his heart – if indeed he has one – you look after his prize possessions, his dogs.'

She nods slowly. 'Yes, that is true. I suppose I am unique in that respect. The fact is, his animals trust me, and he places great store in their judgement. It is almost a religion with him. Plus, I am very skilled at what I do, and he knows he couldn't get anyone better. However, while his dogs trust me completely, he does not. I was always watched, my movements restricted, and it's fair to say my relationship with him was always that of master and very lowly servant.' She lowers her eyes, her expression crinkling into one of disgust, and adds, 'Among other things.'

'I understand,' I say, 'and I'm sorry.'

I glance at Larson, who has been sitting quietly on the edge of the sofa, listening, and see his face melt into an expression of utter shock at this last statement. He catches my eye and with a struggle recovers himself, thankfully keeping his mouth firmly closed.

'Just to be clear,' I persist, managing to keep my voice even, 'you are absolutely sure that the person we're looking for can't possibly be a female?'

'I'd stake my life on it,' she replies. She looks up at me with a sad smile. 'I probably already have.'

Larson breaks his silence. 'Something's happened, hasn't it? What is it? Has someone else been hurt?'

'I'm sorry, son,' I say, getting to my feet. 'I can't tell you much right now.' I turn to Teresi. 'Thank you, Jenny. You may have been more help than you know. I'll be in touch. In the meantime, I need you both to take extra care. Make sure you're not seen, and don't answer the door to anyone except me or my boss, DCI Helston. Do you have everything you need, for now?'

'We'll be fine,' Larson says. 'There's plenty of food – and drink.'

Teresi nods her agreement. 'Don't worry, Inspector Crow. We'll be very careful, I promise you.'

I head for the door, and Larson follows. 'Can't you tell me anything?' he asks.

I gesture for him to keep his voice down. 'Sillitoe has disappeared,' I tell him. 'Her phone has been on her coffee table for anything up to two days, but she isn't there. So if Teresi is right, and our bent copper is male ...'

'Oh, Christ!' he says.

'Exactly,' I reply. 'We might have been barking up the wrong tree – if you'll pardon the pun. If that's the case, it means Polly is missing and might already be dead. But if Teresi was an exception to the rule, and she's telling the truth, Sillitoe might have been another. We're pretty sure Polly doesn't know where you are, but the safest thing is to assume we've been compromised, and Kyriaku might know you're here.'

I give him a minute to let this sink in, and to his credit, he takes a deep breath and gives me a nod. 'I understand.' He hesitates, and then adds, 'What about Rosie? Can you tell her something – anything? If I call her, she's bound to pick up that there's a problem, just from the sound of my voice. You know how it is.'

I think back to my awkward conversations with Chrissie and give him a pat on the back. 'Yeah, son, I know how it is. I'll call her. I don't want you to worry about anything but staying safe – you and our guest in there, okay? One thing though – Major Teresi knows the score. If push comes to shove, you could do worse than follow her lead. For now, though, this information is just between us. I'm not saying I don't trust her, but we need to tread very carefully. Do you still have access to the feed from Weston?'

He nods. 'Yes, on my laptop.'

'Good. Keep your eye on it, and if anyone turns up over there, see if Teresi can identify them. As soon as I know anything else, I'll let you know.'

I'm halfway through the door before he asks, 'And what about you? According to Jenny, this Alastor, Kyriaku or whatever his name is, has you on his wish list. Are you sure you should be wandering about without an escort?'

I bite down the caustic comment that's on the tip of my tongue. He's right, of course, and even my being here is a risk, not only to me, but to him and Teresi as well. 'Don't you worry about me, son,' I say finally. 'You do your job, I'll do mine, and with a bit of luck, we'll all come out of this smelling of roses.'

I jab the button and jump into the lift before he can reply, and head back down to the basement and the tradesman's exit. I'm on my way back to my car, parked a few streets away, when my mobile rings.

'What is it, Grace?'

It takes her a while to reply, and when she does, it's in a voice that is unsteady and close to a whisper. 'Al, get over to the infirmary right now. I'll meet you at main reception.'

I start to ask her what's going on, but she's hung up, and I'm talking to the air.

24

Grace is waiting for me at the reception desk. She's white as a sheet, and when she sees me and takes a step, it's unsteady. I rush forward to take her arm, and realise with a shock that she's been crying.

'Jesus Christ, Grace,' I mutter, guiding her towards the nearest chair, which happens to be in the café next to reception. 'What the bloody hell's happened?'

She shakes her head. 'Give me a minute, Al. God, I could do with a slug of something. Would you mind grabbing me a double espresso? I don't suppose you've got a hip flask in your back pocket?'

'Sorry,' I reply. 'It'll have to be caffeine. Stay there, and take some deep breaths.'

When I get back to the table with two strong black coffees and a couple of sugar-hit cookies for good measure, she seems to have recovered herself, and there's a little more colour in her cheeks, much to my relief. She gives me a weak smile.

'Sorry about that. It's just, I never thought I'd be going through this again, not after …'

'After what?' I interrupt. 'For fuck's sake, Grace!' I realise I've raised my voice, and make an effort to stay calm. 'Listen, ma'am. You're my boss, and if you flake out on me, I'm on a hiding to nothing. Just tell me. Whatever it is, I can cope. Who's been hurt, and what are we doing here?' I push her cup towards her. 'Drink your coffee, and take your time, okay?'

She nods and swallows a mouthful. 'It's Polly, Al. Dear God, if you'd seen her when she was brought in …' She sucks in a breath. 'She's in theatre now, and the doctors say it's touch and go. When the ambulance got to her, she wasn't breathing, but they managed to get a pulse. If she survives, they tell me she will lose a leg for sure, and she'll be disfigured for life. It's a miracle she's still alive. She's been in surgery for two hours, and it's not over yet. All we can do now is wait and hope she pulls through.'

I realise suddenly that her former comments must have been referring to the night I was shot. 'Not after you' was what she had been about to say. I swallow down the lump in my throat, and instinctively reach out and take her hand. At any other time she would have pulled away, but not now. 'It will be all right,' I say. 'Grace, listen to me. I came through, and so will Polly. We're a tough bunch of bastards, and Polly is one of the toughest. She'll pull through, I know it.'

She nods and takes another sip of her coffee. 'Yes, she might,' she says. 'But if she does, what is she coming back to? A ruined career? A prison sentence?'

'Neither,' I reply. 'And definitely not prison. She isn't the informant, Grace. Teresi said that all Kyriaku's contacts were male, and he would never have used a female, not even a police officer. Whoever our bent copper is, it isn't Polly Sillitoe. And unlike me, if she pulls through there won't be any brain damage. She will be just as good a police officer as she's ever been – and she's bloody good. If I were you I'd take her in a heartbeat, leg or no leg. She's a fighter, and she'll make it. Just you wait and see.'

It takes a moment for this to sink in, and then Grace asks, 'You're sure she's not the one we're looking for?'

I try to sound confident. 'I'm sure. But how was she found? And where?'

'An anonymous call,' she says. 'They reported a body, south of Bristol, in the woods near West Harptree. The medics were alerted first, and when the ambulance got there, they realised they were dealing with a police officer and got us out there. At first they thought she was dead, but one of the paramedics found a pulse. Another minute and it would have been too late.'

'And what happened? Do you know?'

'It looks like Medusa happened – or Kyriaku did, to be more accurate. She was mauled by at least one large dog, possibly two, according to the consultant, but we won't know for sure unless ...' She catches herself. '*Until* she wakes up and can tell us. That isn't likely to be for a good while.'

'You say it was an anonymous call. Has anyone listened to it – from our lot, I mean?'

She shakes her head. 'Not yet. I thought maybe you could get down to the call centre and go through it, see if it gives us any clues. It's a long shot, but you never know. I'm not moving from here until Polly's out of surgery and we know what her chances are. Christ knows how long that will be.'

'I'm on my way,' I tell her. 'Stay here, get yourself something decent to eat, and I'll call you if there's anything worth pursuing.'

She nods, but not very convincingly. On the way out I stop at the counter, order a bowl of soup and point at Grace. 'Don't let her go until she's eaten it,' I tell the youth at the till. He eyes me suspiciously until I flash him my warrant card.

'Right,' he says. 'Whatever you say, Inspector.' I feel his puzzled gaze follow me all the way to the exit.

THE SHIFT SUPERVISOR ushers me into her private office at the call centre and gestures for me to sit at her desk.

'The call came in at 10.32,' she says, drawing up a chair and sitting beside me. She taps at her keyboard for a few seconds, and the file comes up on the screen. 'I don't know what it can tell you.' She shrugs. 'Clearly a young male, possibly early twenties, scared out of his wits by the sound of it.'

She clicks the 'play' button and sits back while I listen. She's right. The voice is high-pitched, but definitely male, and terrified. The call handler tries to insist he stay on the line, but after giving the location and screaming for an ambulance, the line goes dead.

'He didn't give a name,' the supervisor says, shaking her head. 'The call couldn't be traced – either he turned his phone off straight after, or destroyed the SIM.'

'Don't worry,' I tell her. 'I know exactly who it is.'

She frowns, but says nothing as I get up and thank her for her time.

I'm at the door when she says, 'There is one more thing, Inspector Crow. When the crew got there, they found your officer wrapped in a blanket, and with a crude tourniquet round her right thigh. It looks like whoever he is, he tried to help her, realised it was beyond him and ran off after calling the ambulance. He might actually have saved her life. Without his actions, she probably would have bled to death.'

On the way back through the corridors, I call Grace with the news that I know the identity of the caller and have a pretty good idea where he might be. Thankfully, she sounds a little more collected.

'You go,' she says. 'I'll be fine here – and thanks for the soup. You were right – I just needed food.'

'No problem,' I reply. 'Just stay put, and I'll get back to you as soon as I learn anything.'

I'm several miles south of Bristol when my phone rings again. Without looking, I jab the button on the dash, praying it isn't Grace with bad news. It's not her voice on the other end of the line. Despite the clear effort to stave off panic, the clipped tones of Gerard Hall-Warner are unmistakeable and almost cause me to swerve off the road.

'Inspector Crow? It's Edwin. Can you come to the house? It's urgent – I ...' There's a brief silence, and then, his voice soft, almost pleading, 'I don't know what to do.'

'I'm already on my way,' I answer him. 'I'll be with you in around five minutes. Is Edwin with you?'

'Yes. He's in his room, won't come out. I've tried to talk to him, but he won't say a word. I've never seen him like this. It's worse than you could possibly imagine, Inspector.'

'I doubt that,' I mutter under my breath, and then, louder, 'Believe me, sir, I can imagine quite a lot. Just make sure you keep him there until I arrive.'

'Don't worry, Inspector. His door is locked – he made me give him the key – and there's no other way out. But please hurry. He might listen to you. I'm afraid he might harm himself if someone doesn't get through to him, and it's clear I'm not getting anywhere ...'

His voice trails off, the panic dissolving into despair. However much I dislike Hall-Warner and those like him, I can't help but feel a twinge of sympathy when I think of Rosie and the five years I spent trying vainly to connect with a daughter who refused to believe I didn't throw her stepfather off a balcony. I blink and force my attention back to the road, realising that I'm already approaching the long driveway leading to the Hall-Warner family seat. The Honourable Gerard is outside, pacing up and down and almost crushing his spaniels underfoot. He rushes towards the car as I draw up to the front steps.

'He's upstairs,' he says as I come to a halt and step out onto the gravel. 'Third floor, the last door on the left. Inspector, he was covered in blood when he arrived. I don't know if he's hurt – he wouldn't talk to me, just ran upstairs and locked himself in. He might be bleeding to death up there for all I know ...'

He's rapidly reaching the point of hysteria, and with an effort I push down the urge to slap his face. I do, however, grab his shoulders to hold him still, and wait until he stops struggling and looks me in the eye.

'Mr Hall-Warner,' I say, as evenly as I can manage, 'I need you to get a hold of yourself and calm down before we do anything. You're not going to do your son any good in this state. You understand me?'

For several seconds he just glares at me, muscles tense, fists clenched, but I keep my grip on him until he finally deflates and gives me a curt nod. I let him go.

'Good. Now listen to me. The blood on your son's

clothing isn't his. As far as I know, he isn't hurt, just very scared, okay?'

His face floods with relief, but it's short lived. 'Then whose blood is it? Do you know?'

I nod. 'The chances are it belongs to a police officer who is currently in the infirmary fighting for her life.'

'Oh, Jesus,' he whispers. 'You're telling me that Edwin ...'

I stop him with a gesture. 'If I'm right,' I tell him, 'young Edwin tried to help her, and that's how he got covered in her blood. He covered her with a blanket and tied a rough tourniquet round her leg. I'm told he may well have saved her life.' He opens his mouth, but again I hold up a hand. 'You have to understand, he's still in one hell of a lot of trouble. I'll have to arrest him. At the very least he'll be charged for his involvement in the attack, and with a number of other serious crimes.'

Hall-Warner lets out a long breath and shakes his head. 'I understand, Inspector,' he says quietly. 'Dear God! How could it have come to this? He had every advantage, the chance to do something really great with his life, and now ...'

I decide not to answer his question. The Honourable Gerard has enough on his plate to be going on with, and I'm fairly sure he's not the type to go in for self-recrimination. Besides, from his point of view, things are only going to get worse.

'I'm afraid that's not all,' I say, seeing no point in sugar-coating the next piece of bad news. 'Edwin might be scared of the police, but he's absolutely terrified of what his friends in the gang are going to do to him when they find out he didn't dump a dead body. I have to impress on you that he is now in very real danger – and in all likelihood, so are you. They are bound to find out he's here, if they don't know already, and they'll come for him, and for you too, just to make thing neat and tidy.'

I watch as this sinks in, and to give him credit, he pulls himself together and nods. 'All right, Inspector. What do you want me to do?'

'I'm going to go up and talk to him. With a bit of luck, he'll listen and let me in. I want you to make sure all the doors and windows are locked, then stay downstairs, and do nothing unless I ask you to. Okay?'

He nods again.

'Has he had the chance to clean himself up – shower, change of clothes, anything like that?'

'I don't think so. There's no facility in his room, and he went straight up there.' He quirks his mouth in a bitter smile. 'Don't worry, Inspector. I'm sure you'll find all the evidence you want, assuming you can get past the door.'

'I'll get past the door,' I say. 'You may not realise it, but I have a way with words.'

I leave him to ponder, and head upstairs. A part of me is longing to grab the fire extinguisher halfway along the landing and smash the lock to pieces, but now isn't the time. I summon every vestige of self-restraint and knock softly on the door.

'Eddie? It's Inspector Crow. You know me, son, and you know I'm not going to lie to you. Your dad's not here. I'm alone, and I just want to talk to you, nothing else, I promise. Are you going to let me in?'

There's a faint shuffle from somewhere in the room, but no reply.

'Okay,' I go on, forcing calm into my voice. 'I'm going to tell you a few things, and I want you to listen to me very carefully.' I pause, and again, there's silence. I plough on.

'First, you need to know that Inspector Sillitoe isn't dead. She's in surgery, and I'm told that it's thanks to your actions she's still alive. You saved her life, son.' As I'm saying this, I'm praying it's still true. 'Second, it's not going to take a genius to work out where you are. Kyriaku will be coming after you – and very likely for your father as well. You need to make a decision, Eddie, while you still can. You either talk to me or to him. I think we both know which you would prefer.'

I hold my breath and wait for perhaps a full minute before I hear the soft click of a key turning in the lock. I count to ten, turn the knob and slowly open the door. Edwin Earnest Icarus Hall-Warner is hunched in the far corner of the room, arms round his knees, shaking with terror. For a brief second I imagine a five-year-old Eddie stuffing his small body into the wardrobe to escape the attention of his overbearing father. The ugly Victorian wardrobe is still there. The only thing that's changed over the years is that Eddie's grown too big to fit into it. He's made no attempt to clean himself up. His hands, face and clothing are still streaked with what I assume is Polly Sillitoe's dried blood. Gerard is right – there's more than enough evidence to link his son with the attack, and certainly with transporting and aiming to dispose of the victim. Right now, though, compiling Eddie Hall-Warner's charge sheet is the least of my concerns. I'm looking at a kid who's petrified, in way over his head and, whatever my feelings about him and his family, is in dire need of protection.

I take a step forward, and he presses himself even further into the wall on the other side of the bed.

'It's all right, son,' I say, and pull out my mobile, not wanting to give Eddie the chance to lock the door on me again if I step back outside. I call his father's number and tell him to bring up a couple of heavy-duty rubbish sacks and two mugs of sweet tea and leave them outside the door. I close the door, relock it, and perch myself on the end of the bed.

'Okay,' I say as he eyes me warily, 'first things first. Do you have a dressing gown, something you can cover yourself with for the moment?'

He nods and points to the wardrobe.

'Good,' I say. 'I want you to get undressed and put your clothes in a pile. We'll need to take them away. I'm afraid I can't let you wash just yet. We need to take some samples first. Do you need to use the bathroom?'

He shakes his head.

'Okay. You'll feel a lot better once you're in something clean. Then we can talk.'

He hesitates a moment and then slowly gets to his feet and starts to strip off. There's a shuffle outside the door, followed by a soft knock. 'Thank you, Mr Hall-Warner,' I say, without opening the door. 'Just leave everything outside and go back downstairs. I'll let you know if we need anything else. Meanwhile, keep an eye on your driveway, if you would. If you see anything unusual, call me.'

I wait until his footsteps have died away down the landing, then open the door and retrieve the two plastic rubbish bags and, as I'd requested, two large mugs of tea. When I turn round, Eddie has dropped the bloodstained clothes in a heap on the floor and wrapped himself in a black towelling bathrobe ludicrously emblazoned with the family crest. I hand him one of the bags, and without waiting to be asked, he stuffs the clothes into it. I pass him a mug, and he takes it like a man who's been lost in a desert. I realise then that his silence isn't a deliberate ploy – he's been so parched he simply hasn't been able to talk.

He gulps half of it down despite the risk of scalding his throat, and finally manages to say, 'Thank you.' It's a husky whisper, but it's progress.

'Don't worry, son,' I tell him. 'You've done the right thing. I won't pretend things are going to be easy, but the best thing you can do now is tell me everything you know. If you can do that, I give you my word, I will do everything in my power to protect you, and so will my boss. If you decide not to help us, I think we both know your father will be arranging a funeral before too long. I'm not going to press you. It's your choice, Eddie. But you need to make it right now. You understand me?'

He swallows, and after a second's hesitation, he gives me a nod. 'Help me,' he says, still struggling to speak, and bursts into tears.

25

It takes forty-five minutes for the unmarked van I've requested to arrive, bringing with it a trio from forensics, ready suited in disposable overalls, and a squad of other police officers kitted out in armoured vests and carrying firearms. The part of my message containing the words 'low-key' clearly didn't make it onto the chief constable's action plan, owing mainly, I suspect, to the influence Gerard Hall-Warner is still able to wield. Once word gets out about young Eddie's involvement with a serious criminal gang, however, Gerard's career as a right-wing campaigner for law and order will be well and truly over, much to everyone's relief, not least, I think, the chief constable's.

One of the AFOs, a stocky man draped with enough lethal hardware to rival the gold medallions round Shark Johnson's neck, strolls up to me and gives me a respectful nod.

'Inspector Crow? Sergeant Hallam, sir. My team has been asked to escort you and one prisoner directly to the chief constable's offices. Two of my officers will remain here with the forensic team.' He lowers his voice and adds, 'And to prevent the father making a nuisance of himself.'

'You mean, "for his own protection", Sergeant,' I correct him, struggling to keep the smile off my face despite the circumstances.

'Of course, sir. My apologies.' He puts a hand to his mouth and coughs to hide the grin, and then becomes serious again. 'I'm afraid we haven't been told very much – only that there has been a threat to life, and the priority is to get you and Edwin Hall-Warner to Portishead in one piece.'

I glance across at the van they arrived in, and realise I would probably have done better to request something less conspicuous and more manoeuvrable. Sergeant Hallam catches the look and smiles.

'Don't worry, sir. We've arranged an alternative form of transport. Hopefully, if anyone's watching, they'll be following the van and not us. In my experience, the best way to keep a low profile is to have something high profile to hide behind.'

As he's speaking, one of the forensic team emerges and comes across to us. 'We've finished with your boy, Inspector,' she tells me. 'You can take him whenever you're ready.' She turns to Hallam. 'We'll need another couple of hours here. I'll let you know when we need a ride.'

'At your service, ma'am,' he replies. 'Just remember to stay clear of the windows if you can manage it. We don't want anyone popping off at you by accident.'

'Don't worry, Sergeant,' she says a bit huffily, 'we know what we're doing.'

She stalks back inside, and Hallam jerks his head towards an archway to one side of the main house, leading, I assume, to an inner courtyard and probably garages or a stable block. At the same time, he gestures to his team, and four AFOs get back into the van, two in the back and two in the front. The van sets off down the drive towards the main road.

'There are two cars down by the gate,' he explains as we head off through the arch. 'It should make for quite a show. If anyone's out there watching, they'll hopefully be following the van, not us.'

As I thought, there's a small cobbled courtyard on the other side of the arch, and beyond that, an exit to the rear of the house. Waiting in the courtyard is an old, battered Land Rover, behind which is hooked a trailer loaded with straw bales. The driver, a young farmhand in his mid-twenties, complete with tweed cap, neckerchief and Barbour jacket, wouldn't look out of place on stage with the 1970s West Country band the Worzels. When he sees us, he grins and tips his cap.

'In the back, if you wouldn't mind, sir,' Hallam says, and at the same time another AFO appears on the other side of the courtyard, guiding a handcuffed Hall-Warner Junior in front of him. As we all squeeze into the back of the vehicle, I note that the rear windows have been blacked out. Young Edwin presses himself into a corner, eyes flitting fearfully from one to another of us. 'Relax, lad,' Hallam tells him. 'You're quite safe with us. Mind you,' he adds, 'try anything and we're quite likely to blow your head off.' He finishes the sentence with a genial smile and a wink, which tips Edwin's colour from sickly grey to chalky white.

Hallam turns to the driver. 'How's it looking out there, Morris?'

'Clear as far as I can tell, boss,' Morris replies. 'I followed the regular route the farm manager gave me. If anyone is watching, as far as they are concerned, I'm just a yokel going about my usual business.'

'Good. Even so, keep your weapon handy. You never know. Let's get going – the decoy should be hitting the main road about now.'

'Sir,' Morris replies, and crunches the Land Rover into gear.

Hallam turns to me. 'I'd hang on to something if I were you, Inspector. We'll be going across a few fields before we get to the road, and it could be a bit bumpy.'

After fifteen minutes or so of being jolted and buffeted across one deeply rutted field after another, I'm starting to feel a bit queasy, and Edwin is looking so ill Hallam empties out a canvas tool bag and thrusts it into his lap. 'If you're going to puke,' he says cheerfully, 'make sure it goes in there. Throw up anywhere near my boots and I might just shoot you anyway.'

Thankfully, five minutes later the Land Rover grinds to a halt under a stand of trees.

'There you go, boss,' Morris announces. 'The car is just on the other side of the copse.'

'Good work,' Hallam says, leaning forward and clapping his colleague on the back. 'Make sure you finish the route you've been given – take your time and keep your eyes open. If you see anything odd, radio it through. Better safe than sorry.'

'Will do, boss,' he answers as we all pile out, and the Land Rover rattles off back towards the field.

Hallam leads us in the opposite direction, the other AFO bringing up the rear, and we emerge, to my relief, onto a tarmac road, where a Mercedes fitted with privacy glass is waiting.

'We should be okay from here, sir,' he says. 'Whoever it is we're dealing with, they'd have to be bloody good for us not to have picked them up.'

I get into the front passenger seat beside him, Edwin and the other AFO in the back. 'They *are* bloody good,' I mutter, half to myself, as we head off towards Portishead.

CHIEF CONSTABLE GOSFORD shakes his head, loosens his tie and pours us both another coffee. His secretary has also thoughtfully provided a plate of assorted pastries, but neither of us has an appetite.

'I don't suppose you've heard anything from the infirmary?' he asks.

'No, sir.'

There's a long silence, and then Gosford jerks to his feet and starts to pace the carpet between his desk and the more informal leather armchairs where, surprisingly, he's invited me to sit.

'Damn it, Crow!' he explodes at last. 'We've got to get these bastards before another of my officers ends up in the morgue.'

'Yes, sir,' I agree, my eyes firmly on my bone china coffee cup.

He glares at me for a few seconds, then sighs and sits back down. 'I'm sorry, Inspector,' he says, running his fingers through his thinning widow's peak. 'I know this is a very personal matter for you, in more ways than one. You're doing a great job, and I want you to know it hasn't gone unnoticed.'

'Thank you, sir,' I say warily, wondering what's coming next. The first rule of dealing with the chief constable is never to take things at face value. I'm in a comfortable chair, drinking coffee that probably costs more per ton than my salary, looking at a plate of cakes that wouldn't look out of place at the Ritz. None of these things bode well.

He finally gets to the punchline. 'What are your thoughts on Edwin Hall-Warner, Inspector?'

'My thoughts?'

He lifts his cup to his lips, lowers it back to the saucer without taking a sip, and after twisting it round a couple of times puts it on the coffee table, all the time avoiding my eye. 'He's been involved with this Kyriaku character for some time, by the look of it,' he says, finally looking up. I nod and wait for him to get to the point. 'So,' he goes on after an uncomfortable pause, 'he'll have witnessed quite a lot that can be useful to us, and from what I've been told, he probably doesn't realise just how useful he could be.'

'If you're saying he's an idiot, sir,' I reply, 'I completely agree. But as for being useful …' I shake my head. 'I'm not so sure. The kid's scared witless, and he's not so stupid that he doesn't realise he's heading for prison, and once inside, the gang are going to get to him, however much we'd like to believe they won't. As long as that threat's hanging over him, he won't say a word – whether we like it or not, they are a hell of a lot scarier than we are, and he knows it.'

'Which is why,' Gosford says, spearing me with a look that dares me to disagree with him, 'I intend to offer him witness protection.'

'What?' For a moment, I'm too shocked to say anything sensible. When my thoughts do scramble back together, my first impulse is to grab the chief constable by his pristine lapels and shake him until his expensively veneered teeth rattle. Thankfully, I restrain myself and take a few deep breaths before making any further comment. 'Sir,' I say, as quietly as I can manage, 'you do realise that this miserable little shit assisted in the murder of one police officer, and possibly a second, if Polly Sillitoe doesn't make it? And you're suggesting we turn him loose with a new identity to live the life of Riley somewhere else in exchange for whatever feeble snippets of information he cares to give us? I'm sorry, sir, but if you'll forgive my saying so, you must be out of your mind!'

He gives me a stiff smile. 'At least I can count on you to speak yours, Inspector Crow,' he replies, sitting back and relaxing a little. 'I can assure you that I would want something far beyond "feeble snippets", as you put it. Any deal would be dependent on putting away not only Kyriaku, but the other thugs he's brought with him. We wind up the whole operation, or Hall-Warner gets nothing. I take your point about his involvement in the attacks on DS Brent and DI Sillitoe, but for the moment we have no evidence that he contributed towards Brent's death or Sillitoe's injuries. We only know he drove the car that was involved in the hit-and-run, and that he may have been tasked with the disposal of the bodies after the event. Don't forget, he did call an ambulance when he realised Sillitoe was still alive.'

'Don't worry, sir,' I growl. 'I haven't forgotten.'

'Good. And believe me, Inspector, if it comes to light that he was directly involved in either case, any deal will be well and truly off the table. I give you my word on that.'

My reply is cut off by the phone on Gosford's desk. He picks it up, listens for a minute or so, grunts an acknowledgement and comes back to the coffee table, but doesn't sit down.

'That was DCI Helston,' he tells me. 'DI Sillitoe is awake – and she's asking for you.' He catches my look of surprise and shrugs. 'You'd better get over there. There is one more thing, though.'

'Yes, sir?'

'The Hall-Warner boy seems to trust you. When you've finished at the hospital, come back here. You'll be the one doing the interviews.' He pauses, his expression softening a little. 'Take as long as you need – Hall-Warner won't be going anywhere. And please give my good wishes to Inspector Sillitoe.'

I swear my way out to the car park, wondering how the hell I'm going to get back to the infirmary when my car is on Gerard Hall-Warner's driveway. I'm about to go back to reception to request a cab when Sergeant Hallam strolls across the tarmac and greets me with a cheery wave.

'Your car's just round the corner, sir,' he says good-humouredly. 'I thought you might be needing it, so I got one of my lads to drive it over. Hope that was all right?'

'More than all right,' I say, wondering how someone who spends his days wandering around bristling with lethal weapons can be so cheerful. 'Thanks – I appreciate it.'

'No problem.' He takes a couple of steps and turns back to me. 'Thought you'd like to know, me and the squad are on standby. The chief seems to think we could be moving on that Greek bastard before too long.' He grins. 'After what he's done to you lot at West Hill, I can guarantee we've been busy polishing some very special bullets – ones that never miss. You can tell that to your DCI when you see her. Good luck, Inspector.'

As I make my way over to my car, I realise I'm rubbing the almost invisible indentation in my forehead that is the only remaining outward evidence of the bullet Kyriaku fired into my brain.

26

Sillitoe has been placed in a side room off the ICU. Grace meets me in the corridor outside, looking as if she needs a hot bath and a very long sleep.

'She came round an hour ago,' she says, massaging her temples with index finger and thumb. 'She's not out of the woods yet, but at least she's off the immediate danger list.'

'That's good news,' I reply, guiding her to a chair before she falls down. 'Gosford told me she was asking for me. Why? Do you know?'

She shakes her head. 'No. She's pretty out of it, Al, what with the morphine and everything else. But she was very insistent and got agitated when I told her you were over at headquarters. The consultant reckoned the only way to calm her down was to let you in for a few minutes. Are you okay with that?'

'Of course. Look, why don't you go home and get some sleep? The only thing I've got to look forward to is an interview with Edwin Hall-Warner, and the longer he's left to stew, the happier I'll be. I'll stay here and hold the fort.' I glance at the PC sitting on a chair outside Sillitoe's door. 'She's got protection, and I'm here. There's nothing more you can do, and you need to be away from it for a while. If anything happens, I'll call you, I promise.'

I stay in the corridor until I'm sure my DCI has gone down in the lift, then turn to see a woman in scrubs waiting for my attention.

'Inspector Crow?'

I nod.

'I'm Dr Pelham, your colleague's lead surgeon. She's been through one hell of a trauma, but she's managed to get over the first hurdle. It won't be plain sailing, but the prognosis is a lot better than it was a couple of hours ago. Did DCI Helston tell you she'd been asking to see you?'

I nod again. 'Did she say anything else – anything about what happened?'

'Not that I'm aware. She was only awake for a short while, and she's sleeping again now. If you'd like to sit with her, that's fine. You can stay as long as you need to. Don't expect too much, though. She's on a pretty strong cocktail of drugs, so might not be too coherent when she wakes up again.'

She leads me past a row of beds, the occupants obscured by a medley of tubes connected to ranks of monitors beeping and flashing into the dimly lit ICU. For a moment I freeze, remembering the weeks after the shooting, mostly spent tangled up like a giant prawn in a plate of spaghetti. I take a deep breath, grit my teeth and walk on. The PC gets wearily to his feet when he sees me coming.

'Relax, son,' I say, patting his arm. 'How about you stretch your legs and get us both a coffee? I'm sure the patient will be safe with me for half an hour.'

'Yes, sir. Thank you, sir,' he replies, trying to mask a yawn, and goes off on his errand.

Dr Pelham gives me a nod and leaves me at the door. As I turn the handle, I realise my hand is jerking wildly, another legacy of my brain injury, and one I have, in recent months, begun to control. I close my eyes, focus on my breathing and wait for the tremor to pass. Then I open the door and step into the room.

At first, I can't see much. The blinds are closed, and the room is in near darkness, illuminated only by the dim light from the monitors and several flickering coloured lights that make the area surrounding the bed look like a grotesque Christmas decoration. An armchair has been thoughtfully placed beside the bed, and I sink into it, careful not to disturb the mass of wires pumping drugs and life-giving fluids into Polly Sillitoe's frail body. Half her face is hidden beneath a thick layer of bandages, the lower half of her body protected by a metal frame under the blanket. I reach out and gently squeeze the part of her hand not bristling with needles.

'I'm here, Polly,' I whisper to her unconscious form. 'Take your time – I'm not going anywhere.'

I jerk awake to find a nurse fussing over the bed. She glances at me and smiles.

'You look like you needed that,' she comments, checking the monitors and tubes, replacing bags of goodness knows what.

I push myself up in the chair, almost knocking over a paper cup of freezing cold coffee, dutifully left by the PC guarding the door. 'How long have I been asleep?'

She shrugs. 'A few hours. Don't worry, you haven't missed anything. We have an alert at the nursing station to tell us when she wakes up. It shouldn't be long now. Why don't you stretch your legs and get some fresh coffee?'

'A few hours?' I blink into the gloom, trying to clear my head. 'Shit!'

The nurse raises an eyebrow, but says nothing, and leaves me to gather myself. I realise I'm hungry, and stick my head out the door to find the uniformed PC has transformed into a female in plain clothes. I recognise her as one of the new DCs on Sillitoe's team.

'Sir,' she says, standing crisply to attention and searching my face anxiously for any news of her boss.

'It's all right,' I tell her. 'There's no change yet.' I give her my debit card and send her down to the café to root out coffee and sandwiches – for both of us, on my tab – and close the door again. The side room has its own small ensuite, and I spend a few minutes freshening up. Back in the room, I lift the blind an inch with my finger – it's dark outside and drizzling. I decide I've been asleep for at least five hours. I check my mobile – no missed calls or messages, which thankfully means nothing else has gone horribly wrong. When I turn back to the bed, Sillitoe's eyes are open, and she's watching me.

'Hey, Polly.' I move quickly to her side and take her hand. 'Welcome back.'

She tries to smile, but the bandages won't let her. She gestures with a finger to the water carafe on the bedside cabinet. I pour water into a paper cup and hold it to her lips.

'Well,' she says when her mouth is moist enough to talk, although a little groggily through the haze of pain medication, 'I guess that's my career totally fucked.'

'Jesus, Polly!' I manage a weak grin. 'That's bollocks, and you know it.' I put a finger to the scar on my forehead. 'At least you've got all your brain left. I'll bet a year's salary you get to be the first bionic chief constable within the next ten years.'

Her eyes flash the brief smile her mouth can't quite manage, and I feel her give my hand a light squeeze.

'I got it all wrong, Al,' she says, shifting her gaze to the cage humped over the empty space where her left leg used to be. 'I fucked up completely. Al – I'm sorry.'

'Sorry for what? Whatever you were doing, Pol, you must have thought it was the right thing. The only mistake you made was not having backup. It's the first rule, you know that. Never go into a compromising situation unless someone's watching your arse.'

Her head moves a fraction in a nod. 'I know. But I thought ...'

I can see her tiring, but I also know she won't rest until she's got it off her chest. I give her an encouraging nod. 'It's okay,' I say. 'What is it you want to tell me?'

'When Vicky Brent was killed,' she goes on, 'I figured out there must be an informant in the station somewhere. Vicky was good – very good. I knew her from training, and she would never have given herself away. One of us must have betrayed her.' She hesitates and then spits it out. 'I thought it was you, Al. I'm so sorry ...' She sinks back into the pillow, gasping for breath. 'Jesus Christ, my leg hurts. And the doctors say it isn't even bloody well there!'

I reach for the call button, but the nurse is ahead of me, bursting in and shooing me outside before I can take a breath. The DC on guard chooses that moment to return to her post, and holds out my debit card and a paper bag.

'Ham and mustard, sir,' she says. 'I hope that's okay. And

black coffee. I wasn't sure, so I put sachets of milk and sugar in the bag.'

'Perfect,' I assure her. 'And you'll be pleased to know your DI is awake. When I go back in, I'll recommend you for a promotion – but only if you've managed to sneak a muffin in there as well.'

I'm rewarded with an uncertain smile. 'It's a flapjack, I'm afraid, sir. Good news though about Polly – sorry, I mean DI Sillitoe, sir.' She blushes and looks uncomfortably at her shoes.

It takes me a minute to catch on. 'What's your name, Detective?' I ask.

'DC Robbins, sir,' she replies, blushing even more, then adds, 'but everyone calls me Robbie.'

'Well, Robbie,' I say, taking her arm and giving it a brief squeeze, 'I think Polly's going to be just fine.'

At that moment the nurse emerges and nods to me. 'You can go back in now, Inspector. Just fifteen minutes, and then she needs to rest.'

'Thank you,' I say, and turn back to the DC. 'Make sure you eat those sandwiches, Robbie. If you're going to sit there all night, you'll need to keep your strength up.'

Back at Sillitoe's bedside, I decide it's time to speak plainly. 'Did you know,' I ask her, 'that you were caught on CCTV, following me down to the wildlife sanctuary?'

Her eyes widen. 'No – damn! I should have been more careful.'

'Bloody right you should,' I say, but follow up with a small grin. Now isn't the time for recriminations. 'We also clocked you down at the bungalow in Weston, doing an impression of a *Gardeners' World* presenter with the old lady.'

'Shit! Don't tell me – you thought I was the snitch, right?

The truth is, I was pissed off at being cut out of the loop, and Vicky had told me Eddie Hall was involved somehow, so I was tailing him in my spare time. I wanted to bring something to Grace that would get me back in. I was following Eddie when I spotted you down by the sanctuary and got curious. I mean, you haven't been down on the estates for a good while, and Kelvin Draper's been your informant for years.' She looks away, embarrassed. 'I thought Grace was setting you up to take your old job back, and was pushing me out, so I wanted to find out what you were up to.'

'So you listened in to our conversation,' I prompt.

She nods. 'And then another thought struck me. Maybe there was another reason for you being there. Maybe you wanted to know whether Draper was reliable from the gang's point of view – whether he knew too much to be safe. Next thing, Draper was dead. You can see how that looked?'

I suddenly see the whole scenario. Truth be told, Polly probably drew the same conclusion I would have done in her shoes.

She sucks in water through her straw and goes on. 'I had nothing to take to Grace except an admission that I'd been messing around on my own time, and making any sort of allegation against you would have left me in the shit, so I decided to keep following Eddie and hope some evidence came up. That's how come I got to the bungalow. I showed the old lady your photo, but I doubt she'd have remembered her own face, never mind anyone else's. I did manage to have a good poke around her garden though, and clock the loose fencing behind that shed. I should have come clean then, reported it, and taken the flak for acting without authorisation.'

'But you didn't,' I point out.

'No, I didn't. By this time I was obsessed with finding the evidence I was sure was there somewhere that you had been got at, and were informing on us. Then I realised I'd missed an opportunity to link the gang with the bungalow, maybe get a few more solid identifications. So I went back. I'd noticed a few dog ends – fags and joints – by the old lady's garden seat. I went back a few days after the first visit and collected them. That time, I went out the back way through the fence, and I noticed this high window overlooking the whole garden. It was the perfect spot for a surveillance operation, so I noted it down as something else I could suggest to Grace when the time came.'

I can't help bursting into laughter at this. 'Jesus, Polly,' I manage, 'you really didn't know we were there already? We've got the whole thing on video – you're the star of the show!'

'Fucking hell!' She manages a resigned smile. 'Never mind getting back to work. I'll probably be fired before I get out of intensive care. So all this time, I've been trying to follow you, and you've been tailing me? Jesus Christ!'

'That's about the size of it, yes,' I reply. 'No wonder Kyriaku's lot take us for a bunch of bloody idiots.'

'Who's "we",' she asks, 'and what have you been doing?'

'Ah,' I say, smiling. 'So you haven't been able to follow me everywhere?'

I quickly fill her in on the meagre progress of our investigation, Larson's involvement, and Major Teresi's extraction from the gang, taking care to stick to the barest details. Finally, I tell her about Edwin Hall-Warner, ending with, 'I'm sorry to have to tell you this, but you may have him to thank for your being here and not in the morgue.'

'Bloody hell,' she hisses through clenched teeth. 'That's all I need – owing that little shit a favour!'

It's good to hear a little spark in her voice, but I'm very aware that the full horror of what's happened to her hasn't sunk in yet – and if she's anything like me, it will take a while. Right now, there's a veil of morphine between her and the events of the last twenty-four hours, and even though there's vital information sitting behind that veil, I'm not going to be the one to break through it – at least not tonight. I do risk one question, though.

'Polly,' I say gently, 'did you tell anyone else what you were doing – that you suspected me, or someone, of passing information? Think carefully. It's important.'

Her brow furrows as she tries to think back, and after a minute or so she tries to shake her head, but the bandages around her face won't allow it.

'No,' she replies finally. 'I didn't tell anyone, not even ...' She hesitates and finishes, 'Not even my team.'

Not even DC Robbie Robbins, I guess she was about to say. I ask again. 'You're absolutely sure? You didn't mention anything to anybody, in the force or outside?'

'No,' she says again. 'I'm sure, Al. No one.'

There's more I need to ask, but her eyes are starting to close, the morphine tugging at her consciousness. I squeeze her hand and get to my feet. 'It's all right, Polly. Get some sleep. I'll come again when you're feeling a bit stronger.' By the time I finish the sentence, she's already asleep.

Outside the room, DC Robbins is still perched on her chair, tense and watchful. 'I'll ask the nurse if you can go in and sit with her for a while if you like?' I tell her. 'I doubt anyone is going to mount an attack on intensive care, at least not tonight.'

The young officer nods. 'Thank you, sir, I'd like that.'

I have a quick word at the nursing station and head off down the corridor, chewing absently on the ham sandwiches as I go. Back in my car, I take my phone off silent and check my messages again. There's one from Grace – she's gone home to get some sleep, but call her if there's anything urgent. 'Sleep well, Grace,' I mutter to myself. The second is from the chief constable's secretary. The interviews with Edwin Hall-Warner have been put off until the morning, and can I get down to headquarters for 9am? I let out a relieved sigh and dial Larson's number.

'Everything's quiet here,' he says. 'There's been no movement in Weston, according to George. We're watching a movie and then turning in for the night. I'll check the feeds again last thing.'

'Good,' I reply. 'I want you to go through DI Sillitoe's phone records for the last couple of months – landline and mobile, everything from, say, two weeks before the death of DS Brent. I need to know everyone she spoke to, whom she texted, the lot. Can you do that?'

'I'll get onto it first thing in the morning,' he says, and then, 'You sound as if you need some sleep. Is everything okay with you?'

'Fine, son,' I tell him. 'Don't worry about me.'

I hang up and flick the ignition. Suddenly, the thought of going back to my house – dark, silent and filled with the memories of the weeks I spent in a room just like the one Sillitoe is in now – fills me with dread. I pull out of the car park and head towards Clifton.

27

The door opens a crack, closes, and reopens after a few seconds of jangling as the security chain is slipped off its hook. Rosie peers out at me, her baby bulk virtually blocking the whole doorway, a look of growing panic on her face. It's only then I realise it's getting on for midnight, and I should at the very least have rung ahead to warn someone I was coming.

'Dad?' She takes my hand and pulls me inside. 'What's happened? Is John all right?'

'He's fine, sweetheart,' I say quickly, starting to think perhaps I've made a big mistake. 'Nothing's happened to him – he's quite safe, I promise you.'

She studies me for a moment and nods. 'But something's happened, hasn't it? You look like you've seen a ghost. Come on in, and I'll put the kettle on. Everyone else is asleep.'

'You mean everyone else *was* asleep!' Chrissie appears on the stairs, fumbling with her dressing gown. 'What the hell do you think you're doing, Al? It's the middle of the ...' She stops, catching sight of my face. Past experience takes over, and she springs into action. 'God, you look terrible. Get in and take your coat off. Rosie, shut the door, for goodness' sake; it's bloody freezing. And never mind the kettle, go and dig out the brandy.'

She joins us in the hall and takes my coat. 'Go into the lounge,' she says more gently. 'I'll be in in a minute. Have you eaten?'

'A sandwich,' I say feebly, 'at the hospital. I'll be fine, really.'

She replies with a contemptuous snort and disappears down the hall into the kitchen.

'Come on, Dad,' Rosie says, taking my arm and leading me, sheep-like, into the lounge. I collapse onto the sofa, and a couple of minutes later Chrissie appears with a bowl of steaming soup and some of Joyce's home-made bread. It's all I can do to hold back the tears.

She gets right down to it. 'Hospital? What do you mean "at the hospital"?'

I explain, and at once she sits beside me and takes my hand. 'Polly Sillitoe? Jesus Christ, Al. The poor girl. I suppose she's lucky to be alive.'

'If you call it luck,' I agree. 'It's just that being back there jogged some memories, that's all.' I shrug an apology. 'I didn't realise the time. I didn't mean to frighten you all.'

Chrissie turns to Rosie. 'You get off to bed, love,' she says. 'I'll sort out the spare room for your father.'

Rosie gives us both a look, raises an eyebrow, and hauls herself to her feet. 'Good night, Dad.' She kisses my cheek and disappears.

Chrissie sits back, sipping a brandy, and lets me eat. When I've finished, she refills both our glasses.

'It's a long time since I've seen you like this,' she says, her brow furrowing with concern. 'It's more than just seeing Polly in the hospital, isn't it? So what is it you're not telling me? Rosie's not here now, and I won't say anything to her if you don't want me to. It will just be between the two of us.'

I shift slightly so that we're facing each other. 'The bastard who did this to Polly,' I say, trying to keep my tone even, 'is the same bastard who murdered Vicky Brent.' She opens her mouth, but I hold up a hand. 'And he's the same bastard who killed Joe Bailey and shot me in the head.'

I wait, watching the real meaning of what I'm saying sink in. Finally, she says quietly, 'And you're going after him. Oh, God, Al ...'

She collapses into me, her head resting on my shoulder. I put my arm around her, and we stay like that, silent, for what seems a long time before she straightens and lets out a long sigh.

'I'm done in, and so are you,' she says, getting to her feet. 'There's no point talking about it now. Come on – you can help me sort out some sheets.'

'I don't need ...'

She rounds on me, cutting off my objection with a glare. 'Don't even think about sleeping on the sofa. If you're in my house, you sleep in a proper bed like a civilised person.'

'I wouldn't dream of suggesting otherwise,' I reply, defeated, and follow her upstairs to the linen cupboard.

My best option is to stay out of the firing line while Chrissie bustles about with the efficiency of a hotel house-keeper and within five minutes has the spare bed made up.

'There,' she says as I sink down onto it and set about removing my jacket and tie. 'You know where everything is – just don't sneak off in the morning before you've had a proper breakfast and said hello to Ben. He's bound to find out you've been here, and he's upset enough with his father away.'

'Fine,' I reply, knowing there's no use arguing. 'And thanks. I really needed to be here tonight – you know?'

She nods. 'I know.' She turns to go, but when she gets to the door, she pauses and says, her back to me, 'Just tell me one thing, Al. Tell me John's safe – that he's not in any danger from this – whatever his name is – this murderer. Because I swear, if any harm comes to him because of you ...'

I move up behind her and gently put my hands on her shoulders. 'Don't worry, he's perfectly safe,' I lie. 'Nothing's going to happen to him. I'll make sure of it.'

Before I have a chance to take my next breath, she's turned around, grabbed me in a tight hug, her face buried in my shirt. I hold her to me for what feels an age, yet at the same time not nearly long enough, until she pushes me away roughly and walks out – but not so fast that I don't see the tears on her cheeks.

I GET to headquarters half an hour before my appointment with Gosford, prior to Edwin Hall-Warner's interrogation. I'm ushered into a plush waiting area and supplied with coffee and biscuits. For once, I'm not in need of either, thanks to my ex-mother-in-law's extravagant breakfast. My mobile rings – it's Larson.

'I thought you'd like an update on DI Sillitoe's mobile,' he says. 'The DCI got it over to me via courier yesterday afternoon, so I've been able to go through her call and text history, emails and calendars – at least the ones she keeps on her phone. It's mostly work stuff, calls to the West Hill numbers or to other officers. In addition to those, there are emails to and from family members – a sister and her parents, by the look of it. The email addresses check out. There are also frequent personal calls and texts to someone called Robbie – a boyfriend, maybe? I suppose it could be a cover for a gang contact?'

'Possibly, but I don't think so,' I reply, wondering if DC Robbins has been holding vigil outside Polly's room since I left her last night. There's nothing to be gained putting him straight on that one. 'Shelve the love interest for now – we can always come back to it if we need to. Anything else?'

'If you say so,' he agrees, with a hint of reluctance. 'There isn't a lot in her calendar either, just " Grangeford, lunch" once a month or so – Grangeford is where her parents live, so that makes sense – a dental appointment three weeks ago, and last week a session with the police mental health service, which I'm assuming is part of the normal routine. There's really nothing else so far, at least not that I've found.'

'Okay. Keep digging, and keep me informed.'

It doesn't hit me until five minutes and two cups of cold coffee later, and when it does, I jump to my feet, proclaiming, 'Jesus bloody shit!' to Gosford's startled PA, who wheels her chair backwards with so much force she bangs her head on the wall. At the same moment, the chief constable himself decides to join the party, and strides through from his office, looks from one to the other of us, and stops dead in his tracks.

'Crow? What the hell's going on here?'

I wave a quick apology to the PA and, without waiting for an invitation, stride past Gosford into his sanctum. He follows me, slams the door shut and is about to launch into a verbal equivalent of throwing the rule book at my head when he sees my expression and simply folds his arms, waiting, none too happily, for my explanation.

'Sorry about that, sir,' I concede, 'but I need you to bear with me. There's something I need before I go in to see Eddie. It could be vitally important.'

Gosford keeps up his impression of a concrete post for another few seconds, then finally takes a breath and walks across to his desk, gesturing for me to take a seat. He does likewise and leans forward, elbows on the mahogany.

'It had better be,' he comments stiffly. 'So what, Inspector, is so urgent you feel the need to frighten my secretary half to death?'

'This may sound a bit of a long shot, sir,' I say to his narrowing eyebrows, 'but I've got a hunch I want to follow up. I assume we have HR files for every civilian employee working in or visiting the local stations?'

'I would be concerned if we didn't,' he replies. 'The vetting process is very strict, as you can imagine.'

'And it applies to everyone – cleaners, caterers, medical staff ...'

'Naturally,' he spits impatiently. 'Where is this leading, Inspector?'

'I need printed copies of the photo IDs of all civilian staff who have regular contact with West Hill station. One of your HR people should be able to pull them off the computer within the next five minutes. If they can't, I'll get Larson to do it. I'd also like copies of the CCTV images we caught of Kyriaku and his associate from that pub in Weston-super-Mare.' He stares at me, aghast, so I add, injecting as much sincerity and urgency into my voice as I can manage, 'It's very important, sir. I wouldn't be asking otherwise.'

He looks me up and down, decides there's a slim chance I might be onto something, and jabs his intercom button.

'Kathy, get me the director of Human Resources. Now!' He releases the button. 'You'd better not be wasting everyone's time, Inspector Crow.'

A moment later his phone rings, and he gives the curt instruction, leaving me to imagine the confused look on the face of the force's head of personnel. We wait for several minutes, and then there's a tap on the door, and a flustered clerk comes in carrying a sheaf of papers.

'These are all the records we have to date, sir,' he says, holding them out. 'The CCTV stuff is there as well.'

Gosford gestures at me. 'Thank you. Give them to Inspector Crow if you would. That will be all for the moment.'

I take the pile and thumb through the images, each captioned with a name, redacted, and role within the organisation. 'Thank you, sir,' I say. 'I think I'm ready to talk to Hall-Warner now.'

'If you're sure you can spare the time, Inspector,' Gosford growls, opting for overkill on the sarcasm. He gets up. 'I intend to listen in on this one. Whatever's going on in your head, it had better be good!'

As we head down to the interview suite, I'm thinking exactly the same thing.

EDWIN HALL-WARNER IS HUNCHED into a chair on one side of the desk next to a woman I don't recognise, but assume is one of the local duty solicitors. On the other side, next to the empty chair set out for me, is a burly detective. As I walk in, he turns, and I recognise DS Benson, a former rookie of mine over at West Hill, now stationed at the local Portishead nick. Last time I saw him, he was pulling the body of a murderer out of Portishead Lock – the murder that ended up in Rosie's arrest as an accessory.

He greets me with a wide grin. 'Morning, boss. All well with you and yours, I hope?'

'Morning, Benson. We're all good, thanks for asking. You?'

'Couldn't be better. My eldest got her degree last October. Financial management, would you believe? If you need someone to look after your pension, just give her a shout – special rates for folks in the job. I'll give you her number later on.'

'Thanks,' I say, smiling. 'I'll bear it in mind.'

I sit down and give my attention to the duo sitting on the other side of the table. Edwin has crumbled into himself, leaning as far away from all of us as he can and staring fixedly at the floor between his feet. He looks like a five-year-old forced to sit through a school governors' meeting to discuss his future. I turn to the brief, who looks so unsympathetic she reminds me of Carol Dodds, the scourge of all self-respecting police officers, and the barrister who, thank God, represented my daughter in her hour of need. The main difference here is, Rosie was innocent. Edwin Hall-Warner is as guilty as hell, and everyone in the room knows it. She gives me a bleak smile.

'Julia Mason,' she informs me. 'I will be representing Mr Hall-Warner.'

I give her a cursory nod. 'I take it your father couldn't run to his usual barrister?' I ask Edwin, who shrinks even further into his seat, if that's possible. Mason snorts, but has the good sense to keep quiet. She's on a hiding to nothing, and she knows it. I give Benson a nod. He goes through the motions and begins the recording.

I offer Edwin a reassuring smile. 'I hope we've been looking after you, Eddie. You've had breakfast and so on? I can arrange some coffee if you like. It's not quite premium quality, but it's warm and wet.'

He shakes his head, still not looking up, and mumbles, 'No, thanks,' at his shoes.

'If you're sure,' I go on. 'I won't keep you long. I just want you to look at a few pictures for me. Do you think you're up to that?'

He finally meets my eye and says, his voice unsteady, a look of pure desperation on his face, 'They'll kill me, Inspector Crow. You don't know what they're like – if I tell you anything, they'll know, and they'll get to me, even here. I can't say anything – I just can't.'

He trails off and bats away a tear, then wipes his nose on his sleeve. His solicitor helpfully digs in her bag and hands him a sachet of tissues. I give her a nod of thanks, wait until he's blown his nose and I have his attention.

'Listen to me, son,' I say. 'I think I know exactly what they're like. The fact is, I know more than you do. For instance, I know that it doesn't matter whether you talk to me or not. They will simply assume that as you are here, you've let something slip, and that you are probably singing louder than Pavarotti. Believe me, the only chance you've got is to cooperate with us. If you do that, we can do our best to protect you. If you don't, you're going to end up in a mainstream prison, and you know what that means.' I pause to let this sink in, and then say, 'Do you really think they won't have realised you tried to help that police officer you were supposed to dump? Your job was to dispose of a dead body, not deliver a vital witness to the police. Your card is already well and truly marked, son, regardless of what you say to me now.'

There's a silence while he thinks this over. Finally, he nods. 'What do you want to know?'

At once, Mason butts in, 'My client doesn't have to tell you anything, Inspector.' She turns to Edwin. 'Mr Hall-Warner, I strongly advise you against giving the police any information at this stage.'

He turns on her with a surprising show of backbone – or panic, it's hard to tell which. 'Okay – and if I do that, I'll be dead by tomorrow morning, so keep out of it. I don't want you here anyway.'

Mason gives me an appealing look.

'That wouldn't be wise, son,' I tell him. 'You should have your legal representative present whenever we interview you.' I don't add that it's for our protection as much as his. The last thing we need is a false accusation of police brutality or a forced confession. I look from one to the other. 'If we're ready?'

I get a reluctant nod from Mason and riffle through the stack of printouts on the table in front of me. I pull out the grainy image of Kyriaku from the CCTV and slide it across.

'Eddie, can you tell me who this man is?'

The sight of the picture makes him turn even paler than he already is. 'Alastor,' he mumbles. 'Everyone calls him Alastor.'

'Does he have another name? Have you ever heard anyone call him something else?'

He thinks for a minute. 'He's got a girlfriend. I saw her once, with his dog. She called him ...' He shakes his head, trying to remember. 'It was Darren or Dario – something like that. He got really angry. I never heard that name again.'

'Thank you, Eddie,' I say, and show him another image, this time of the other driver on the CCTV. 'And this one?'

'His name's Sidaris,' Edwin replies, with a shudder. 'He goes everywhere with Alastor. He looks like some kind of minder, but he isn't.' He gives me a nervous look. 'Everyone's nearly as scared of him as they are of Alastor. He's the one made me run over Karen – I mean the other policewoman, after she was dead. He said if I didn't, he'd do the same to me ...' He chokes up again and pulls out another tissue.

'It's all right, Eddie,' I say, resisting the urge to lean over the table and break his nose. At least now I know the identity of the man who put the frighteners on Shark Johnson and Reggie Perrin. 'You're doing really well,' I say. 'Just a couple more and then we're done, for now. Okay?'

He nods miserably, and I show him a couple of random faces from the personnel files. He shakes his head at each of them. I pick out the third and slide it across. At once, he leans forward, studying the picture.

'You know him?' I ask, holding my breath.

'I don't know his name,' he says, his brow furrowing. 'I've seen him though, a couple of times.'

'Where, and when? Can you remember?'

'He was at the warehouse, the day before – before the thing with the policewoman and the car. He came to see Alastor.'

'You said "a couple of times"?'

He nods. 'He was there again a few days ago. He went to see Alastor, and there was a row – they were shouting at each other.'

'Did you hear what they were saying?' I ask.

This time he shakes his head. 'I heard it – everybody did. But it was all in Greek. I didn't understand any of it. Then it went quiet, and the guy left. He looked scared. I don't know any more, honestly, Inspector Crow. He left, and I didn't see him again.'

'Thank you, Eddie,' I say. 'That's all for the moment. Don't worry, you'll be staying here for the time being, and we'll make sure you're safe. We'll be having another chat very soon.'

I grab my papers and head for the door, leaving Benson to wind up the proceedings. Outside, Gosford is waiting, arms folded, a combination of irritation and puzzlement. I thrust the page displaying the final photo into his hand.

'Well, sir?' I ask. 'I'm assuming you recognise this person?'

He glances at it, and the colour drains from his face. 'Oh, dear God!' he mutters. 'I don't believe it. Davis? Are you sure?'

'Quite sure,' I reply. 'And do remember, sir, when you are explaining to the Police and Crime Commission, that it was your idea to insist all officers have regular sessions with counselling services. Pity the vetting process wasn't a bit more thorough, but I suppose what with budget cuts and all – and someone had to be the guinea pig for a new service like this ...'

'That's enough, Inspector,' he hisses through clenched teeth. 'I want this bastard arrested – now!'

I sigh. 'With respect, sir, perhaps that isn't a good idea?'

To give him his due, Gosford didn't get to be chief constable without doing at least some time on the frontline, and despite years of paperwork and corporate lunches at the golf club, he hasn't forgotten how things work. He rolls his eyes in frustration.

'You're right, of course,' he agrees. 'The minute we lift him, they'll know we're onto their informant. What do you suggest?'

'Try to keep him under observation for now. There's a young DC on Sillitoe's team – DC Robbins. She's bright, inconspicuous and discreet. We could do worse than have her keep an eye on him until we're ready to bring him in. There's also DC Jackson – best if they team up, just to be safe.'

He nods. 'I suppose now we know who's been passing information, we can bring in a few more people. God knows we'll need them. We still need to be careful, though, just in case Davis isn't the only one.'

'Yes, sir,' I say. 'I also think I should get back to the hospital. Sillitoe told me she'd been tailing me for a while – she thought I was the informant. That means she could have followed me to Redcliffe, even if she didn't know why I was there. I intended to ask her, but she's pretty drugged up, and I didn't get the chance. I need to talk to her again as soon as possible. It's clear she was unaware of the surveillance at Weston though, so hopefully she hadn't worked out anything much. She had one of your compulsory counselling sessions a few days ago, and if she let slip any information on her out-of-hours movements, Kyriaku may well start joining the dots.'

Gosford groans. 'Go,' he says. 'Now – and while you're there, I'll get Hallam and a couple of his squad deployed to the safe house. George Saint can stay where he is for the moment, but I'll get an AFO over to him as well, just in case.'

'Sir.'

I head for the door, but Gosford calls me back before I get through it.

'Inspector Crow?'

'Sir?'

'I'm putting you in charge of DI Sillitoe's team. Use them as you see fit. But I'd be grateful if you could try to make sure no more of my officers end up either in hospital or in the morgue.'

28

Thankfully the nurses inform me Sillitoe is awake when I arrive back in the intensive care unit. As I make my way through to the side room, I bump into DC Robbins on her way out, her lips set in a thin line of grim determination. Clearly, Gosford has put her in the picture, and she's out for Davis's blood. She stops and straightens to attention when she sees me.

'The chief constable tells me you're in charge now, sir,' she says, accusation and resentment battling for the upper hand in both her tone and expression.

'Until Detective Inspector Sillitoe recovers, yes, Constable,' I answer stiffly. 'If you think you will have difficulty with that, I'd be happy to support a transfer request. No reflection on your ability, naturally.'

She pales at the suggestion. 'No, sir, I ... of course not, sir, I didn't mean ...'

I take her arm gently and lead her out into the corridor out of everyone's way. 'Listen, Robbie. I know you and Polly are close.' Maybe, I think, too close to be working on the same team, but it's their business, not mine. She changes colour again, faster than a traffic light, this time blushing furiously. 'Believe me,' I carry on, 'we all want the same things – to put away the bastards who did this to her, and to have her back where she belongs, on the job, as soon as possible. We can only do that if we all work together, yes?'

She nods and attempts a weak smile. 'Yes, sir. Thank you, sir.'

'Furthermore,' I say, 'I've just told the chief constable you're the sharpest officer on the team and that if anyone can keep tabs on Donald bloody Duck without being clocked in five minutes, it's you. Or did I get that wrong?'

The determination comes back at once, and she straightens up. 'No, sir. You didn't get it wrong. I'm on my way to meet Daz – I mean DC Jackson – now. Dr Davis is in the hospital today, in an office on the fourth floor. Neither of us has had any dealings with him so far, so he shouldn't recognise us. We'll stay out of the way, though, just in case.'

'Good. I knew I could count on you and Darren.' I smile. 'You'd better get off before he starts thinking you've fallen down a lift shaft!'

'I'm on my way, sir,' she replies, and rushes off, although not without a last, hesitant glance in the direction of Sillitoe's room.

I walk in to find nothing much has changed. The machines are still beeping softly and pulsing away at no one in particular.

'She's been waiting for you,' the nurse hovering at the bedside says, straightening up and giving me a smile. 'One thing about you West Hill lot – you're a load of tough cookies! I hear you had a bit of a brush yourself a few years ago.

According to the matron, you're a legend round here. If this one's anything like you, I think you've got competition!'

'You don't know the half of it,' I reply as she brushes past me to the door.

'You'd be surprised, Inspector,' she retorts, and retreats to the nursing station.

'If it's a competition, I'm buggered if I know who's winning,' Sillitoe says weakly as I take my place at her bedside.

'So far I'd say it was a draw,' I answer, giving her hand a squeeze. She still looks pretty terrible, but a little more alert than on my last visit. 'Listen, Polly. There's something I need to tell you, and I have a feeling you're not going to like it. I wish I could leave it until you're feeling a bit stronger, but I'm afraid it won't wait.'

'You mean this isn't a social visit? Al, I'm disappointed.' Her mouth can't quite manage a smile, but there's a touch of humour in her eyes.

'You've been seeing that counsellor the chief constable sent over to West Hill, yes?'

'You mean Donald "the Duck" Davis? Yes. Not by choice – at least not at first, but after a couple of sessions, I started to think maybe it wasn't such a bad idea. It's tough sometimes, you know, what we do, and offloading at home – well, let's just say it doesn't make relationships any easier.'

'I won't argue there. So you and Robbie Robbins didn't discuss the job outside of work? Not ever?'

Her eyes widen. 'How the hell ...?'

'Didn't take a genius. She's been hovering outside your door more or less ever since you were brought in. So you never discussed your suspicions about me, or your movements out of hours with her?'

'No. Never. I didn't want to involve her – I was going off-piste, and it might have put her in an awkward position, especially with the DCI. She's just starting out and doesn't need to be given the black spot before her career's got off the ground.'

I nod. 'Fair enough. But what about Davis, in those mental health sessions? How much did you tell him?'

There's a long silence. Then she closes her eyes and mutters, 'Shit!'

I give her a minute to mull things over. 'I'm sorry, Polly,' I say, really meaning it. I remember only too well the guilt that followed me – still follows me – after Joe Bailey's death, and the constant niggle that perhaps I made a mistake, could have done things differently. Polly Sillitoe did precisely what I would have done, and if she'd been right, she would be a hero right now. It's a fine line, I reflect, between getting a medal and winding up in a coffin. 'Take your time, and just tell me everything you can remember from the last session you had with him. When was it, and what was the conversation?'

'It was Friday,' she says. 'Friday evening. I had an appointment for nine o'clock.'

'In the evening?' I interrupt. 'Didn't you think that was a bit odd?'

She screws her eyelids together. I know that feeling. 'I should have, Al,' she says eventually. 'I really should have. But I was so taken up with finding out what you were doing, I didn't think. I was so convinced you were the informant, and you and Grace have always been close. If it came down to it, my word against yours, she wouldn't listen to me unless I had hard evidence – shit, I was being such a fucking idiot ...'

'No,' I tell her. 'No, Polly, you weren't – or at least if you were a fucking idiot, we all were. Don't forget, we were thinking the same thing about you. Medusa has had us chasing our tails, and whether they planned it or not, they've had all of us looking in the wrong direction. But not anymore. Go on – what happened when you met up with him?'

'I told him about my suspicions. I mean, I couldn't tell anyone else, and Christ, I needed to tell somebody! I couldn't say anything to Robbie. She would have wanted to help out, and I couldn't put her career on the line. We haven't known each other that long, and it would have been unfair, and the truth is, I really like her, you know? It's early days, but I don't want to lose her, not over this.' She pauses and then says bitterly, 'When she starts to understand what's happened, I probably will anyway. Who wants to live with a cripple? And a cripple with half a face? Forget it!'

'In the first place,' I reply at once, 'you won't be a cripple, not if I know you, Pol. And in the second place, DC Robbins is no fool. She knows what's happened, and she's been sat outside your room all this time. In fact, she's tailing Donald Duck as we speak, with Daz Jackson.' I see the look of horror on her face and add quickly, 'You don't need to worry. She's sharp, and she isn't going to take any risks. It's her job, Polly, and if you can't let her do it, she shouldn't be on your team.'

She lets out a long sigh. 'You're right of course. And yes, she's sharp – she'll be after both our jobs in a few years' time. Anyway, I should have realised something wasn't quite right, but at the time I was at home trying to get all the paperwork in order on the Draper murders. I was planning to throw a sickie the next day and didn't want anyone chasing me for loose ends.'

'A sickie? Why? That's not like you.'

Her lips quirk into something resembling a smile. 'To tail you. I was hoping to pick up something I could take to Grace, convince her to let me follow it up. I felt I needed to talk it over with someone to get things clear in my head, and it had to be someone outside the station, because if I was wrong about you, it meant the informant was someone else, and I didn't know who to trust. Don Davis was an outsider, and all the sessions were confidential, so it made sense – or seemed to.'

'And once you'd talked it over, you decided to carry on with the plan?'

'Yes. I followed you down to the harbour, but then I saw you meet up with Grace, and realised I might have made a terrible mistake. Either you and Grace were in it together, or something else was going on. Having both of you taking backhanders from the mob was impossible, so I figured it must be an undercover job.'

'You figured right,' I say. 'But wait a minute. You say you were down at the harbour on Saturday? Did you take your mobile? Can you remember?'

She frowns. 'What kind of question is that?' Suddenly, she starts to shake, so violently I'm convinced she must be having some sort of seizure. I'm a whisker away from thumping the emergency buzzer by the bed when she gasps, 'No – it's okay, Al. Just leave it – please?' I start to object, but she reaches out with an effort and grasps my hand. 'I'm all right. It's just that ...'

'Just that what?'

'I remembered. They took my phone. They took everything, and I thought, thank God it's only the spare one, and then ...'

Her chest begins to heave again as she fights for breath, trying to fend off panic.

'Listen to me, Polly,' I say firmly, squeezing her hand as hard as I dare. 'You're okay. I'm here, and you're all right. I'm not going anywhere, you hear me? You had your spare phone. Why? Focus on the question – forget everything else. Why didn't you take your work phone?'

'The battery was dead. I forgot to charge it up. I've got an old pay-as-you-go that I keep topped up just in case. I put the work mobile on charge and took the other.' Her expression changes as she realises the reason for my question. 'You had a trace on it. You bastard – you had a tracker on my phone!'

'And you would have put one on mine if you'd thought of it,' I shoot back, but with a smile. What I don't say is that if she'd taken that mobile with her, we might have picked up what was happening and got her out. Now just isn't the time.

'Believe me, I thought of it,' she replies. 'I just didn't have a technical whizz-kid in my pocket, and I would have had to go through the procedures.'

'So you saw me with Grace down on the harbour. Then what?'

'I took a step back. I grabbed something to eat and then staked out your house. I saw you come back and waited until you went out again. I was curious – if this was an official operation, I wanted to know what was going on. I guess I should have left well alone, but I didn't. You went down to Redcliffe and into a block of flats. I parked in the multi-storey, walked across to the apartment building, and that's when they jumped me. After that ...' She shudders again. 'I don't remember much. Just the odd snatch here and there, and then waking up like this.'

The queasiness in my stomach that has been growing

since she mentioned the counselling appointment congeals into a solid icy lump. She was followed to the apartments where Teresi and Larson are holed up. If they were following her, the chances are they saw me too. Another thought follows – perhaps the only reason I'm not either in the morgue or in the bed she's in now is that they took her first. It could so easily have been me. The final and worst realisation is that they know where my son-in-law and Jennifer Teresi are. Maybe not the exact apartment – the block has just short of a hundred flats, and there's no way of knowing which one from the outside. It's only a matter of time, though, and not a lot of time. It could already be too late.

'What is it?' she asks, and I realise I've groaned out loud. She didn't stay at the harbour long enough to see Larson and Teresi make their escape, so naturally, she had no idea why I was visiting those flats. Kyriaku, though, wouldn't have known that, and would have assumed she knew where his former dog handler was.

Now isn't the time to make her feel worse than she does already. I shake my head. 'Nothing. Don't worry. I have to go – there's something I need to do. Just try to get some rest, okay?'

Back out in the corridor, I pass an agitated elderly couple scurrying towards ICU, the man supporting his wife, who is leaning against him, dabbing her eyes with a tissue. She bears a striking resemblance to Sillitoe – her parents, clearly. At least, I think, she's going to have people around her in the coming months. She's going to need all the support she can get, especially when the memories begin to surface and the nightmares start.

The lift door opens, and a uniformed officer steps out,

the padding of a Kevlar vest visible under his jacket. I have no doubt there's a concealed weapon, too. He gives me a nod.

'There's a van been sent down to Redcliffe, sir,' he tells me. 'We've got officers on the front and rear entrances, and we'll send someone up to sit with your witness. Your boss has let them know to expect us. Nobody will get in or out without being seen.'

'I'm sure you're doing an excellent job,' I reply, trying to sound convincing, and managing not to add, 'seen by whom?'

That's when it hits me that my next move is one I can't make. Showing up anywhere near the Redcliffe apartment would be nothing short of stupid. I might as well be carrying a tourist guide's umbrella and shouting 'This way to the safe house!' After what Sillitoe has just told me, even getting into my car in the hospital car park is a risk. The lift door opens, but I let it go, take a couple of slow breaths, and set off for the stairs, fishing my mobile out of my pocket as I go.

There's no reply from Larson, just twenty seconds of the ringtone cutting to the answering service. I'm about to leave a message when Grace's number pops up on my screen. I pick up the call.

'Stay where you are,' she orders before I've had a chance to get a word out. 'You don't set foot outside that hospital, do you hear me, Al? I've got an armed officer on the way, and you don't go anywhere without protection.'

'I wasn't intending to,' I assure her. 'I'm going to get a decent coffee. Tell them I'll meet them in the ground-floor café.'

'Good. Come straight over to West Hill. I want to know exactly what Polly's told you before we go any further.'

'Yes, ma'am.'

I've just reached the ground floor when my phone pings. It's a text message from Larson.

All fine. Nothing new.

That's it. I swear under my breath. I'm going to have to have a serious chat with my son-in-law about professionalism and communication. I get myself a coffee and settle in to wait for my chaperone. I'm just taking my first bite from a bar of something containing mostly sugar when my phone demands my attention again. It's Rosie.

'Dad? Have you spoken to John?'

'I got a text from him just now. Why?'

'I got one, too,' she says. 'I tried to call him an hour ago, and he didn't reply. I just assumed he was busy with something. Then I got a text, and it doesn't make sense.'

'What doesn't? What did he say?'

'It says, *Sorry I haven't been in touch. Everything's fine. Don't wait up, Honey xxx.* Dad, I'm worried. I mean, "Don't wait up, Honey?" John would never say that – it's awful! I tried ringing him back, but he didn't answer.'

Suddenly, my hand is trembling, and I feel my legs start to freeze. If I hadn't been sitting down, I would have fallen over. I've let my irrational prejudice blind me to what's really happening. Out of the corner of my eye, I see a woman in uniform, like her colleague decked out in a bulletproof vest, a helmet wedged under her arm, making her way to my table.

'Don't worry, sweetheart,' I say to Rosie. 'I'll find out what's going on and get back to you as soon as I've spoken to him.' I hang up, struggle to my feet, hoping I can stay upright and not embarrass myself, and head for the uniform.

'Sergeant Taylor,' the woman says. 'I've been told to ...'

'Fuck what you've been told,' I snap. 'Follow me, Sergeant, and do as I say.'

'But ...'

'Get on the radio and tell your boss to send a message through to the AFOs at Redcliffe. Tell them to get up to the penthouse and break in if they have to – now! Meanwhile, you're with me, and don't even think about arguing.'

'Yes, sir,' she replies, blinking in confusion, but she falls in and follows me as I make for the car park as fast as my unsteady legs can go.

She holds out an arm to steady me, but I bat it away. It's not until I get out into the open air of the car park that I realise I haven't got a clue where I'm heading, or what the hell I'm going to do next. I come to a sudden halt, and Sergeant Taylor, taken by surprise, ploughs into me, almost knocking me flat. At the same time, there's a buzzing noise in the inside pocket of my jacket. It isn't my mobile – I fumble for the source of the sound and dig out another phone – the burner I was given by Shark's gang. There's a message. It simply says, *Get in the car.* What car? I show the message to Taylor.

'This is a car park, for God's sake,' I mutter, waving an arm at the miserly space provided by the infirmary for patients and visitors, bursting at the seams with vehicles of every conceivable description. 'I'm a policeman, not a bloody psychic!'

'Perhaps it means your car, sir?' she suggests nervously.

'Somewhere to start, I suppose,' I say, and trudge across the tarmac. My car is where I left it, still has all its tyres and, as far as I can see, has the same number of dents and scratches it did when I parked it. When I'm around five metres away, I click the remote and realise it isn't locked. Taylor and I exchange a look, and I curse my stubborn refusal to use the fancy high-tech saloon Grace provided me with – the additional stress of dealing with an unfamiliar vehicle seemed a step too far. With hindsight, it might have been a really stupid decision.

'Wait here, sir,' she says, and edges towards it, one hand slipping inside her jacket towards the pistol in its holster under her right arm. I ignore the instruction and stay a pace behind her. She flattens herself beside one of the rear doors and peers inside, jumps, and is about to draw the weapon when I see what she's looking at and grab her arm.

'Stop!' I hiss. 'It's all right, Sergeant; you can put that thing away.'

Clive Gingell is sitting on the back seat, arms folded, staring out at us with a self-satisfied smile.

29

'Okay, Clive,' I growl, twisting round in the driver's seat so that I can give him my most withering glare. 'What's so bloody urgent that you thought breaking into a police officer's car was in any way acceptable behaviour?'

'This ain't a car,' he replies with a smirk, completely undaunted. 'It's a pile of crap. And you ain't even got anything worth nicking in it – fucking tosser.'

Taylor, in the passenger seat, has enough presence of mind to accept the situation as perfectly normal, deciding now is the perfect moment to check the roadworthiness of her firearm. She gives the barrel of the pistol a quick polish with her sleeve and tests the sight by pointing it between Gingell Junior's eyes. He gapes, eyes out on stalks, and sits back, arms folded. 'Nice shooter,' he comments uncertainly.

'Only the best,' she replies, 'and before you ask, dead accurate up to fifty metres, so don't even think of trying to run for it.' She emphasises the statement with a predatory smile.

'I wasn't,' he says, 'and you can't shoot me if I haven't done nothing.' He drops his gaze, shuffles, and mutters, 'Mad bitch,' under his breath.

I'm about to point out that nobody has time for polite conversation when Taylor's radio crackles, and Sergeant Hallam's distinctive voice fills the gap, grim and urgent.

'Flo – is Inspector Crow with you?'

'I'm here,' I say at once. 'What's happening?'

'We had to break into the flat,' he replies. 'It's empty. Looks like they left in a hurry, and probably not under their own steam. No sign of a forced entry, though – apart from ours of course.'

'How long ago?' I ask. 'Do you have any idea?'

'Not that long. They had eaten breakfast by the look of the kitchen, and the kettle was still slightly warm. I'd say two hours, maybe three. No more than that, and certainly not since we got here an hour ago. Looks like we missed them by a whisker. I'm sorry, Inspector. The SOCOs have just arrived, for all the good that will do.'

'Any sign of injury or a struggle?'

'There's no blood anywhere as far as I can see, but I guess it's up to the SOCOs to try to work out the sequence of events. Your lot are sending a team across to do a door-to-door, try to find potential witnesses. That's about all we can do here. I'll keep you updated as soon as we have more information.'

The radio goes dead. My hands are shaking as if I'm having an attack of the palsy, and I grip the steering wheel so hard I think I might bend it out of shape. 'Shit!' I manage through gritted teeth. 'Shit, shit, shit!' My son-in-law and our star witness are very likely next in line to be a killer Doberman's afternoon snack, and it could take days to find the warehouse Teresi mentioned. It could be anywhere in the countryside between Weston and Bristol or Bath. The area is sparsely populated and huge. And Teresi is the only one who could have taken us there. 'Shit!' I say again, trying to ward off the despair that is threatening to take over my body as much as my mind. A shrill, insistent voice breaks through the fog.

'Hey, Bird Man. You ain't listening. I said that's why Shark sent me. "Tell the Bird you know where they've gone," he told me. He said to take you. I mean, this is all the thanks I get, a fucking gun in my face, so if you don't want to know, I've got better things to do. But he said to tell you, so I'm telling you. I can take you, okay?'

I turn to Clive, hardly daring to hope. 'Are you serious? You know where they are?'

He nods. 'Are you fucking deaf? That's what I said. Shark said to show you, but if you're not interested ...'

He yanks the door handle, but I reach back and grab his arm. There's no way either of us will catch him if he makes a run for it. He's way too streetwise. 'You want me to tell Shark you wimped out?' I ask him.

He glares at me and slumps back in his seat. 'You're just a bastard pig, same as all the rest,' he grumbles.

'Maybe,' I agree. 'But unlike all the rest, I'm the bastard pig who's asking you to show me where Kyriaku's taken my daughter's husband. I'm also the bastard pig who will owe you a favour if you do, Shark or no Shark. Do we understand each other, son?'

'I'll have to sit in the front,' Clive says after some hesitation.

I raise an eyebrow at Taylor, who frowns, but gets out to make room for Clive to scramble over the gear stick into the front, while she takes her place behind him, keeping one hand firmly on her weapon, now back in its holster under her jacket.

'Okay, Clive,' I say, starting the engine. 'Lead on – and if you know what's good for you, don't even think about messing me about.' Somehow, I manage to get my limbs under enough control to drive without hitting anything on the way out, although my stomach feels like I've swallowed a block of ice. Clive's directions take us out of town, south towards the Mendip Hills.

'Sir,' Taylor ventures, 'I'm not sure we should be ...'

'Get hold of Hallam,' I tell her. 'Relay our position and tell him to get his team on the road and, if they can, to follow at a discreet distance. Then ask him to alert DCI Helston.'

'Yes, sir, but ...'

'Don't bloody argue, Sergeant. Just do it!'

She heaves a huge and disapproving sigh, but pulls out her radio and starts to mutter into it. A minute later the inevitable call comes through from Grace.

'Al? What the bloody hell do you think you're doing? You get your arse back here right now if you want a job to come back to. Do you hear me?'

'Not a chance, Grace,' I reply, gritting my teeth and accelerating onto the M5. 'They're pulling out, I can feel it. Kyriaku knew he was blown the moment we snatched Teresi. He's overstepped the mark, Grace. He's not only got us after him, he's failed to subdue the local gangs, and if what Teresi says is true, his obsession with these dogs has got his bosses' backs up. He's between a rock and a hard place – but before he leaves, he wants his revenge on Teresi, and my son-in-law is caught up in it. I'm with the only person who can get me to where they are before it's too late, so you can sack me if you like, but before you fill out the forms, tell Gosford to find me some backup, and have them ready to move as soon as I get a location.'

'For Christ's sake, Al ...' There's a pause, then, 'Hang on, it's George.' I hear a short, muffled conversation, and then she's back. 'Looks like you're right. George has got three of them at the bungalow, clearing the shed. I'll get a load of uniforms over there to round them up, and I'll tell the chief constable to hand control of Hallam's team over to you.'

'Thanks, Grace.'

'Don't thank me, Al. Just don't fuck it up, and don't take any unnecessary risks.'

She hangs up without waiting for a reply, and Clive tugs my sleeve, points to the exit sign. We're just south of Weston-super-Mare, heading for the expanse of the Somerset Levels and its maze of narrow, often single-track roads, many bordered by deep, water-filled irrigation trenches known locally as rhynes – treacherous for drivers unfamiliar with the landscape, especially after dark. I glance at my watch – it's getting on for mid afternoon. On the one hand, the levels are dotted with old, abandoned buildings and peat diggings – perfect places to hide. On the other, they are, as the name suggests, flat. Anyone keeping watch can see a possible threat coming from miles away.

As if mirroring my thoughts, Clive says, 'We got to go careful now. If they see us, we're dog meat.'

'I get it, son,' I reply. 'You got any suggestions?'

He nods. 'There's a place not far away from here. We can stay there 'til it gets dark. Then we have to walk.' He glances at my pavement shoes and grins. 'Looks like you're going to get your feet wet, Bird Man.'

'Wait 'til it gets dark? Son, that's two or three hours away.'

I can't bring myself to voice my worst fear – Larson and Teresi could well be dead by then, if they're not already.

'It won't make no difference,' Clive says, reading my expression. 'They don't do nothing 'til it gets dark. That's when he turns up, and things happen. If you want to get him, you have to wait.'

'You know that for sure?' I ask.

He shrugs. 'I've been down here watching for Shark. The big bastard ain't there yet. And when somebody gets wasted, he's always there.'

'Okay.' I've suddenly got something else to rage about. 'You're happy with that, are you? Shark Johnson sends you to do his dirty work, knowing what will happen if you get caught? Too scared to come himself, is he?'

He rounds on me, jabbing an accusing finger into my arm. 'You're a fucking arsehole. You don't know nothing. Shark makes sure I'm all right. He looks after us – me and the twins.'

'The twins?'

'Molly and Pete. Our ma don't do nothing – not since her crap boyfriend beat her up and she lost the kid she was having. She turned into a head case after that – never goes out, not even to the shop down the road. Pete and Molly were babies then, and I've been looking after them since. Shark makes sure we've got money and food and stuff, and when I'm not there, he sends someone to get the twins to school – they're six now. He says, if anything happens to me, he'll see them right. So you don't know what you're talking about.' He points at a turning coming up on the left. 'Go down there, and shut the fuck up.'

I follow both instructions, taking a left turn, and silently mulling over Clive's story. Once again, I'm struck by the parallels between his experience as a child growing up in the modern-day tenements of Bristol and that of Darius Kyriaku in Athens – two bright, streetwise and desperate kids picked up and nurtured by local gang bosses, in debt to organised crime by the time they reach puberty, most often either killers or dead before they are old enough to vote. I stop thinking as Clive gives my arm another sharp poke.

'Over there,' he says, pointing at a derelict construction of rotting wood and corrugated iron set back from the road and half obscured by a dense screen of brambles and weeds that have punched through what was once a concrete yard.

I turn into what used to be the gateway, and bulldoze my long-suffering rust bucket through the undergrowth, coming to a halt in the middle of the yard. At least, I think, our presence will be pretty much obscured from the road. Clive gets out of the car and heads for a gap in the corrugated iron. Taylor, who has been quiet in the back seat, leaps out and tries to grab him, but I hold her back.

'It's okay. He isn't going to run off.'

She gives me a dubious look.

'Get onto Hallam,' I tell her before she can object. 'Give him our position, and tell him to stay at least half a mile back. No vans, no helicopters, just unmarked cars, and not in convoy – they'll stick out like a sore thumb.'

She gives me one of her meaningful sighs and a look that says, *Do you think we're all stupid?*

I hold up my hands. 'Sorry.'

'Sir,' she says, clearly trying to pick her words, 'I know you're worried about your son-in-law, but our clear priority is to pick up Kyriaku and as many of his group as possible. We're already stretching things, especially with that ...' she gestures towards the dilapidated barn, 'that boy. Surely you don't trust a word he says?'

The fragile hold I have on my temper is dangerously close to breaking point. I take several deep breaths and say very slowly and deliberately, 'I think, Sergeant, you need to reassess your priorities. One police officer is dead, and another is in hospital with life-threatening injuries. Our "clear priority" is to extract a third officer and a civilian police employee, preferably while they are still breathing. If you think storming Medusa's base camp with all guns blazing is going to achieve that, be my guest. I've been put in charge, and so your priorities are what I say they are. Do you understand?'

She glares at me, but after a short standoff takes a step back and nods. 'Yes, sir.'

'Good. As for Clive Gingell, yes, I trust him to do what Shark Johnson has told him to do. If he doesn't, his life won't be worth living – if he hangs on to his life long enough. We're fighting a common enemy, and until Kyriaku has been neutralised, we have an agreement – the kind the local gangs will stick to. You'll just have to take my word on that.'

She ponders this for all of five seconds and then says, 'Okay, sir. I'll get onto the team right away.'

'Thank you, Sergeant.'

I leave her to converse with her radio, and follow Clive into the outbuilding. To my surprise, I find him sitting on an old mattress, boiling water in a saucepan on a rusty Primus stove.

'Got some coffee, if you want some,' he offers, rooting around in a cardboard box and pulling out a tin of instant. 'It's crap stuff, and I've run out of milk powder.' After a bit more rummaging, he holds up some pots of instant noodles.

'Or you can have one of these if you like. Only got one mug though, so the bitch will have to wait her turn.'

For a moment I picture him at home, making sure his brother and sister get fed, clothed, and off to school, and most likely sorting out his ineffective mother as well. 'Coffee's good,' I say. 'Thanks. Looks like you've got a good set-up here.'

He smiles fleetingly, then, realising his hard-man image might be taking a bit of a knock, turns it back into a scowl. 'It's my place,' he snaps. 'I found it, and you keep your mouth shut.'

'Don't worry, son. Your secret is safe with me – and I'll make sure Sergeant Taylor doesn't say anything.'

He grunts, sloshes hot water into the mug over a spoon of coffee and holds it out. I take it, and he fills a plastic noodle pot for himself. He's even equipped himself with a rudimentary set of cutlery. I resist the urge to ask which supermarket was the unwilling donor of his food and equipment. It would be a bit churlish under the circumstances.

I sip the coffee, and he swirls the water into his noodles in silence for a minute or two, then says, 'It's good here. You can hear lots of different birds, and at night there are owls and badgers and foxes. If you put peanuts down, sometimes the badgers come up close, and you can watch.'

I wonder if he and the late Kelvin Draper ever swapped notes, but don't get the chance to ask as Taylor squeezes past the iron sheeting into the barn.

'The team is in place, sir,' she announces, raising an eyebrow at the Primus stove and the mug in my hand. 'They're on standby, waiting for your signal.'

I finish my coffee and hand the mug back to Clive. 'Good.

Thank you, Sergeant. You want some coffee? No milk, I'm afraid.'

She looks dubious, but nods. Clive grudgingly spoons some into the mug, fills it from the pan and holds it out.

'Thanks,' she says politely, and goes back outside to keep watch.

Clive finishes his noodles, fishes a smart phone and earbuds out of his jacket, sees my expression and glares, daring me to say what I'm thinking.

'Don't mind me, son,' I tell him, and settle back against a pile of old grain sacks. There's still a couple of hours until dusk, and all I can do now is wait, try to gather my strength, and pray the boy is right, and Kyriaku won't turn up before dark.

30

I've just noticed that the hole I've been digging for hours – the one that doesn't seem to be getting any deeper despite my efforts, is a grave with a headstone I can't quite read, when a cacophony of steeple bells starts up, and I shoot, blinking, into a sitting position and realise I must have dozed off. The pealing bells transform themselves into the insistent trill of my mobile. I shake my head to clear the fog, blink several times, and answer it. Taylor has come back inside, so I put it on speaker.

'We've managed to nick two of them over in Weston,' Grace says, 'and there's a sizeable stash of goodness knows what in that shed. Looks like pretty high-grade heroin, cocaine and a dozen or so firearms among other things. One got away though, and unfortunately it's the one Eddie Hall-Warner identified as the thug who calls himself Sidaris – as dangerous as Kyriaku, if not more so, armed, and probably headed in your direction. He's got a reputation as a survivalist, too – specialises in finding people who don't want to be found.'

I glance at Clive, who is looking distinctly nervous. He nods. 'Shark says he's the main man. He pretends he's a minder, but he isn't. He's a real bastard. Everybody's scared of him, except maybe the dog man. But the dog man's just fucking crazy, so he's not scared of anybody.'

'We'll keep our eyes open, Grace,' I say, and move to the gap in the metal sheets to look out. The light is fading fast. 'We'll be moving any time now,' I tell her, 'and I'll give the order for Hallam's people to move in as soon as I'm sure the whole gang is there and we've located Teresi and Larson.'

There's a short silence, and then Grace says, 'Remember what I said, Al. No risks, and no heroics. Sidaris has probably warned Kyriaku by now, so at the very least they'll be on the alert. We just have to hope they don't realise we know where they are and scatter. We'll be right behind you, and until we're in position, you don't take any action, no matter what you see, you got that?'

'Don't worry, Grace,' I reply. 'I know what I'm doing.' I hang up, put my phone on silent and turn to Clive. 'Are you ready?'

He pokes his head out into the growing dusk and sniffs the air, then nods. 'We have to go careful,' he says. 'There's a moon tonight.' He grins. 'I 'spose that's good for you – you won't tread in so much crap. But we're easier to see, so you and the bitch had better keep your heads down, right?'

'Right,' I agree, and give Taylor a look. She's still looking less than happy, but checks her weapon, turns her radio off.

Clive slips outside, I follow, and Taylor brings up the rear. He leads us away from the road into a network of fields, each one bordered by water-filled ditches. Within ten minutes my trousers are soaked to the knees, my shoes are caked in mud, and I can't feel my feet inside socks sopping with freezing water. I glance enviously at Taylor striding easily in regulation army-style boots, and Clive, who doesn't seem to mind that his state-of-the-art and probably stolen trainers are wet through. After about half an hour, we reach a small copse of stunted trees, and he leads us into it. When we get to the centre, he gestures for us to stop, and puts a finger to his lips. We stand still, listening to the rustles and creaks of the night-time countryside. I'm itching to take off my shoes and wring out my socks, but have enough training to know it's the worst thing I can do – it will only chill my feet even further.

Clive tugs my sleeve, and I bend down so he can whisper. Taylor follows suit, and we huddle under the trees. 'There's someone behind us,' he says, and gives Taylor a look. 'You sure it's not one of yours?'

She shakes her head. 'Not police. Are you sure it's not a fox or a cow or something?'

'I ain't stupid,' he hisses back. 'Just cos you don't fucking know nothing! I know what I'm hearing.'

'How far away, Clive?' I ask, feeling my stomach start to churn again.

He shrugs. 'Close, but not that close. Been there around ten minutes, but not coming closer. Just following.'

'You think it's one of the gang? They know where we are?'

He shrugs again. 'If it is, they'll send somebody else out. They won't risk one of us getting away.' He nudges Taylor. 'Better keep a hand on your shooter, and you'd better be as good as you say you are.'

'I am,' she growls. 'If you don't believe me, try me!'

I feel rather than see his grin in the faint moonlight. 'You're pretty cool for a pig bitch,' he says appreciatively. 'We have to move – unless you can't manage it, Bird Man. You ask me, you're looking a bit shagged out.'

'I didn't ask you, and I'm fine,' I reply, trying to ignore the blocks of ice that used to be my feet. 'What about our friend out there? If he's contacted Kyriaku, we're pretty much fucked as soon as we get to wherever it is we're going. Maybe you should just point us in the right direction and make yourself scarce, son.'

'Fuck you,' is his predictable response. 'Shark said to take you all the way. If you end up getting wasted, I'll be dead meat when I get back. So let's go, yeah?'

He moves silently out from under cover of the trees and in seconds is no more than a faint shadow on the moorland. Taylor and I follow, trying to move as quietly as possible, and keep our footing on the boggy ground. We keep going for another half an hour or so, the hairs on the back of my neck prickling at every step, heart jumping at every rustle behind us in the darkness. I suddenly realise that the terrain has changed. We're no longer trudging across open fields, but on ground that is more uneven, spongy underfoot, the meadowland giving way to a carpet of slippery moss and brambles, difficult to avoid in the almost pitch dark beneath a canopy of spindly trees blocking out the moonlight. Suddenly, the black outline of a building looms up in front of us, and Clive grabs my arm.

'Where are we?' I ask.

'Old peat works,' he replies. 'There are loads of them round here. This is the biggest, and they've set up in one of the warehouses on the other side. There are too many sheds for them to watch them all. They never come into this one, and you can see who comes and goes from inside.'

'And what about our shadow out there? If we get trapped

inside, we'll be like fish in a barrel. I assume he is still with us?'

'Yeah, but not any closer than he was before. And we've got the bitch if he tries anything.' He sniffs. 'Plus, I'm not that fucking stupid. There's another way out in the back wall.'

'Okay. At least we won't be out in the open.' I signal to Taylor, who is standing a few feet away, alert, peering out into the darkness behind us. 'By the way,' I say under my breath as he pushes aside a section of wooden sheeting over the doorway, 'didn't Shark tell you to watch your language? Sergeant Taylor over there might very well end up saving your arse, so do us all a favour and start being a bit more polite, eh?'

'You ain't my fucking dad,' he shoots back, but then shrugs, glances at Taylor and wipes his nose on his sleeve. 'Yeah, right.'

Taylor signs her intention to stand guard just inside the door, and Clive takes me over to the opposite wall and a window, the glass long since shattered, the remaining shards crunching under my feet as I reach it and cautiously look out onto a large complex of buildings, some brick, some a combination of wood and metal – the remains of barns and offices for the extraction and storage of peat. Directly opposite us, some eight hundred metres away and partly obscured by other buildings, is a large, brick-built structure, two stories high. Light is seeping out from several boarded-up windows on the first floor, and on the ground floor the outline of a large set of rolling doors is visible, most likely for the storage of heavy machinery, and a smaller door to the side. There are faint sounds coming from inside, but too far away to make sense of.

Clive tugs my sleeve and points to the left of the smaller

door. At first I see nothing, but then my straining eyes catch a shadowy movement, and a moment later the shadow crosses the area of light trickling out below the door, and solidifies into a human shape before melting back into the darkness.

'They've only got the one lookout,' he whispers. 'Everybody else goes inside. He goes in and another comes out every hour.'

I'm about to reply when he grabs my arm tightly and points again. A large, dark shape slides out of the gloom, silent except for the crunching of tyres on gravel, and comes to a halt next to the door – an electric car, headlights off. The door opens, and I flinch back, blinking as the dim glow of the courtesy light becomes almost blinding in the near pitch dark. An instantly recognisable figure gets out, followed by the muscular, sinuous and terrifying shape of a large dog. To my horror, the dog lets out a loud bark, shattering the silence, and sets off at a run, straight towards us. All three of us freeze, not daring even to breathe. If the animal has our scent, it's all over, and although I'm no stranger to fear in most of its forms, I find myself, for the first time in my life, understanding what it means to be physically sick with terror. Taylor's hand is in her jacket, but she stays perfectly still, not daring to draw her weapon.

Kyriaku lets loose a furious stream of Greek, getting louder as, presumably, he chases after the animal. I risk a glance sideways out the window and catch the shape of the Doberman careering towards us. It's no more than a hundred metres away now, barking madly with excitement. I try not to imagine its slavering jaws, the gruesome effect of its teeth on human flesh. It's halved the remaining distance when suddenly, inexplicably, the creature veers away to the left of the building we're in, and heads for a much smaller brick shed. The barking becomes even more frantic, and we're close enough to hear the scrape of its claws scrabbling against the shed door. Kyriaku catches up with it, still cursing the animal, and there's the sound of a chain jangling as he gets it under control and drags it back towards the warehouse. A few moments later we hear the sound of a door opening and closing, and then silence.

Nobody moves for a full thirty seconds, and then we all heave a collective sigh of relief.

'Jesus bloody Christ!' I mutter under my breath, and turn to Clive. 'You all right, son?'

'What do you fucking think?' he asks, his voice defiant, but I catch the tremor in it.

'Do you know roughly how many are in there?'

'I've never counted more than ten,' he replies. 'Not everybody knows about this place, only the ones he trusts to keep their mouths shut.'

Taylor leaves her post at the back of the shed and joins us. 'Sir?'

I think for a moment and nod. 'Get onto Hallam, Sergeant,' I say. 'Tell him to move his people in, carefully and quietly. We don't want a bloodbath if we can avoid it. If he can get sights around that building without alerting the occupants, we'll at least be able to keep them pinned down. But nothing happens until we know exactly where Larson and Teresi are, understood? If they're in there, it could turn into a hostage situation, and somehow I don't think these bastards are very good at negotiating.'

'What about the one that kid says is following us?' she asks.

'It's a problem,' I agree. 'There's not much we can do

about it, but at least we know whoever it is hasn't given us away to Kyriaku, not yet anyway. If he had, I think we'd be dead by now. Tell Hallam to keep his eyes open, but not to apprehend unless there's no option. I've got a feeling that whatever his agenda is, it's not the same as Kyriaku's.'

I'm pretty certain I know the identity of our shadow. It must be Sidaris. What the bloody hell he's up to, though, is something I haven't yet been able to fathom. My mind goes back to Grace's description – an expert tracker who finds people who don't want to be found. Suddenly, it makes sense. He found us because he was looking for us. He assumed, naturally, that Teresi could give us the precise location of the warehouse, and that a police presence would be around somewhere. He's right, even if it's for the wrong reason. What I can't understand is why he hasn't made any move to get rid of us.

I realise Taylor is talking. 'Anything else, sir?'

I take a deep breath. 'I want to know what the dog found so interesting in that shed. You stay here and cover us. My assistant and I are going to see if we can get inside.'

31

Clive guides me to a loose plank in a far corner of the building. I order Taylor to stay put and keep watch and follow him outside. Our exit is hidden from the warehouse serving as Kyriaku's headquarters by a pile of rusting equipment, and we skirt round it cautiously, Clive skipping round obstacles like a mountain goat while I make slower progress, terrified of snagging my feet on something and bringing both a shower of rusty metal and the local branch of Medusa down on our heads. As we reach the other side of the pile, Clive swats my chest with the flat of his hand, and we come to a halt. The target building is just a few metres away, but to get to it, we need to cross an open space in full view of the warehouse. The moon chooses that precise moment to pop out from behind a cloud, casting a faint light that will make our shadows visible to anyone looking in the right direction. I hunker down behind him, trusting in his better eyesight to judge when it's safe to cross.

While we're waiting, I become aware of two things. First, the scrabbling and rustling noises I assumed were rats and other local countryside wildlife are, without any doubt, coming from the shed we're aiming for. The second, drifting on the light breeze blowing in our direction, is a very familiar smell – old, well-fermented piss, the scent of every underpass and communal corridor in the tower blocks of West Hill. The building we're headed for is a proverbial brick shithouse. Clive reaches back, squeezes my wrist and bolts across the gap. I follow, ignoring the stabs of protest from my long-suffering knees. When this is all over, I think, I'm going to have to get my sluggish body back into condition.

Thankfully, we gain the safety of the back wall of the old toilet block, out of sight, and now that we're close, it's immediately apparent what got Kyriaku's beast so excited. The scrabbling and rustling is much louder, coming from the other side of the door, which is secured by a hefty, newly affixed combination padlock. Behind the animal noises, I also catch a faint hum – a generator of some sort. I glance at Clive, just visible in the moonlight, and gesture towards the padlock. He digs into a pocket and holds up a Swiss Army knife. He studies the lock, feeling round it with his fingers, selects a tool and sets to work. There's no way of tackling the padlock directly, but the hasp and staple are set into an ancient wooden door and frame. Clearly, nobody is expecting a break-in. I get the feeling the lock is more to prevent whatever is inside getting out. He goes for the staple, carefully digging out the wood from around it until he can get his tool underneath to loosen it enough to push it back into the wood, exposing the screw heads that are sunken into the metal. Once he's able to get his penknife to the heads, it's a simple matter of unscrewing them, and the hasp falls away, leaving the padlock dangling uselessly from the door. I gesture for him to stand back, carefully turn the doorknob, push open the door, and freeze.

The block has been half gutted, the smashed remains of the urinals piled up in one corner, and only one of the two sinks remaining on the opposite wall. There are two stalls, doors long since gone, the toilet bowls and high cisterns cracked and broken. The furthest stall is emitting a dull, red glow, giving me just enough light to see my surroundings. Beneath the light is a large, wooden crate, the source of the rustling we heard from outside, but whatever is in it isn't visible behind the planking. In the stall nearest to the door is the unmistakeable shape of a human body, trussed like a chicken, wrists and ankles bound with cable ties linked together by a length of rope behind its back. It isn't moving. In front of both stalls, secured by a long chain stapled to the wall, a large Doberman stands guard, lips curled back to expose the razor-sharp canines, a low, ominous growl rumbling in its throat. The chain is probably just long enough to reach me if it decides to attack. I realise I'm standing a few feet away from an animal in the grip of one of the most dangerous and universal instincts in the world – a parent defending its young.

One look at the dog's undercarriage tells me this is the father. The mother of Susan Chalmers's stolen puppies must be in the stall under the heat lamp, counting on her mate to keep her and the offspring safe. As for the body in the next stall, still and lifeless, there's no doubt about its identity. My terror of the Doberman is matched only by the fact that I might be looking at my son-in-law's corpse. The dog's growl is getting deeper, more insistent, and I see a dribble of foam on its lips. In desperation I force my hand to move, very slowly, to my jacket pocket and my phone, although how I can possibly extract it and key in a number before the animal attacks I haven't quite worked out. I manage to get a grip on it, but it's managed to wrap itself in something else – a piece of cloth. I try to disentangle it, but only seem to get it more snarled up in whatever I've left in there. I'm mentally cursing my slovenly attitude to life, and wondering why the hell I don't take more care of just about everything, when it hits me what it is. As if by divine intervention, the handkerchief Chalmers gave me to wipe coffee off my shirt has wormed its way into my hand. It's a slim chance, but it's the only one I've got.

I slowly pull the cloth out of my pocket and hold it out towards the dog, trying desperately to remember its name. Brook? Bramble? I close my eyes, recalling the conversation. Briar! That was it! I take a deep breath.

'Briar?' I say, crouching down and trying to pitch my voice the way I've heard dog owners speak, a combination of authority and baby talk. 'Here, boy. I'm a friend of your mum's. Come and have a sniff; there's a good dog ...'

I keep on babbling at it in a low mumble, aware that Clive has crept up behind me, peering over my shoulder at the creature, who is still growling, but at least has closed its jaws and is snuffling at the air. It takes a step towards me, pokes its nose into the handkerchief, sniffs, and tentatively licks my hand. I risk stroking it, and at once it nuzzles into me and tries to lick my face. We're friends, I decide, at least for the moment.

I'm telling it what a good boy it is and scratching its ear when there's a groan from the corner, and a movement. Larson is alive and conscious. Light-headed with relief, I raise myself slowly, careful not to spook the animal, and edge into the stall where my son-in-law is trying, unsuccessfully, to sit up. His mouth is trussed in heavy-duty electrical tape, and there's blood trickling down one side of his face.

'Okay, boy,' I say to the dog, who is still glued to my side, but clearly nervous of the new movement. 'Keep still,' I hiss to Larson, and then, to Clive, who is still behind me, 'You got that army knife handy, son?'

He slides it into my hand without a word, the blade already selected, and I cut through the cable ties on Larson's wrists and ankles, then help him to sit up. The ties have bitten into his flesh, tight enough to cut off the circulation. 'Take a deep breath,' I tell him, and rip the tape off his mouth.

'Jesus!' he manages to mutter through parched lips.

I look around and see a tap in the wall. Suddenly, it makes sense – a small, relatively draught-free building, a portable generator and a water supply make for a perfect place to keep a litter of puppies out of harm's way. Briar has evidently decided we're not out to harm his little family, and has lain down next to his mate, who is busy guiding her brood to her milk supply. I root around in my pockets and bring out another, clean handkerchief.

'See if that tap works,' I tell Clive, handing it to him together with his knife. 'Soak this, and we can clean him up a bit.'

He does as he's told, and Larson tries to take it, but the blood flow is still making its way to his fingers, so I hold it for him while he sucks some moisture into his mouth.

'Thanks,' he says, once he's able to talk. 'Christ, my head hurts!'

Clive soaks the handkerchief again, and I set about mopping the blood off his face. There's a lump the size of a duck's egg on his left temple.

'Somebody gave you a pretty good whack on the head,' I tell him.

'You don't say,' he replies. 'Where the hell are we?'

'If you really want to know, we're in the middle of nowhere, in a urinal with a bunch of stolen dogs, right next door to a warehouse full of armed drug dealers and psychotic killers.'

'Fine,' he says, blinking to clear his vision. 'Where's Jenny Teresi?'

'In the warehouse is my guess,' I say, 'if she's still alive.'

I'm about to ask him what he remembers, when Clive thumps me in the back, and at the same time Briar lifts his head and lets out a low, menacing growl. A moment later a figure who looks like he's been practising for the next Mr Universe contest looms in the doorway, brandishing a large pipe wrench. My first thought is, *Thank God it's not a gun.* My second is, *Where the fucking hell is Taylor?* I don't have to wait long for the answer. The hired muscle takes a step forward, swinging the wrench, and several things happen at once. Briar's snarl rises in pitch, and the dog takes a leap forward. It doesn't quite reach its target though, as the chain it's attached to isn't quite long enough, and it's yanked back. It's enough to distract Kyriaku's guard for a few vital seconds though, and before I can process what's happening, Clive has darted forward and buried his blade to the hilt in the back of the man's hand. He drops the wrench with a furious howl, which is cut short as he realises there's a gun barrel digging into the base of his skull.

'On the floor,' Taylor instructs him. 'Now!'

He doesn't argue, and drops flat. Taylor follows him down, gun in one hand, cuffs in the other, and secures his hands behind his back, the knife still buried in one of them, its point protruding from his palm.

In the brief silence that follows, Clive pipes up. 'Can I have my knife back?'

I hesitate, unsure of the medical wisdom of pulling the thing out, but Taylor has no such qualms, and after a brief examination extracts it with a sharp tug, which draws an agonised groan from the prisoner, wipes it on the man's trouser leg and tosses it in Clive's direction.

'Better give it a rinse and dry it before you fold the blade back,' she advises him. 'You don't want it to rust.'

Our captive doesn't make another sound, although he's gritted his teeth, and there are beads of sweat trickling down his forehead. Taylor, with professional efficiency, tears a strip from his shirtsleeve and uses it to roughly bind the wound, then goes on to search his pockets, retrieving a burner phone and a two-way radio – no firearm, I note with some surprise. Maybe Kyriaku doesn't fully trust his own people.

'We've got around forty-five minutes if the relief guard runs to time,' she says. 'Long enough to try to get a look at what's going on in there.'

'What about Hallam's team?' I ask.

'They should be in position by now, six officers four hundred metres behind us, and four marksmen up ahead, one trained on each side of the warehouse. There are two paramedics with the main group, and an ambulance standing by back on the main road.'

I turn to Larson. 'How are you feeling, John? Do you think you can walk?'

He nods and struggles to his feet, unsteady, but upright. He doesn't look good.

'Get a couple of the AFOs up here,' I tell Taylor. 'We need

to get Larson to a medic, and Clive out of the firing line in case things turn nasty.' I jerk a thumb at our unwelcome guest. 'They can deal with him, too.'

She gets onto her radio, and a minute later two black-clad officers emerge silently out of the gloom, alert, weapons drawn. Briar lets out a warning growl, and they come to a dead stop, waiting while I do my best to reassure the animal, praying he doesn't start to bark. Luckily, I seem to have become canine flavour of the month, and he quiets down again.

I point at my son-in-law. 'He needs medical treatment,' I say. 'Right away. And I want you to look after this boy. We wouldn't have got here without him.'

'Fuck off!' Clive puts in. 'I ain't going nowhere with them pigs. I'm staying here.'

'Do as I say,' I tell him, 'unless you want me to tell Shark what a pain in the arse you've been.'

'Fuck you,' he replies, but grins. 'As long as you tell him I saved *your* arse. You wouldn't have got that fucker without me.' He points to Kyriaku's goon glowering at us from the urinal.

Clive puffs out his chest proudly, and I don't know whether to laugh or cry. A kid who measures his worth by his knife skills is probably already a lost cause. 'You'll do as you're bloody well told,' I say. 'I'm not going back to Shark with a body bag, you understand me?' He gives me a contemptuous snort, but a glance at the two automatic rifles waving vaguely in his direction makes his mind up. He shrugs, pockets his knife, and moves over to join his escort.

One of the duo supports Larson, while the other roughly hauls the gang's lookout to his feet. 'Come on, kid,' the second one says to Clive, and together, the five of them troop out, leaving me, Taylor, and Susan Chalmers's dogs alone in the toilet block.

'Right, then,' I say to Taylor. 'Let's go and see what's going on in there. Tell Hallam to move his people forward – we might need them in a hurry. I just hope you're right about the guard changeover. I don't want them spooked until I know for sure where Major Teresi is. Nobody takes further action without my signal, okay?'

'Okay, sir,' she says, but hesitates.

'What?' I ask.

'What if she is in there, and it's not possible to get her out?'

I give her a long, hard look. 'Then we think of a way to make it possible,' I say, and start for the door. It's a fair question, but the thought of having to make that decision is one I can't afford to give room to if I want my mind, not to say my body, to keep functioning.

Taylor pockets the thug's burner and radio and follows me out. The side of the warehouse facing us has three windows on the ground floor, all blacked out except for a small square of dim light trickling through a gap in one of the panes at the far left of the building. There is also a light at one of the first-floor windows, filtering through the slats of a venetian blind and casting a striped shadow on the ground off to our right. I point at the ground-floor window. Taylor nods, and we make our way, keeping low, to the end of the warehouse and the patch of light. We reach the window without incident, flattening ourselves against the wall. I'm about to stick my neck out – literally – and peer through the nine-inch pane of dirt-streaked glass when Taylor grabs my arm and points to the shadow of the venetian blind. The slats are moving. We both freeze as whoever is up there parts the slats, and the outline of first a hand, then a head briefly appears, then disappears as the slats are released. A second later the shadow is gone as the light in the upper room is switched off. I let out a breath and cautiously peer through the window.

I count eight men inside the warehouse, a large, open space, no chairs or any other furniture apart from units of shelving and stacks of what look like oil drums stacked against the walls. There is hardly any noise, just the low murmur of subdued conversation. Kyriaku isn't among them. Teresi, however, is, standing between two of the men, one of them holding a pistol to her stomach, her arms pinned behind her by the other. She looks unharmed, and not particularly fearful. Her expression is blank, unreadable. Either she's drugged, or one hell of a lot braver than I am.

Suddenly, the place falls silent, and the little assembly moves back, leaving an empty expanse of concrete in the centre of the room. A door opens at the far end, and Darius Kyriaku finally makes his appearance, the dog padding quietly at his heel. It's the first time I've been able to take a good look at the man who murdered one of my closest friends and put a bullet in my brain. I've seen a fair few killers in my time, most, thankfully, serving life sentences. They range from a sixteen-year-old who knifed a fellow pupil on the way home from school, through an assortment of gangsters and armed robbers, to an eighty-year-old woman convicted of fatally poisoning her estranged husband to prevent him cutting her out of his will. Contrary to popular myth, however, a true psychopath is a rare creature – a phenomenon the average policeman may come across once in a lifetime, if at all. Tall, attractive, fastidiously dressed in what looks like a long, made-to-measure cashmere overcoat, polished boots more than likely handmade, and fine leather gloves – an ensemble that probably cost more than my annual salary – Kyriaku oozes charisma as he steps forward into the space, his acolytes moving even further back to give him room. For several seconds I'm mesmerised, but then, for the first time, I see his face clearly and, handsome as it is, I feel a sudden shiver of revulsion. There is no expression there – the eyes might as well be chiselled from marble. There's going to be no negotiation, no compromise with this man. My desire to see the bastard in a courtroom, answering for the death of Vicky Brent, the injuries to Polly Sillitoe, and most importantly the shooting of my sergeant Joe Bailey, will very likely never be fulfilled. The concept of surrender just isn't a part of his mindset.

At a gesture, the two men holding Teresi release her and push her forward. Remarkably, she is still showing no outward fear, but steps confidently into what is looking ominously like an arena, smiles at Kyriaku, and says something in Greek. He responds with a humourless smile of his own and answers in the same language.

'Tell them to be ready,' I hiss over my shoulder at Taylor, and feel her move back a couple of paces to pass on the message.

I keep watching. The exchange between Teresi and Kyriaku, separated by the length of the central space, continues, barely audible through the glass. Apart from their voices, there is no other sound or movement. Then, with a suddenness that makes my stomach lurch, Kyriaku snaps an order to the dog, and it leaps forward, almost faster than my brain can process, towards Teresi, teeth bared, flecks of foam spitting from its jaws. For a vital second I'm frozen, unable to move or speak. The animal crouches, preparing to leap on its prey, but then something inexplicable happens. Teresi hasn't moved an inch, is still standing straight, relaxed, her eyes fixed on the Doberman. As it rears up, she lets out a piercing whistle, and the animal stalls mid-spring, falls back on its haunches and sits, motionless, like a puppy expecting a treat. Kyriaku simply stares, rigid with fury. Teresi whistles again, a different sound, low and soft. The dog turns, lets out an ominous growl and launches itself, snarling, straight back towards its master. In the split second before it leaps, I see Kyriaku's eyes widen in disbelief. Then he starts to scream.

'Now!' I shout to Taylor, who snaps the order into her radio.

All hell breaks loose. Several windows shatter at once, and the building starts to fill with smoke. Dark shadows with rifles and gas masks flit past me into the warehouse. I start after them, but Taylor grabs my arm and gestures for me to wait. Neither of us have protection from the gas. I hear another pane of glass break somewhere above us, followed by a single rifle shot. Then the only sounds are the muffled voices and movements inside the building as the firearms squad goes about its business.

The relative calm doesn't last long. Within a couple of minutes the yard is full of flashing blue lights as a convoy of marked and unmarked police cars and two ambulances pile into the yard in front of us. Grace leaps out of the leading car as it comes to a halt, and I trot over to join her.

'Thank God!' she comments, then, 'Looks like we've got them, Al. Great job!'

'What about Larson?' I ask. 'Is he all right?'

'He'll be fine,' she replies, giving me a pat on the shoulder. 'He's in one of the ambulances, but the paramedics say there's no sign of concussion, and it's mainly superficial cuts and bruises. He's a very lucky man, considering what could have happened.'

I heave a sigh of relief. 'And Clive?'

She laughs. 'Gave us the slip. He's well on the way back to West Hill by now – probably stolen someone's bike for the journey.'

'Tell the local uniforms to go easy if they catch him,' I say. 'If it weren't for him, I'd have a pipe wrench buried in my skull, and Larson would be in a body bag.'

'Noted,' she says, still grinning.

The smoke inside the warehouse is starting to dissipate, and first out is Teresi, coughing, but otherwise unhurt. I watch as she's conducted to one of the ambulances, and as the door opens, I catch sight of Larson, pale, but looking a hell of a lot better than he did half an hour ago. He looks up, sees me and gives me a weak smile. I nod and try to wave, but my hand is shaking too much, the relief that they are both still with us starting to take over. The gang members come next, herded into a waiting van, which pulls away as soon as the last one is inside. There's no sign of Kyriaku. I remember the rifle shot and swear under my breath.

'I suppose I'll never get to look that bastard in the eye now,' I comment bitterly.

'Oh, I wouldn't be too sure,' a voice says behind us, and I turn to see Hallam striding up to us. At the same time I hear the distinctive regular thump of a helicopter rotor overhead, rapidly coming closer. 'Air ambulance,' he says. 'He's in a bad way, but he's conscious. You can read him his rights if you like.'

He jerks a thumb behind him, and I see two paramedics coming out of the warehouse carrying a stretcher. Together, Grace and I walk over to it and look down on the face that just half an hour ago was capable of inspiring such fear among some of the worst criminals I've had the misfortune to come across. Now, a deep gouge has torn through the right eye, ripped the flesh from the cheekbone, left the ear hanging by a thread. It's awful to look at, but not quite as awful as the remaining, undamaged eye, which is staring up at us with a look of pure hatred.

'I'll leave the honours to you, Inspector,' Grace says.

I take a deep breath. 'Darius Kyriaku, I'm arresting you for the murders of Detective Sergeant Joseph Bailey and Detective Sergeant Victoria Brent, and the attempted murder of Detective Inspector Polly Sillitoe. You do not have to say anything ...'

I manage to keep my voice even until I've completed the caution, and the paramedics whisk him away to the helicopter, accompanied by an armed officer.

'I heard a shot,' I say to Hallam.

He nods. 'The dog – bullet clean through the head. And before you ask, it wasn't us. There was someone on the roof. They're not there now, and we've got officers looking, but I doubt they'll find whoever it was, at least not tonight.'

'You won't find him,' I tell him. 'My guess is he'll be well out of the area by now.'

Hallam turns to go, but stops and roots in his pocket, coming up with a smart phone. 'We found this on one of the gang,' he says, handing it to me. 'Looks like it belongs to your boy over there.' He jabs a thumb towards the ambulance. 'I think his wife's been trying to get hold of him.'

I look at the phone – there are at least a dozen missed calls, several from Rosie, and the most recent from Chrissie's number.

'Shit!' I say, and pull out my own phone, which has been

on silent for the last couple of hours. My missed call list is the same. I go over to Larson, sitting in the back of the ambulance, ring Chrissie's number and put it on speaker.

'Al? Where the bloody hell have you been? And where's John? Rosie went into labour more than an hour ago. We're at the infirmary. Never mind what the two of you are doing, just bloody well get here, now!'

'You'll be quicker in one of the squad cars,' Grace says, and calls over the nearest uniform while I get Larson onto his feet. 'Don't worry about anything here. It's all more or less wrapped up, and we've got a van coming from the RSPCA to take care of the dogs. Just go!'

For once, neither Larson nor I are going to argue.

32

'For goodness' sake, Al, sit down! You're driving me mad!'

'Sorry,' I say, perching myself back on the plastic chair next to Chrissie. 'Are you sure everything's okay? We've been sitting here for hours.'

'An hour and a half,' Chrissie corrects me. 'And I've been sitting – you've been wandering up and down the corridor like a lost dog.'

I wince at the expression, but don't say anything – it wouldn't help.

She smiles and takes my hand. 'I was in labour more than eight hours with Rosie. Do you remember?'

'I remember you suddenly developed a craving for sausage rolls and had me running up and down to the hospital canteen every five minutes.'

'That was just to get you out of the way. The midwife hid them all in a plant pot and handed them out to the nurses afterwards.'

I'm trying to think of a suitable response to this when the

door to the delivery room opens and the midwife sticks her head out.

'You can both come in now,' she says, beams, and disappears back inside.

Chrissie and I look at each other, and I see my own nervousness reflected in her expression. I squeeze her hand. 'Come on – better do as the woman says.'

Our daughter and son-in-law are sitting together on the bed, looking exhausted but deliriously happy. Between them, the new addition to the family is all but invisible, bundled in blankets.

Rosie beckons to us. 'Come and meet your granddaughter,' she says, grinning. 'Eight pounds and twelve ounces.'

We join them, perching ourselves on the bed and peering at the new arrival, who seems to be taking things in her stride, two curious blue eyes flitting from one face to another. Rosie lifts her up and holds her out to me.

'Want to hold her, Dad?'

I take the little bundle gingerly, marvelling at the tiny, perfectly formed mouth and nose, the little fingers reaching up to curl around my thumb. 'She's beautiful,' I manage, feeling a lump rising in my throat. 'Have you decided on a name yet?'

'We think she sort of takes after you,' Larson pipes up. 'So we thought Alexandra – if that's okay with you?'

I STUMBLE into the chief constable's office feeling distinctly jittery after a night spent in Chrissie's lounge, talking over old times and wetting the baby's head with more cups of coffee than I can count. Major Teresi is already there, together with Grace, and Hallam, who is just finishing his report. Gosford greets me with an unusually warm smile.

'I understand congratulations are in order, Inspector,' he comments, gesturing to a chair. Thank you, Sergeant Hallam, that will be all.'

'Sir,' Hallam replies, and gives me a wide grin on his way out.

'Major Teresi was just describing her version of last night's events,' Gosford goes on. 'Major, perhaps you would like to fill in some of the details for Inspector Crow?'

'Of course,' she replies as I take my seat. 'I expect you were a little worried when you learned we were no longer in your safe house.'

'You could say that,' I agree. 'So what happened?'

'I knew Kyriaku would track us down eventually,' she says, 'but he wasn't the only one looking for us. We got a message telling us an armed unit was being dispatched, so when a person came to the door claiming to be one of your officers, we had no reason not to believe him. He had identification and was in uniform, so we opened the door.'

'Let me guess,' I interrupt. 'It was Sidaris.'

She nods. 'By the time I saw his face, it was too late. He put a gun to Mr Larson's head and threatened to kill him if we didn't do as he said. He had a van outside and made me drive to the place they were using in Weston to store their drugs. Your team must have missed us by minutes. When we got there, he locked us in the back, tied and gagged, and left us there. After he'd gone, I realised something wasn't quite right. If he'd been acting on orders from Kyriaku, he would have taken us straight to the warehouse – getting me back and finding out how much I'd told you would have taken priority over everything else. Half an hour later, he came back, very agitated. He left Mr Larson in the back of the van, but released me and told me to drive again, this time to the warehouse. All the time my suspicion was growing, and when he made me stop at least two miles away, I was convinced.'

'He'd been ordered to eliminate Kyriaku,' I say, the light starting to dawn, 'but Kyriaku was already suspicious of him, so he needed you to get him close enough.'

'Exactly.' She gives me an appreciative smile. 'He had been given two tasks – to get me back, preferably alive, probably to use as leverage against the Athens police, or dead as an example.' She shudders and carries on. 'His second order was to stop Kyriaku. However, Sidaris is a clever man. Unlike Kyriaku, he prefers not to kill himself. His victims almost always die at the hands of others, or in a manner that can be explained as some sort of accident. No one has, so far, been able to point a finger directly at him. His plan was to use me as a distraction. Up to that point, he'd kept your daughter's husband alive both to have some control over me, and to avoid being the subject of a murder hunt himself – he wanted all the guilt to fall on Kyriaku's head. He intended to do away with Mr Larson and dump the body at the warehouse, where he would simply become another victim of the mad Greek assassin, hand me over, and take out Kyriaku once everyone's attention was on me. However, that presented problems for him. Given the number of gang members in the warehouse, there was a big risk of being brought down before he could get himself out. He was also tipped off by your informant that the police were closing in, and if arrested, he would be unable to deny a direct charge of murder. So I offered Sidaris a deal. We both knew that once Kyriaku had me back, he would set the dog on me – it's what he does. But I spent five years with that animal, and that time wasn't wasted. In many ways, Charon was as loyal to me as he was to his master. I'd trained him to obey my commands as well as Kyriaku's. I told Sidaris I would use those commands – but only if he agreed to leave Mr Larson alive. That was the deal. If I failed, he could always kill him anyway, and still go after Kyriaku.'

'You were taking a hell of a risk,' I comment.

She nods. 'True. I was not at all sure Charon would choose to follow my instructions rather than his master's. I'd never had the chance to test it. Sidaris thought it was worth the gamble, though. He knocked Mr Larson unconscious, dumped him in the outhouse with the other dogs, and I walked into the warehouse, pretending I had escaped from the clutches of the British police. I wasn't believed, of course – I didn't expect to be – but it got me where I needed to be, and the rest you know.'

'And now,' I finish for her, 'the man who murdered your father is likely to spend the rest of his life in prison. There is one thing I don't understand, though. Sidaris was ordered by his Medusa bosses to eliminate Kyriaku, so why didn't he let the dog finish him off? Why shoot it? It doesn't make sense.'

'It makes perfect sense,' she answers. 'Even if Kyriaku makes it to court and through the trial, he won't live very long once he gets to a prison, no matter what you do. Medusa will see to that. But in his whole life, the only things that have mattered to him have been his dogs. The loss of Charon will have broken him completely, and the short time he has left will be spent in the knowledge that he was betrayed by the one creature he trusted. In the meantime, even if you manage to catch Sidaris – which you can guarantee is not his real name anyway – you might possibly charge him with one or two minor offences if you manage to find enough evidence, but murder? Any good lawyer would simply point out that he grabbed a gun belonging to one of your officers and was trying to save Kyriaku's life. If anything, his position within the organisation will be strengthened. They appreciate ingenuity, but even more, they like their senior operatives to have a clean police record.' She shrugs and gets to her feet, holds out a hand. 'It was a pleasure to meet you, Inspector Crow. If you will excuse me, I need to go and complete my report for the Athens police department. I'm sure you will be receiving a message from my superiors, thanking you for your cooperation.'

'What about Davis?' I ask, when Teresi has left.

'In custody,' Grace says. 'He claims he was forced into it, and I suppose he was, to a point. Medusa got hold of him when he developed a minor drug habit at university and got into debt; from what we've been able to gather – gave the habit and his career a bit of a leg up, and of course demanded payback once he could be useful. According to him, they threatened to take it out on his wife and children if he didn't play ball. We're checking it out, but either way his career's finished, and he's looking at the inside of a cell. The only question is, for how long.'

'I'm sure you will have the opportunity to read all the reports, Inspector,' Gosford puts in, with some impatience. 'Meanwhile, there is another matter we need to discuss.'

I groan inwardly. 'Another matter, sir?'

The chief constable clears his throat and gives Grace an uncomfortable glance. She returns the look with a noncommittal smile.

'I'm sure you will be pleased to hear,' he says, fixing me with a stare that dares me to contradict the statement, 'that we have finally been able to acquire sufficient funding to station a detective superintendent permanently at West Hill.'

'I see,' is all I can reply, looking at Grace, who simply raises an eyebrow. 'I'm sure that is good news, sir.' My main thought, however, is that the last thing West Hill needs is another bloody pen-pushing idiot coming in and buggering up a system that has pretty much worked up to now.

'Indeed,' Gosford agrees with a frosty smile. 'I am also very pleased to be able to tell you that DCI Helston has accepted the post, effective immediately.'

That piece of news does bring me up short. On the one hand, nobody deserves it more than Grace. On the other, it means I'm going to have to deal with a new DCI, most likely a fast-track graduate with more acne than brain matter and no clue how to deal with the kind of problems West Hill presents to even the most experienced officers. For once, retirement is starting to look reasonably attractive.

'Congratulations, ma'am,' I manage. 'Jesus bloody Christ!'

Gosford coughs again, looking even more uncomfortable. 'However,' he continues doggedly, 'DSI Helston has made her acceptance conditional on a specific request. I understand, Inspector, that you are eligible for promotion to DCI. DSI Helston firmly believes that you are the best person to fill this role, and ...' He hesitates, grits his teeth. 'So do I,' he finishes, and turns his gaze to the grain in the mahogany.

'What do you say, Al?' Grace asks, giving me a wide grin. 'You up for it?'

For a moment, I'm too stunned to say anything. Finally, I get my mouth in line with my brain and say, 'I would be delighted, ma'am, but I'm afraid I do have one small condition of my own.'

Gosford's head jerks up, and he manages the verbal equivalent of a splutter. 'A condition, Inspector?'

'If I am to take up the post of DCI,' I explain, 'I'm going to need a halfway decent DI to work with. I am happy to accept, on condition that once she is fit to return to work, DI Sillitoe's position is made permanent.'

Gosford looks from one to the other of us and makes the wise decision to withdraw from the battlefield. 'Agreed,' he mutters, 'although that will be dependent on the outcome of any disciplinary procedures – we take a very dim view of loose cannons, especially in the senior ranks. Now, if we can get back to normal business, I've had a request from Mrs Chalmers. Lovely woman – I used to play golf with her late husband, you know. The RSPCA are returning her dogs to her this morning. All, I should add, in perfect health, thanks to your excellent work, DCI Crow. She has asked for you to be present so that she can thank you personally. I would take it as a great personal favour if you could attend.' He looks at his watch. 'It's eight thirty now. The animals are being returned at nine. You should be able to make it if you leave right away.'

'Of course, sir.'

'Do you mind if I break the news to Polly?' Grace asks as I reach the door. 'She had a good night, apparently, and it will give her something to keep her spirits up.'

'Go ahead,' I say, 'and tell her I'll drop in to see her later.'

I have a distinct spring in my step as I head across the car park. Generally speaking, sometimes, life isn't all that bad.

. . .

It's a warm, sunny day in early June. Most of the local villains are taking time out from their usual unsavoury occupations to lounge around the West Hill estate car parks, playing loud music and smoking dope. I've decided to follow their example and take some of the copious leave I'm owed to help Rosie with Ben while Larson is away at some sort of IT conference in London, and Chrissie and Joyce are enjoying the sights of southern Italy.

'He's not finding it easy,' she tells me as we stroll through the park to pick Ben up from school, taking turns to push two-month-old Alexandra's buggy. 'I suppose I should have expected a few problems. He's had us to himself for six years. He loves little Alex of course, but he's finding it very hard to share our attention with her.'

'He needs something to focus his own attention on,' I say. 'If our plan works, it will be perfect. Good thing your mother is away, though.'

Rosie laughs. 'Don't worry about Mum. Once she gets used to the idea, she'll love it.'

We arrive at the school gates just as the pupils start streaming out onto the pavements, the primary children in brown uniforms, making them look like a swarm of giant ants fanning out into the street, jumping into waiting cars, greeting parents or older siblings who have made the journey on foot. We stay on the other side of the road, clear of the melee, watching for Ben, and as we wait, I catch sight of an older boy with a bike, dressed in the green uniform of the comprehensive school next door. He makes his way to the primary entrance and is met by two children of around Ben's age, a girl and a boy. He sets the girl on the saddle of his bike, and with one arm protectively around her, the boy on the other side gripping the girl's hand, the little group make their way to the corner and disappear. For good or ill, Shark Johnson is making good on his promise, and Clive Gingell is finally getting an education in more than drug dealing and knife work – something Social Services haven't managed to achieve in the last six years.

'Here, Dad,' Rosie says, thrusting Alex's buggy into my hand, and rushes over to collect Ben from the gate.

'Grandad!' Ben lets go of Rosie's hand and launches himself at me with enough force to break a kneecap.

'Hey, Ben,' I say. 'Fancy tea at my place today?'

'Yeah,' he replies, beaming, but in less than a breath his face falls, and he gives his mother a sulky glance. 'Do Mum and Alex have to come?'

'I think your mum's a bit too busy today,' I tell him. 'Besides, I need your help with something, so I thought maybe you could come along and give me a hand. How about it?'

At once, he brightens up again. 'Sure,' he says, and adds, trying to imitate his father's voice, 'No sweat, kiddo!'

Rosie gets in an eye roll just before I do. Rosie sets off back across the park, and Ben follows me to my car, parked a couple of streets away from the mayhem that is the school run. Back at the house, I unlock the door and put a finger to my lips. We stand in the hallway, listening, and are rewarded with a scuffling from the lounge.

'Grandad,' Ben whispers, 'there's someone in your house.'

'You're right,' I whisper back. 'You want to go and see who it is?' He gives me an uncertain look. 'Go on, it's quite safe.'

His brow furrows, making him look comically like his father, but he takes a few steps forward and opens the lounge door, then freezes for a full five seconds before turning back to me, mouth open in disbelief. Before he can say anything, though, a little black bundle comes skittering out the open door, letting out a stream of high-pitched squeaks and yaps, tangling itself round our ankles and lashing Ben's legs with its tail. I grab the bundle and take it back into the lounge.

'Say hello to Bluebell,' I say, depositing the wriggling puppy back in her playpen. 'I'm going to need a bit of help looking after her. Do you think you're up to it?'

Ben isn't listening. Already, he's lying flat on the floor of the pen, laughing and tickling the ears of the runt of Susan Chalmers's litter of Dobermans. I have a feeling that whatever Chrissie thinks about it, I have, for once, made the right decision.

ABOUT THE AUTHOR

H J Reed lives and writes in Bristol, where she graduated with a PhD in psychology and began a long career lecturing in psychology and criminology, both in mainstream universities and in the prison education system. Her evenings were spent writing novels and short stories in various genres and styles, and pondering on the strange workings of the criminal mind. After a number of publication successes, she gained an MA in creative writing and went on to teach literature and the arts. Now, she is able to follow her lifelong passion and write crime fiction full time. When she is not writing, she can be found being taken for long muddy walks by a middle-aged, temperamental toy poodle, or in far-flung foreign cities thinking up new plots.

Did you enjoy *The Killing Ground*? Please consider leaving a review on Amazon to help other readers discover the book.

www.hjreed.com

ALSO BY HJ REED

DI Crow Series

Her Last Chance

The Killing Ground

Printed in Great Britain
by Amazon